Programmed to Steal

Tony C. Franklin

Published by Tony C. Franklin, 2023.

PROGRAMMED TO STEAL

First edition. December 15, 2023.

ISBN: 979-8989614714

Written by Tony C. Franklin.

Chapter 1

Friday, 5:00 a.m. Fayetteville, Arkansas

Jess sat alone on her sofa with her laptop on her knees. "I'm coming for you," she said aloud. The only light in her duplex came from the screen of her laptop as it flickered shadows on the wall around her. She had been on her computer since two a.m. and had been searching for this information for months. A friend of hers was abused when he was a child. Videos were made, pictures had been taken, and Jess made it one of her missions in life to find those pictures and videos and get them off the internet. She meant to bring the culprit to justice, if possible.

She had kept her promise. Now her eyes burned and her head ached as she fought through the exhaustion. She was tired of searching a hidden world of the most unthinkable perversions. Tired of seeing pictures and videos of adults abusing children. It had been a semester of difficult classes. But she'd kept her promise.

Jess was a hacker. For the past several years she had used her skills to do good. She searched the deepest most protected depths of the dark web for child pornography. When she found a website or gained access to someone's files, she used advanced facial recognition software to look for her friend. The sites and files she found were turned over to The Center for Missing and Exploited Children. The center then worked with the FBI and local police to bring down the child pornography sites.

Until this morning.

This morning, after months of searching, she located the right site. She had found over a hundred pictures and videos of her friend.

"I got you, you bastard!" she said in a harsh whisper. "I finally found you," she whispered as tears of triumph, anger, and frustration rolled

1

from the corners of her eyes. She closed her eyes tightly, trying to stop the tears.

The pictures and videos disgusted her and made her stomach roll from the things she saw. Seeing the pictures explained why Benji didn't let people into his life easily. It explained a lot of his quirks. In high school, she thought they would become boyfriend and girlfriend. But he was wired differently, and she had settled for being his friend. His only close friend.

She methodically copied the website onto an empty one-terabyte thumb drive. She purchased a picture from the site and immediately transferred it to the thumb drive. Then using a software program that she and her friend Mike had been working on for the past six months, she tracked down the owner's financial accounts.

The websites and files she'd found were all saved to online servers. Finding out who owned the files wasn't easy, but Jess usually had little trouble. Finding where the perverts lived was the hard part, and she usually left that to the FBI. What she wanted today was their banking information, and getting this was usually very difficult.

That financial information from the picture she purchased led her to names and numbered accounts. All the names were fake, or shell corporations, of course. But she didn't care. Her face was flushed with anger and now that she found what she was looking for, she was striking back for her friend and all the other children being abused.

By noon, she had destroyed five child pornography websites and cleaned out the pedophiles' bank accounts. She hadn't expected much money, but it was there, lots of money, and she was in the mood to punish someone. She didn't need the money. She intended to turn it over to the FBI on Monday morning. She did not see herself as a thief, but more as a vigilante.

"This is going to hurt."

Jess smiled with satisfaction. She was graduating from college in two days. She had fulfilled a promise to an old friend, and now she wanted to see her boyfriend, Mike.

Jess had wanted to be more than Mike's friend months ago. But Mike had insisted they focus on schoolwork and not date. At the time, she had agreed, wanting to finish her bachelor's degree, find her friend's abductor, and complete her personal software project.

She had asked Mike to help with her software project for three reasons. The first was selfish: she wanted to stay close to him. Second, his knowledge of banking and programming was a huge help in her recent endeavors. Third, he had caught her searching for child pornography files and websites last semester. Jess had expressed her motivations about protecting children but Mike couldn't understand at first and had walked out on her.

A few days later he apologized and said, "Jess, two wrongs don't make a right."

She responded, "Unless the second wrong is called revenge."

He nodded and said, "That's what I needed to hear," and presented her with a plan. It was a daring plan, a potentially dangerous plan, and she had implemented it this morning. That also brought them together as boyfriend and girlfriend.

Chapter 2

The aroma of dark-roasted coffee, vanilla, and cinnamon filled the air. The sound of coffee beans grinding could be heard in the background. The barista watched the counter while he cleaned up from the morning rush.

Coffee shops are a good place to buy a little motivation from a cup or collect your thoughts before attacking the mall. But they aren't the safest place to use the free WIFI. Benji knew this because he was the one they needed to fear.

Five customers were using the WIFI in Starbucks that morning. Two young ladies were sitting at a table shopping Wish and Amazon while chatting away. They were checking clothing prices online before heading to the Promenade to shop. Benji lurked behind her laptop waiting for a purchase to be made.

The third was trolling Facebook. The fourth was checking her bank card balance using her Samsung smartphone. The fifth was Benji, and she was slouched in the corner, hiding behind a laptop recording everything the fourth lady did on her screen. If the other customers looked at Benji they would see a blonde girl with a notebook and a laptop who appeared to be studying.

Using modified software that allowed computer techs to take control of a computer and make repairs over the internet, Benji invaded people's electronic devices and their privacy. She recorded the lady logging into her account. Benji captured her login ID, her password, and saw the balance on her account.

Using a split screen, Benji had been monitoring the other two young ladies who were shopping on Wish and Amazon. She decided they weren't buying anything online today. She had gathered the critical credit card information from two other patrons that morning. She had their card types, both Visas. She had the card numbers, their expiration dates, and the security numbers from the back of their cards. If more people used a VPN, she would have to find a real job.

The secret was to not get greedy. Benji scribbled some notes into a notebook, closed the laptop, slid it into a worn canvas and leather backpack, and left the coffee shop.

In the parking lot, Benji noticed the woman from Starbucks following at a distance. Benji got into a white minivan advertising internet and computer repairs. A glance in the rearview mirror confirmed the woman watched from behind two rows of parked cars. But Benji knew she couldn't see into the van.

Benji settled into the driver's seat. Reached for the box of tissues between the seats and wiped the minimal lipstick and eye shadow off her face. Scanning the parking lot to make sure no one was watching, she reached up and pulled the blonde wig off, revealing a young man with a thin face, high cheekbones, and short blond hair. Benji was no longer a blonde woman, but a young man with blond hair. He started the minivan and drove away.

Benji felt both masculine and feminine at different times. He was, he knew, bi-gender. Some days he was a woman and other days he was a man. This was an oversimplified way of explaining it. Some indigenous tribes like the Lakota and Navajo, would call him a dual spirit, and view him as a third gender. To begin to understand his gender had taken years of therapy. Even now, he couldn't fully understand his feelings. He knew that dressing feminine didn't help his dysphoria. But it did help him hide his identity; he only needed to hide his activity a little longer. He was also asexual. The lack of sexual attraction, he attributed to his childhood. Things that had happened to him during his childhood made him see the world in a way that often brought tears to his eyes. A world that needed compassion and retribution at the same time,

His mother had told him, there are strong people and there are weak people. The strong live, and the weak die.

"How do you become strong?" he had asked her.

"Through suffering," she had answered. "You can see yourself as a victim for life, or you can see yourself as a victim one time. Some people blame their behavior on a single incident that happened long ago. They wallow in self-pity their whole life and want people to feel sorry for them. Other people see a similar incident as a one-time occurrence and they become stronger because of it."

He thought she had been right about seeing yourself as a victim. Unfortunately for her and Benji, she never overcame being a victim herself.

Benji returned to his apartment. He lived a few blocks off the University of Arkansas campus in Fayetteville. He found David, his neighbor's eight-year-old son, sitting in front of his door. He and David had become friends over the six-month period they had been neighbors. Benji kept extra snacks and drinks in his apartment in case David was hungry. He sometimes helped him with his homework or they just sat and talked. David's mom was a waitress and had been an opioid addict. She tried to stay clean and had stayed away from the drug for the last six months. But in times of stress, she would resort to using again. Benji had a nagging feeling she would overdose someday, and he feared he wouldn't be there for David. He felt a need to protect the child. He knew, personally, the kind of predators who would take advantage of a kid like David.

"Why aren't you at school, David?" Benji asked him.

"Mom didn't wake me, and I can't wake her up," David said.

A knot formed in Benji's stomach. The thing he feared seemed to surge from his stomach to his throat. He unlocked his apartment door and put his thumb on the back of his phone to unlock it and handed it to the boy. "David, I want you to go into my apartment and call 911, okay? I'll go check on your mom."

"Is she going to be, okay?" David asked.

Benji knelt to be at the boy's height and put his hand on David's shoulder. "I don't know David, but I sure hope so."

He pushed the door open and motioned David inside.

"Make the call like we practiced," Benji said.

Benji took about four steps to the apartment next door. He opened the door and the contrasting smell of stale food and air freshener hit him at once. He forced the bile in his throat back down as he swallowed. The silence was frightening. The layout of the apartment was identical to his but decorated much nicer. It had a woman's touch, with family pictures, and vases of artificial flowers scattered around the room.

He went to the bedroom and found his neighbor lying on her stomach, facing away from him on her bed wearing shorts and a tank top. She looked like she was sleeping peacefully. He thought he saw her breathing. He called her name. "Lyndsey?" There was no reply. He stepped to the bed and shook her shoulder.

"Lyndsey, wake up."

There was no reply. He held his fingers against her neck and could feel a pulse. Thank God, he thought. He didn't want David to lose his mom that way. It brought back too many memories of losing his own mom. He heard sirens in the distance. He turned and walked out of the apartment, closing the door behind him. He found David in his apartment on the couch crying.

It was going to be a long afternoon, Benji thought. He would be late for a visit with a friend, but she would understand. He had to protect David and the child needed him.

***

The lady who had been checking her bank account in Starbucks was FBI Special Agent Renee Henderson. The account was an FBI account. It was set up to catch thieves who trolled free WIFI locations for customers accessing accounts or shopping online. She could tell by the blinking of the screen on her pre-programmed phone that someone had accessed her phone remotely. The problem with the sting she was working on was that she couldn't tell who accessed her phone, and it might be a year before anyone used the account information that was stolen. That was why she was there though. To identify and stop the thief. Over a thousand credit card identities had been stolen from this geographic area in the last year. When her phone stopped blinking, she looked up to see the young blonde woman packing her stuff.

The FBI agent followed the woman at a distance and saw her get into the van. But she was shocked when she saw a young man drive away. She overcame her shock in the nick of time to catch the license plate number. Unfortunately, she parked too far away to follow the van.

Chapter 3

Every Friday, at one thirty in the afternoon, The Bookkeeper ran a report to send to his clients. His job was to maintain accounts of emergency funds for some of the largest crime organizations in the world.

Only he knew where the money was and how to get it. He had conceived this idea over twenty years before. His oldest client had expressed concern about keeping all his money in real banks. It could be traced, and seized by law enforcement agencies. The Bookkeeper had suggested a solution, and before he realized it, he was in business.

His system set up shell corporations and anonymous accounts in tax havens all over the world. They paid him well to watch over these accounts. On several occasions his clients were arrested and their funds frozen. They contacted him, and he arranged to provide them with fake loans of their funds to use for legal defenses and to live on. Since it was their money, no interest was charged on the loans and whether they paid it back was their choice. He made sure they had money when they weren't supposed to have money.

He had planned well, though. Expecting that something like this might happen someday, he had purchased the best forensic software that wasn't on the market. The U.S. Government developed this software for various government agencies. It tracked terrorist accounts. It was also used to trace computer actions back to their source. He conducted most of his business in tax-haven countries. He stored most of his software and information in a cloud-based computer system located in Paris. There were duplicate backups in the Cayman Islands and Washington D.C.

The software program, which he had nicknamed Guardian, was always running in the background. It could follow most transactions made from his accounts, provided he entered the account information into his computer. It tracked it electronically wherever it went.

The Bookkeeper knew the NSA had written the software and used it to track the accounts of terrorist organizations. Some of his clients were terrorist organizations, but he had been assured the NSA was not watching him handle his money.

Never in twenty years had anyone touched the accounts but himself. Today was different. Today was the day someone had dared to track his accounts. They stole his money, one hundred and fifty million dollars of the over five hundred million he managed. He was angry, but like a boxer before the fight, he was anxious to try out his software program. He had paid five million dollars for the program, and it had better work.

It did work. It took thirty minutes to track his money from fifteen accounts through five financial institutions around the world. It all stopped in one account in Hong Kong. Then it disappeared. The money was withdrawn from the account without a trace.

It wasn't his money, but he thought of it that way because it was his job to watch over it. He wanted to know who had found the money and who had the balls to steal it.

After fifteen more minutes, he had the IP address of the computer that had transferred his money. After a few more minutes, he had all the information he needed. He picked up his smartphone and placed a call.

"I need a favor," he said. A lot of people owed him favors. They would even kill people to pay off those favors. The name rang a bell in his memory. He'd known someone by that name long ago.

Chapter 4

There is an old Yiddish saying, 'Man plans and God laughs'. Mike had talked to his faculty advisor earlier that afternoon; the FBI wanted his resume. He hadn't scheduled any interviews through the career placement office during his last semester of college. He knew what he was going to do when he graduated. The plan was to go back home with his best friend and roommate, take over the family business, and grow it into a huge international success. But now, he thought, God was laughing because an intriguing option had been thrown his way.

He sat at his desk in the bedroom of his apartment and wondered about his future. Most graduating seniors spent part of their last semester updating and changing their resumes. Then they interviewed for the job that would be the first step in their career. Mike thought he already had the next step. That was until he had the interview with Special Agent Carson of the FBI.

Mike's advisor had set up the interview. The FBI needed graduates who understood international finance and who were good with computers for their Cyber Crimes division. Mike was an international finance major, with an interest in computers. It was a plus that he could speak two foreign languages and had a 3.95 GPA. Special Agent Carson had explained that they needed people who could help them track money. Drug money and terrorist money moved around a lot. It was hard to shut down these operations when the money could not be tracked down. The FBI needed young graduates, like Mike, who were patriotic, smart, and most of all, computer literate.

"Your country needs you, Mike. Yes, I know it sounds corny, but it's true," Agent Carson had said.

He had decided to find out more. Submit the resume. Do the second interview, and then decide what he would do.

"Mike, are you going out with us tonight? Graduation is in two days. It's time for you to relax and finally have some fun," his roommate, Bobby said.

"I don't have time to go out, I have a resume to work on, and I have to study for my last final," replied Mike.

Bobby stepped into the doorway of Mike's bedroom. "Man, you've had three dates the whole time you've been in college."

"Four!" Mike moaned with his hand over his face. "I came here to get my degree, not to party. Besides, what does having four dates have to do with going to a party?"

Most of the women he met at college had turned him off. They seemed to be there to major in catching a husband, not in getting a real degree. The ones who were there to get a real degree didn't seem to notice guys at all. They were like him, focused on their classes. Mike hadn't been looking for a girlfriend or a potential wife and never thought about it until he met Jess.

"Yeah, well, I came here to party and I'm getting my degree the same day you are," laughed Bobby. "Angela is bringing Jess. When's the last time you saw her?" Bobby asked, grabbing Mike's attention.

Mike didn't tell Bobby that he and Jess considered themselves dating now. They had lunch last week. It was a working lunch, though, not a date. Their schedules had not worked out so they could see each other during finals, but they'd kept in touch.

Jess was about five feet six inches tall; she was thin with all the curves a young lady was supposed to have. But she didn't show them off like most young women. She considered herself a computer nerd. She dressed the part, often wearing baggy jeans or even sweats, but she didn't look like one. She had long curly blonde hair and beautiful blue eyes. Eyes that looked right through him and seemed to read his every thought.

He smiled, remembering the first time he had seen her. She was a cute blonde who seemed out of place in a computer programming class. He had noticed her on the first day of school. He then found himself sitting beside her in the computer lab after class. He offered to help her that first day, but it turned out that she knew her stuff and had helped him. After that first day, they sat beside each other in class and the computer lab. They talked about their assignments and what they thought the professor expected. She was right most of the time. He had, at first, attributed it to her being a computer science major, unlike him. But when it came to programming, she was a genius.

Two of his four college dates had been with Jess, and they had remained very close. They decided to cool the dating to focus on classes and a personal programming project that he was helping her with. They texted each other several times a day on an app that Jess had written during that class. He had wondered at the beginning why Jess would need his help at all. She explained that writing computer software was easy, but making sure it did exactly what it was supposed to do was the difficult part. So, she wrote code and he researched and inserted the detailed information and checked the output. If Jess was attending the party, it meant she'd completed the project. And it was time to test the program.

Now that they were both graduating, it was also time for him to tell her how he felt about her. He hoped she felt the same way. He was pretty sure the feeling was mutual. They each had had one more semester left and they had both promised themselves that they would get their degrees. They would avoid the other distractions that college and being around thousands of other young people their age could cause. They may not have dated, but they had regular lunches and talked every day. Jess was a talented programmer and was thinking about graduate school.

"Mike, I'm leaving in twenty minutes."

"All right, all right, I'm hitting the shower. Don't leave without me."

Mike reminisced as he took his shower. He and Bobby had been best friends since grade school. They were both good-looking, athletic, and made good grades. Both were over six feet tall and about two hundred pounds, mostly muscle. Bobby was the outgoing one, which was surprising considering he was half Black and half Cherokee and attended an almost all-white school. In high school, he always asked girls out on dates and usually got the girls to go out with him. Sometimes, he could even talk the ones with boyfriends into going out with him. That got him into several altercations with jealous and protective boyfriends. Mike was the smarter one, but not by much. He was equally at home in a locker room full of jocks or a classroom full of computer nerds. While Mike focused on his studies, Bobby and Angela studied together and spent time doing the things that young couples do when they are in love.

Angela was Mike's little sister and Bobby's girlfriend. She was also the only girl who had ever managed to keep Bobby in a monogamous relationship for more than two weeks. That was saying a lot since they had been together ever since Angela had started college two years ago. Mike believed there had been something going on for much longer, though. Because she was his little sister, she had often played with Mike and Bobby as children and hung out with them as teenagers. Angela had always said she was lucky to have two big brothers looking out for her.

Back in high school, they had dreamed of playing football in college. But the scholarship offers that they knew would come to them by the dozens, never came. Their coach told them that it was hard to get scholarship offers for players on teams that only managed to go 5-5. He said winning is impressive, losing is not impressive, and being average is even worse. But things had worked out. They had started a small business in high school together, and it generated enough money to pay their way through college without having to borrow student loans.

Twenty minutes later, as they walked out of their apartment, Mike's phone buzzed. He read the text message from a professor and frowned.

"That's strange!" he said to Bobby. "Dr. Haygood texted me saying I need to be in his office at 7:30 a.m. tomorrow if I want to graduate. I haven't had him since I had that class with Jess last semester."

"Maybe Jess will have an idea about what's going on," Bobby replied.

"Why would she know?" Mike asked, as his phone buzzed again. He looked at his phone to see that Jess had texted him on their private app.

"Shit! Jess got the same message."

He texted her back that he got the same message and they would talk at the party. He would see her in a few minutes.

***

Jess was in her car in front of Angela's dormitory waiting for her, when she got the text from Dr. Haygood. She had no idea what was going on. She wasn't guilty of cheating or anything like that. She didn't need to cheat. She didn't think she was a genius, but she wasn't afraid of a little hard work either. Her parents had taught her early on that work came before play. And the smarter you worked, the more time you had to play. She texted Mike to tell him about Dr. Haygood's message. She was more than a little surprised at Mike's response that he had gotten the same message. She was happy that he would be at the party, but something was going on. She didn't know what it was, but it wasn't good to be threatened with not graduating.

Angela came jogging out of her dorm, waving at Jess with one hand and holding her dress down with the other before Jess could think about it anymore. Angela opened the car door, took one look at Jess, and asked, "What's wrong?"

"Get in. I'll tell you on the way."

Jess wanted to see Mike. She never meant to fall in love, but she and Mike had too much chemistry. They both agreed that too many students didn't come to college to get an education as much as they did to party. Getting their degrees was a priority for them. They had accomplished that now, so why not see where this attraction took them?

Angela was very pretty and resembled her brother if you looked closely. She was tall for a woman, five foot ten inches, with the lean athletic body of someone who stayed very active. Jess and Mike had spent a lot of time together last semester and had often eaten lunch together with Angela and Bobby in the student union. She had enjoyed those lunches and the feeling of closeness that the three of them shared. They were family. Mike and Angela were brother and sister and the two of them had known Bobby since grade school. Because Mike accepted Jess as a friend, they accepted her as well. Angela had become something like the little sister she never had. Angela was living in an on-campus residence hall, while the other three all lived off campus. Jess had made it a point to have lunch with Angela once a week to keep up with her and Mike.

Jess explained the text to Angela on the way to the party at the student union. She was confused, but not worried. What confused her was why Dr. Haygood wanted to meet with her and Mike at the same time. Angela suggested that it might have something to do with the project that she and Mike had been working on all semester.

Jess looked at Angela and asked, "How did you know about that? Dr. Haygood shouldn't know about it either."

Angela replied, "I'm not dumb, nor am I deaf or blind. I can see that you two are in love, and my brother spent a lot of time programming this semester and wasn't taking a programming class. Also, he's never had two dates with the same girl before and continued to stay in daily contact with her."

Jess looked at her, dumbfounded, and said, "I see." She turned to keep her eyes on the road and said, "He's never had a second date with anyone but me?"

"Never!" Angela replied.

Jess smiled and decided not to hide her feelings anymore. They had gotten closer recently, but they hadn't made any commitments.

They made it to the student union, where the graduation party was before the guys did. It was a sunny day with a nice cool breeze, so they waited out front for them and listened to the strains of Bruno Mars playing in the background.

The students joked that this was the pre-party. It was the university's way of trying to keep students from leaving campus and getting drunk. They managed to get a lot of students to come because they gave out a lot of prizes and gifts every year. But, by ten o'clock, over half of the students in attendance would leave and go to Dickson Street and Greek parties. The real parties. It was also a semi-formal party, meaning that guys were expected to wear at least a tie and sports coat, and the women were expected to wear dresses. The reasoning behind the attire was to get the graduates ready for the formal attire of the workplace. Although, American society is much less formal now.

Mike and Bobby found the women waiting by the fountain in front of the student union. The guys wore their khakis and blue blazers with white button-down shirts and blue and maroon ties respectively. Jess wore a stylish little black dress, fitted to show all her curves. Angela wore a knee-length red dress. Angela ran to Bobby and gave him a quick kiss while saying hi to her brother. She quickly turned with Bobby's arm around her to watch Mike and Jess. They walked to each other, embraced, and kissed passionately enough to make Bobby say in a joking manner, "Get a room!"

Mike and Jess looked into each other's eyes and smiled. It was like a whole conversation had passed between them without a word. She knew they would not keep themselves away from each other any longer.

"We need to talk about Haygood," Jess said. "But let's go inside and see if we can have a little fun first."

After they signed into the party, they walked around the student union, signing up for door prizes. They could also play games at which they won tickets to for chances to win more prizes. All four used most of their tickets for a chance to win the latest iPad. Eventually, they ended up in the ballroom. The ballroom was decorated with black and gold streamers and "Congrats,

Grads" banners. They moved to a corner of the dance floor away from the booming speakers where they could hear each other's loud whispers.

After a couple of dances, a slow song came on and Mike pulled Jess closer. He leaned his head over until his cheek touched her hair. She had dreamed of him holding her like this for a long time.

He spoke softly. "I hate to spoil the fun, but what is going on with Dr. Haygood?"

"Let's enjoy this dance first. Okay?"

Her body wanted to hold him close for a very long time. But her mind was a tornado of scattered thoughts about Mike, Haygood, graduation, and her plans for graduate school. Mike didn't argue, though, and leaned down to kiss her on top of the head. She looked up into his eyes and kissed him passionately.

The slow song ended. The DJ started playing *Old Town Road*, by Little Nas X and Billy Ray Cyrus. Mike and Jess looked at each other. Mike shook his head and led Jess across the dance floor to the door. They found the refreshment table and while Mike got two cups of punch, she selected several cookies for them to share. They worked their way outside to the balcony which overlooked the school's sports complexes, affording a view of the football stadium and the colorful landscaping around the ticket booths. They found a location away from other students and took a few minutes to drink their punch and eat a cookie.

They sat in silence, holding hands for a few minutes, staring at the stars that were becoming visible over the school's football stadium. Jess took her phone out of her little clutch purse, turned it off, and laid it on the table.

She looked over at Mike and mouthed the words, "Let me see your phone."

He handed her his cell phone and she promptly turned it off and laid it on the table beside hers.

Then she whispered, "No one, not even Google, can hear us now."

***

Mike raised his eyebrows at her. Jess told him to scoot his chair closer to hers. He wasn't sure how he could get much closer, but somehow, he managed to do it. He put his arm around her shoulder, thinking this was what she wanted when she leaned her head on his shoulder. Whenever they were together, they would talk about anything and everything. It felt odd being quiet for even a little while. But he could tell Jess was thinking hard because she was biting her lower lip like she did when she was stumped by a programming error. When she finally spoke, she had a strange tone to her voice.

"Look down the balcony and tell me what you see."

He said, "I see five couples and one guy standing at the rail."

Before he could continue, Jess said, "Exactly, I saw that same guy when I left Angela's dorm, again in front of the student union, in the ballroom, and now here.

"I believe he's following me. Mike, this afternoon, I found a tracer on one of the emails we were sending back and forth. That's why I haven't sent anything back to you. The programs are finished and I think someone else knows about them and wants them."

Mike asked, "Is that what Haygood wants?"

"I don't know," she replied.

"Wait! You said programs, as in more than one?"

She nodded. "They are almost identical, except that one has a lot more encryption and password protocols than the first."

Chapter 5

The Bookkeeper smiled and caressed his beard. His software program had traced the theft of his money back to a college student in Fayetteville, Arkansas. His contacts had people there and he was assured they would have her picked up and talking within the hour. He would have his money back within twenty-four hours and life would go back to normal.

The Bookkeeper felt the need to relieve some of the stress he was feeling. He smiled to himself. He knew just the thing.

The man had only one vice. It was true he liked to sip a good bourbon every now and then, but he could do without that. His real vice was something much worse.

He stood up from his computer and walked to his fireplace. Under the mantle was a button. The button released a secret door beside the fireplace which led to a hidden hallway. The hallway had two doors on the left and two doors on the right.

The two rooms on the left consisted of a playroom and a film studio. The first door on the right held a small bedroom. The second door hid a stairwell.

He went to the bedroom and unlocked the deadbolt on the door. The young boy in the bedroom was around eight or nine. He had long black hair down to his shoulders. He sat on the single bunk bed wearing pajamas that were too large. He looked up from his coloring book when The Bookkeeper entered the room. He did not speak until spoken to. That was the first rule Johnny was taught. There were lots of rules, with complete obedience being the primary one.

The Bookkeeper had bought the boy from his drug-addicted mother two months ago for two hundred dollars. He had learned years ago that buying kids from their parents was much easier and safer than kidnapping them. Parents never admitted to selling their kids.

"Hi Johnny, how's the coloring today?"

***

Johnny knew he could talk now. "Good," he replied.

Johnny knew what was coming. It was easier to do what the man wanted than to fight or argue. He still had bruises from his last beating two weeks before.

"Would you like to do me a favor, Johnny?" The Bookkeeper asked.

Johnny didn't want to, but he nodded his head yes. He usually gave Johnny a treat when he did what he wanted.

"Would you like for me to suck your lollipop?" Johnny asked.

"That would be fine Johnny. That would be really fine."

Chapter 6

Benji's eyes were red and his face was puffy. He had spent most of the afternoon with caseworkers from the Department of Human Services. They were taking David to a foster home. He would have liked to let David stay with him. The case workers even considered it until they got a call from their office. David's mother had slipped into a coma and they weren't sure she would survive the night. That made David a ward of the state. David did not want to go, but Benji promised he would check on him.

He was now at the NWA Psychiatric Hospital. He had missed his afternoon appointment to visit with his friend Staci. Normally, it would have been a week before he could return to see her. But the case worker from DHS had called and explained why Benji couldn't make it there on time.

Staci was like a sister from a part of his life that neither of them wanted to remember.

"What's wrong Benji? You've been crying."

He nodded.

"My neighbor overdosed today. I've looked after her son several times when she had to work late. DHS came and took him away. That's why I missed our afternoon appointment."

Staci said, "I see, were you close to her?"

"No, nothing like that," Benji replied. "I was close to David. He was like me when my mom was using. He needed an adult he could depend on. Strangely enough, that was me."

"Benji the savior strikes again," she said, placing her hand on his and smiling at him.

27

He looked at Staci, sitting at the table across from him. He had found her in St. Louis; she had been near death from drug use and beatings from her pimp. She had been in this hospital for eighteen months going through rehab and counseling.

Their meetings were in the open room where a nurse could monitor them. However, the nurses paid them little attention after the first three or four months. They had learned bits and pieces of Benji and Staci's dark story and admired them for fighting to overcome the abuse they had gone through. Benji knew he was her only visitor.

"Benji, thank you for finding me and saving me. I don't know how you have paid for this, but thank you."

Benji smiled. He wouldn't tell her how he had paid for it. Staci was beautiful now that she was getting well. Her pixie haircut made her eyes look large and her lips appear full. He still remembered the frightened little girl who cried herself to sleep in his arms. He was sure she remembered him trying to be brave and crying too.

"Don't worry about it. I graduate this weekend," Benji said, changing the subject.

"They told me you can leave whenever you feel comfortable. I have a few job interviews set up for the next few weeks so I will be out of town. But when I come back, we can get you out of here. You can live with me until you find a place of your own."

"I'm almost ready, Benji," she said. "I still have nightmares. I want to work with the psychiatrist on ways to deal with them. Then I'll be ready."

They talked a little longer, hugged each other, and said goodbye. He hated the short visits but understood the reasoning behind them.

Chapter 7

Laying on the table in front of them, both Mike and Jess's cell phones turned themselves on.

"What the hell?" Mike said.

"And then there's that!" Jess pointed to the phones. "Mine first did that two hours ago when it locked up and I turned it off. There must be some kind of tracking program on our phones. If I turn it off, it will come on again in ten minutes."

"Let me get this straight. There are trackers on our emails, there may be trackers on our phones, and people are following you. What have you gotten into, Jess? What have you gotten me into?"

He leaned back away from her and looked her straight in the eyes.

"And don't forget, Dr. Haygood is threatening to not let us graduate," she said and sighed heavily. "Mike," she said. "Look at the guy leaning against the rail."

Mike looked and now saw two guys leaning against the rail. They appeared to be talking, but they kept glancing in their direction. Mike thought fast. Could the guys be a coincidence? If it wasn't for everything else that Jess had told him, he would have said yes. Earlier, he was thrilled that they were finally getting together. Now, he was feeling weird, he didn't know what he felt. Upset? Maybe. Afraid? Definitely! At this point, he wasn't willing to take a chance. Jess still had a lot of explaining to do.

There were two sets of double doors leading to and from the balcony. One door was right behind the guys leaning on the railing. It led right back into the party. The other set of doors was a few steps from where he and Jess were sitting, and they led into the food court. Out of the eight vendors, he could only see Starbucks and Pizza Hut still open. He hoped there were other vendors open. And a lot more people.

"We have to get out of here," Jess said.

Mike grabbed his phone and said, "Leave that to me, or rather Bobby and Angela."

He was already texting Bobby and Angela. *Wingman. Need distraction. Nd u 2 on balcony. 2 guys on the rail, meet @ Bens 1 hr. Ditch ur phones b4.*

Jess read the message as he typed and hit send.

"Will they understand that?"

"They'll understand. I'm more worried about when they will get the message, so we will have to wait and be ready. You might want to take your heels off."

She had barely gotten her shoes off, when Bobby staggered through the doors backward, yelling, "What the hell, Angela?"

Mike and Jess started to move, but not before Bobby ducked a thrown water bottle. The bottle hit one of the two guys in the back of the head. Angela screamed something about him looking at other girls.

"Damn, that looked real! I've only seen them fight one time before," Mike said, as they ducked through the door.

The food court vendors shared a large common seating area. It had tables and chairs and little islands with trash cans and fake plants and trees for decoration. There were restrooms and a locker area on one side in the middle of four vendors. Across from the restrooms, between the other four vendors, was an exit door used for deliveries. About forty people were in the food court. Not as many as Mike had hoped for.

Mike said to Jess, "Give me your phone, I'll meet you at the delivery exit."

She gave him a quizzical look, but she gave him her phone. Then she headed for the exit, while he ran to the lockers. They were the kind you put your stuff in and took the key with you until you came back to get your stuff later. They were used often because students didn't want to carry all their books around while they were eating lunch with their friends. He found an empty locker and tossed both phones in. He yanked the key out and dashed across the dining area. The door closed behind him and Jess.

Jess grabbed Mike's hand. "My car is over here in the M lot."

"No," Mike said. "We'll take the bus. There's probably some kind of tracker on your car by now as well."

She squeezed his hand, looked at him, and said, "Now, I'm really getting scared."

"Put your shoes back on."

He took his blazer off and draped it over her shoulders and they headed to the bus stop in front of the student union. It wasn't cold outside, but those men would be looking for a man in a blazer, not a white shirt. And in the growing dusk and the light of the sidewalk lamps, it would be difficult to tell that Jess had his blue blazer on over her black dress. It was a small difference, but sometimes that was all it took.

They stood against the building, away from the bus stop, thinking in silence. The bus they were waiting on ran every five minutes. It should be there soon, but not soon enough, they felt. Two minutes seemed like an eternity. As soon as they saw the bus coming, they moved to the curb. They let two girls off the bus before getting on. They took a seat in the middle of the bus and on the side away from the student union. Mike hoped they had managed to escape the two men.

The bus they rode made a loop around the campus. The main campus was on one side of the route. Apartment complexes and businesses that depended on the student population were on the other side. Jess leaned against Mike and apologized for getting him into this unexplained mess. She looked up at him expectantly, waiting for him to say something. He remained silent, not able to voice his thoughts, with so many running through his head. He gave her a quick smile and a gentle kiss on the forehead and put his index finger over his lips indicating she should be quiet for now. After their escape, he knew she wanted to talk, to get everything out in the open. He had a good idea of what was going on now, but he had no idea how to deal with it. He hadn't planned for something like this.

After four stops, they got off the bus. Jess asked, "Where are we going?"

"A little place called Ben's Bar and Grill. Bobby and I are friends with the owner's son. They converted a huge old house into a bar and restaurant. The bar is on the first floor, and the restaurant seats its guests in several different rooms on the second floor. There's a good chance we can get a quiet room upstairs where we can talk. We eat there often, it's two blocks from campus and about a block from our apartment. Their menu brags of the best burgers in town and beer as cold as your ex's heart."

He looked down at Jess to see that his last comment brought a smile to her face. "I don't know about you, but I'm starving," Mike said.

They turned up the sidewalk to the front of the restaurant. It had a wraparound porch that served as a kind of lobby when the place was busy. It was nearly nine, so while the bar was packed, there was no one waiting for tables upstairs.

Mike opened the door for Jess and followed her in. His friend Ben, or more accurately, Ben Jr., was working as the host that evening. Ben looked up to see Mike and Jess.

"Good evening, Mike, your party is waiting for you upstairs in the steamboat room."

Mike stopped immediately and nervously said, "My party?"

"Yeah, man! Your sister and Bobby got here a few minutes ago."

Ben must have seen the relief show on both faces because he began to chuckle. "Come on, I'll walk up with you."

Before he moved, he looked at Jess and gave a big bow. In his best, or worst, British accent he said, "Good evening, my lady, Benjamin Franklin Matthews, Jr. at your service. Ben to you and my close friends. If Mike doesn't treat you like a gentleman, let me know, and I'll take him out back and whip him into shape."

"Now, Ben, you know you couldn't take me," Mike said. Ben was about five foot five and might weigh a hundred and fifty pounds. He knew what Ben's response would be.

"Of course, I could, Mike. Me and my two bouncers would have no trouble taking you." Ben laughed and headed upstairs ahead of them near the end of a hall. It must have been a child's bedroom long ago, before the place became a bar and grill. The room was decorated with pictures of steamboats and even had an old steamboat whistle standing in one corner of the room. There was just enough room for a table and chairs to seat six people, even though it would only be used for four tonight.

Angela jumped up immediately upon seeing them. She stepped forward to hug them both and ask about the guys at the student union.

"Jess thought one of them was following her today. So, we thought we would use a distraction and shake him."

Bobby jumped in then and said, "They were following you, all right. As soon as they got out of the way of our little fight, they looked where you had been, and took off running. They ran straight to the food court and lost you. We followed them and watched one pull out his phone and they both took off toward the restrooms."

Angela picked up the story. "One of the guys went into the men's room and the other one stood outside the ladies' room until the first one came back."

"It didn't take them long to figure out that you dumped your phones in the lockers and took off. They must have been tracking your phones somehow. One of them ran out of the food court back toward the ballroom, while the other one ran out the delivery door on the other side," Bobby added.

Angela took up the story again. "That's when we headed straight to the car and came here. Where did you two go?"

Their waiter showed up then, to take their drink orders. The guys ordered a local favorite craft beer, and the women ordered diet sodas. Angela wasn't twenty-one yet, and Jess didn't want her to be the only one not drinking beer.

"Go ahead and bring us four classics," Mike said.

"What's a classic?" Jess asked.

Angela responded first. "Only the best hamburger and fry combo in the world. Now, you two tell us what is going on."

***

Angela and Bobby looked at Mike. Mike looked at Jess and she sighed. She knew she could trust them, but she couldn't tell them everything.

"Okay! I promised myself I would never tell anyone this while I was in college. Please don't tell anyone what I'm about to tell you. People treat me differently when they know."

Mike raised his eyebrows and asked, "Know what? I know you're very smart, gorgeous, and I don't want to ever go another day without being with you. Nothing you say can change that."

Jess blushed. "A lot of people say the same thing, but after a while, the fact that my father was a millionaire changes the way they view me. They begin thinking I should buy them everything they want because they think I'm rich. My parents started out poor and saved their money. They managed a struggling construction company, put a little money in the bank each year, grew the company a little each year, and became wealthy."

"Sort of a *Millionaire Next Door*," said Bobby, mentioning a book Mike's dad had made them read after starting their business in high school.

"Exactly!" Jess replied with a relieved smile on her face.

"But Jess," Mike said, "we already knew that much."

Jess continued, "Just before my dad passed away, he created a trust fund for me with a million dollars in it. It's managed by a trust company until I turn twenty-five or graduate from college. I don't have complete access to it, but people still think of *me* as a millionaire."

She looked at Mike with a hopeful expression.

Bobby spoke up. "Don't worry about Mike, he doesn't like money! Remember Bridgette?"

Mike hung his head, and his sister smiled and said, "Oh, yeah!"

Bobby said, "She was a girl from high school. Her father owned the franchise for some fast-food company and had ten to twelve stores. She was very pretty, very popular, very rich and she knew it. And." He drew the word out for emphasis. "She wanted Mike for her boyfriend."

Mike looked up and finished the story. "She was a bore! She could only talk about herself and what she had bought or was going to buy."

Angela added, "Our parents taught us that money can't buy relationships. It might fix a lot of problems, but it will never fulfill you like a good relationship will." She looked Jess in the eyes, hoping she understood her meaning.

Bobby broke the ice. "But it can buy a lot of classic combos."

Right on cue, the door opened to their private room and their waiter brought in their food.

There were four plates piled high with fries. The long thin kind that little kids liked to play with and dab into piles of ketchup and hold up high and tilt their heads back and lower the fries into their mouth. The waiter served the ladies first, then the guys, and finally set four empty plates in front of them.

Jess looked at the plate of fries with her mouth wide and then the empty plate and asked, "Where's the burger?"

The others laughed, and Mike showed her by picking up some of the fries from his full plate and putting them on the empty plate. "Hidden under the fries, my dear."

After eating a few bites and after the waiter left, Bobby asked, "So how does being a millionaire have anything to do with Dr. Haygood, or the guys following you tonight?"

Jess set her fork down. She looked like she had lost her appetite.

"It doesn't. But I had to tell you that, so I could tell you the rest of the story."

She picked up her fork, stabbed a long fry and held it up, and eyed it for a moment before taking a bite and chewing it.

She took a sip of diet soda, glanced at Mike, and said, "I wouldn't tell you this if I didn't already feel like part of your family. All the time we spent together last semester tells me I can trust you."

Mike put his hand on hers and smiled. Jess smiled back at him.

"Here we go," she said. "When I was two years old, my dad's construction company was having a rough year. He barely kept it running. He was outbid on every project. Then he won two bids to build two big strip malls. He had never done anything that big, much less run two large projects at the same time. He went to his bank to borrow money and they turned him down because of his lack of experience and lack of collateral. He tried several banks and they all turned him down for the same reason. One of his old high school buddies owned several pawn shops and several quick loan places. The kind of place you go to borrow money at high-interest rates. Dad invited his friend to lunch one day and told him the situation. His friend said he couldn't legally loan him that kind of money through his business. But he took a business card out of his pocket, wrote a number on the back of it, and gave it to my father. He told him that if he would cut him in for ten percent of the profit, he could use that to finance his construction projects. It was a numbered bank account in Belize, with ten million dollars in it. My dad asked him if he could think about it and let him know the next day. His friend said sure."

She stopped long enough to take a bite of her burger and sip her diet soda before continuing.

"Soon after that, my dad's friend was killed in a joint DEA and IRS bust. They confiscated everything except the foreign bank account. My dad waited two weeks for the Feds to come knocking on his door. They never came, and he used the money and built the two strip malls and many other projects. That was twenty years ago and the money stayed there until yesterday."

Mike stopped with a fry halfway to his mouth and asked, "What happened to the money yesterday?"

Jess looked at him with a little fear in her eyes. "I moved it. Using the software that you and I wrote."

Chapter 8

"Shit!" Bobby said. "Y'all wrote a program to steal ten million dollars?"

"Closer to twenty million. My dad repaid his debt to his high school friend. He didn't know what to do with the ten percent cut. So, each time he completed a project, he deposited it back into the numbered account. And I didn't steal anything. I moved it to protect it. Someone, besides my mom and I, has been checking on the account. I think they were planning to steal it."

"Whose money is it then? Where did it come from?" Angela asked.

"Did your dad's friend have any heirs? Who else knew about the money? And again, how does this relate to Dr. Haygood and these two goons?"

"I'm getting there," Jess said. "Newspaper reports said the guy was a money launderer for drug dealers. He used pawn shops and small loan businesses to move lots of cash. So, the money was probably drug money. I've found no information about who the drug dealers were or anything. According to my mother, my dad and his friend talked about their daughters. We believe he has a daughter, but we've never found her."

Jess stopped to take a sip of her soda. She started again. "On who knows about the account. I would guess that the bankers would have known since Dad used it as collateral, but it's been years since he used it. It's possible that our attorney or the CPA firm that we used knew about it. I'm not sure."

She stopped as if thinking about other possibilities and then shook her head.

"I have no idea what Haygood wants. I've used my student account from last semester to gain access to some of the coding resources we used."

"I've done that, too, especially the security information," Mike added.

They all sat in silence thinking of questions and possibilities. Angela was always good at asking the tough questions. She had a way of getting down to the core of the problem. Angela, Mike, and Bobby had evaluated countless paper topics and debated politics many times. They schemed up many schemes in their childhood. It was Angela who always asked the obvious questions and then started to drill down to the less obvious.

Angela asked, "What are you two going to do about your phones? You can't use them if they are being tracked."

"Temporary burner phones, for now?" Mike replied, more as a question than as an answer.

Jess added, "I think our emails are being tracked also."

Mike said, "A new email account could bypass that. But you wouldn't have access to your school emails or other personal emails."

"Enough!" Angela said. "We still don't have a good idea of who we," she hesitated, looking at Jess, "really you, are dealing with. You're assuming this is about the money. But it may not be about the money at all. Could it be about your app? Is there anything else you haven't thought about yet? Is it possible the other guy was following Mike and Bobby?"

Jess had a blank look on her face. "I don't know."

Angela looked at Mike and then Bobby, "Did either of you notice the other guy before you got to the student union?"

Bobby said, "No, we were running late, and then Mike got the text from Dr. Haygood. So, we were pretty distracted. Didn't notice a thing. We were flying low and trying not to mow any pedestrians down."

Angela poked Bobby in the ribs and said, "This is serious. We know that you're being followed. We've all seen the two guys. Jess is certain her emails are tagged, and your phones have trackers, as well. That means that mine and Bobby's may also. That's why you wanted us to leave them behind. Right?"

When Angela stopped, Jess added, "Mike suggested we take the bus, because my car might have a tracker on it."

"Shit! What about my car?" Bobby asked.

"Let's hope not," Mike said.

Angela gave everyone a hard look that said *let's hurry up and get out of here.* "What we don't know is who they are and why they are following you. Or, if it has anything to do with Dr. Haygood."

"How do we find out?" Jess responded.

Mike had his right elbow on the table and pointed his index finger in the air.

"First, we need our phones back. Angela, we need you and Bobby to go get our phones."

He dug into his pants pocket to get the locker key out before continuing.

"When you open the locker, turn the phones off. You'll have about ten minutes before they turn themselves on again. Jess and I will take the bus to the computer lab next to the campus police station. We will meet you there."

The campus buildings that had computer labs were closed. They were locked by 1:00 a.m. and didn't open again until 7:00 a.m. The police station was open twenty-four hours a day, seven days a week, and the computer lab was also. Mike figured no one would bother them there.

"You two go ahead. I'll get the check and see you there. Jess and I'll try to come up with a plan on the way."

As they were getting up from the table, their waiter came in and closed the door. He said, "Ben said to tell you that two guys are downstairs asking about you. As soon as I walk out of this room, he will have the bouncers throw them out. He said to leave through the kitchen and you can settle the bill later."

Bobby grinned, reached over, and slapped the waiter on the back.

"Thanks, Mike over there will be sure and tip you well for your help."

The waiter looked confused for a minute, then shrugged and grinned. "Turn right, the stairs are on the left, you'll come out in the back of the kitchen." The waiter turned and left.

Mike said, "Let's stick with the plan. It took them over an hour to find us. Let's go."

They slipped out the back door, and Bobby and Angela went to his car. Jess and Mike walked toward the bus stop. There were two men in dark clothing following them.

Chapter 9

Mike glanced at Jess in the dim light from the street lamps and said, "Now it's my turn for a little confession. Angela, Bobby, and I own part of a small business, with my parents owning the rest. Remember the touchscreen calendar in my apartment? And the electronic photo screens that changed pictures frequently?"

"Yes."

Mike continued, "We own the patent for the calendar, and have agreements in place for the photo frames. We distribute them in the US, and across much of Europe. It was Angela's idea and Bobby and I put it together. My parents run the company for us. We have a pretty good net worth. But not a lot of cash flow after paying business expenses, paying college expenses for the three of us, and paying our parents to run the business."

"So, my trust fund doesn't bother you much," Jessica observed.

"Not at all," he replied, squeezing her hand. "We don't tell many people about our business either."

"Good. How do we find out what's going on?" she asked Mike.

"Did you try to find out who tagged our emails?"

"Yes, and I didn't find anything. It's like it sends a blind carbon copy and then immediately deletes the record."

"Did your dad ever try to find his friend's daughter?" Mike asked.

"He must have," Jess said. "I was two or three then, so I obviously don't remember. But I can ask my mother. I'll call her tomorrow morning. I do know my dad used the money for his projects. He continued to pay ten percent of each deal into the account when he used it. He must not have found anything. There were either no heirs or he couldn't find anyone."

"Mike, I need to tell you something else," Jess said.

They reached the bus stop and Mike turned and drew Jess into his arms. He peeked over her shoulder before bending to kiss her. After softly kissing her lips, he moved his mouth up to her ear and whispered, "We have company."

She hugged him tighter and wondered what she had gotten them into. Mike chuckled, "My mistake, it's a couple of frat boys out for a jog."

He didn't see the two shadows get into a car following along behind them with the headlights off. After the scare, he forgot that Jess had been about to tell him something.

They remained silent on the bus ride. Jess leaned her head against Mike's chest and he wrapped his arm around her. It would have been a pleasant ride if they could have enjoyed the time they were spending with each other. Instead, his mind was asking too many questions, and not coming up with enough answers. If this had been a final exam, he would be failing. There were six stops before they reached the campus police station which housed the twenty-four-hour computer lab. The bus route was a big loop around campus so they had to stop at the student union again. He was surprised to see Angela stick her head through the doors of the bus, look for them, and get on when she spotted them.

She handed Mike his phone. "Someone broke into the locker. Jess's phone was gone. Mine and Bobby's were still there in another locker. Bobby has gone to Walmart to get us some cheap burner phones. We thought it would be safer if we all used different phones for a few days." She hesitated for a few seconds before continuing. "It looks like they are only interested in Jess and what's on her phone." She looked at Jess. "You're part of the family now, so we are all in this together." Before Jess could say anything, Angela looked at her brother. She said, "Mike, you better check your phone."

Mike did as his sister told him. "Whoa!" he replied. There were at least twenty missed messages and calls on his phone. All were from Dr. Haygood. They all said, "Mike where are you? Have you seen Jess? Call me immediately!"

Jess and Angela were looking on from both sides. Jess looked like she was getting sick. "Call him, I need some answers. *We* need some answers!"

Mike dialed the number from the last call, which was five minutes earlier. He never heard the phone ring on his end. Dr. Haygood answered the phone with a quick, "Hello?"

"Dr. Haygood? This is Mike."

Dr. Haygood answered with a voice that sounded both relieved and worried. "Are you okay? Do you know where Jess is? Where are you?"

Mike had put the phone on speaker, loud enough for the three of them to hear.

"We're fine. Jess is with me. We are on a transit bus on our way to the computer lab next to the campus police station. What's going on Doctor Haygood, what's the urgency?"

The doctor made muffled sounds and then he said, "Good, good! That's actually the safest place for you to be tonight. You are in danger. Mainly Jess, but you also, as long as you are with her."

Jess spoke up then. "Dr. Haygood, what's going on?"

His response surprised them all because he shouted, "Just go! I'll meet you there in a few minutes." He hung up on them.

Jess stared at Mike's phone. Angela jumped into analysis mode. "He sounded very concerned. He did say you are in danger and that you are headed to a safe place. He also said he would meet you there. So, maybe. you can get him to talk there."

Jess asked, "Can we trust him?"

Mike spoke up. "We don't trust anyone, other than the four of us! We need answers, and we start with him."

The bus stopped half a block away from the campus police station in a cloud of diesel smoke and the hiss from air brakes. It was a short walk, almost to the end of the block, then across three double rows of parked cars in a well-lit parking lot. Angela took the lead with Mike and Jess following. Since it was a Friday night, and most students weren't using the computers for school work, the student gaming club took over most of the computers. This meant that the parking lot was full. They cut across the parking lot in a single file line, with Mike in the rear, instead of walking to the end of the block to reach the sidewalk that led to the building. They were cutting through the second row of parked cars when an older model black Buick stopped close to the cars in front of them and blocked their path. Mike heard footsteps behind him and turned.

The second man, from the Student Union, was behind him raising a pistol in his right hand. Mike never considered what he did next. There was no conscious thought about being shot or hurt. He knew he needed to protect himself, his sister, and Jess. There was no training to rely on, there was just his reaction. As the attacker raised the pistol, Mike reached out with his left hand and grabbed it. As Mike started to squeeze the attacker's gun hand, he also swung with his right. The attacker pulled the trigger of the pistol and the hammer fell. It hit Mike's index finger instead of the firing pin, breaking the skin and possibly the bone, causing excruciating pain. As the agony shot through him, it fueled Mike's rage and he hit the guy again and again and again. He pounded him against a student's car, setting off the car alarm.

Angela and Jess stopped where they were. The black Buick had stopped so close to the cars they were walking between, that it barely missed the vehicles. The driver jumped out holding a pistol in his right hand, but he didn't aim it at them. He walked to the front of the Buick and looked at the two young ladies. He started to speak when a car alarm screeched. At the same time, the sound of a car horn and the rev of a small engine came from the thug's left. Jess, Angela, and their attacker all turned toward the car horn. It was an old Honda Civic racing toward the second attacker. The attacker hesitated a second too long before he raised his pistol and shot two times at the oncoming car. It wouldn't have mattered anyway, as the little old Honda slammed into the attacker and the Buick. The attacker dropped the pistol between the two cars and it came to rest at Angela's feet. The airbag had deployed in the little Honda and hid whoever the driver might have been.

The sounds of the car alarm, a car crash, gunshots, and a man screaming in agony brought the students out of the computer lab. The two officers, one white male and one black female, on duty in the station ran out with their hands on their pistols. It was a lot to take in. A head-on collision in a parking lot. A man was trapped between the two cars, screaming in agony, most likely from two broken legs. A blond female standing alone with her hands in the air was looking behind her. The two officers looked confused. As the female officer radioed for backup, Angela stood up holding the pistol the attacker had dropped in front of her. Then Mike stood up holding the pistol from the attacker who came up behind him. The male officer saw the pistols and immediately drew his own. He started yelling, "Drop your weapon! Drop your weapon!" Mike and Angela laid the guns back at their feet and slowly raised their hands in the air.

A third attacker jumped out of the Buick and ran away. Four or five of the computer gamers, who came out to see what was happening, tackled him before he got fifteen feet from the car.

Another computer gamer had approached the Honda Civic. He yelled, "We need an ambulance, Dr. Haygood has been shot."

It was all too much for the two officers to process. The female officer let go of the mic strapped to the shoulder of her uniform and drew her weapon. But she wasn't sure where to point it. The man trapped between the two cars passed out. Without his screams, the only sound was the blaring car alarm.

The female officer shouted, "Can someone shut off that damn car alarm? I need someone to call 911. We need backup, and two ambulances!"

"Three," Mike said. "There's a third man down over here."

One of the computer gamers must have owned the car because the car alarm stopped. The silence seemed to overwhelm everyone until they heard sirens from far away.

Neither officer moved. "What the hell happened here?" asked the female officer, still holding her gun, but not pointing it at anyone.

Angela spoke up. "We were attacked. My brother fought the one who came up behind us. And this car took out the one trapped between the cars." The female officer took charge then.

"Ed, take these three in and lock them in an interrogation room. Then come back and lock up this one over here."

The female officer holstered her pistol. She headed to where the computer gamers were struggling to hold their captive down. It didn't take her long to cuff him and leave him lying face down.

The male officer, Ed, walked around the cars. He kept his pistol pointed at Angela, Jess, and Mike. He moved around behind the car whose alarm had been blaring earlier. The officer stepped around the back of the car, saw the man lying on the pavement, and immediately heaved up everything he had eaten for supper. The attacker's face was bloody. Blood was in his hair. It covered his clothes and the pavement. There was so much blood that it appeared that he had bled to death.

Angela stepped past Jess and Mike. She grabbed the officer by the left arm and turned him away from the man on the pavement. She said, "Ed? You lead the way; we will follow you. We aren't going anywhere. This is the safest place we can be right now. You can put your gun away."

The officer looked at Angela. "Thank you, I'm sorry. I've never seen that much blood before. Is he dead?"

"I hope not. Probably a broken nose and a concussion. He might wake up any time, though."

As they walked away, the officer began to come out of it. He holstered his pistol and led them into the station. The female officer had finally taken charge and sent most of the gamers back to the computer lab. "Make room, I've got ambulances coming."

Angela, Jess, and Mike all looked at the Honda Civic as they walked by. Was he dead? He was supposed to help them find some answers about what was going on. Now, they had even more questions.

The officer led them to an interrogation room. Mike asked if he could wash his hands. The officer almost vomited again when he looked at Mike's hands, but he told him no. That he might need to take pictures of his hands. He left them in the room and went back outside. It had all happened in less than five minutes, but it would take longer than that to straighten out.

They sat quietly for several minutes. They were each trying to make sense of what happened. Angela's phone rang in her purse. She dug it out, looked at the caller ID, and said, "It's Bobby." She answered the phone. Bobby said he couldn't get anywhere near the campus police station. There were a dozen police cars and several ambulances in the parking lot. He wanted to know if she knew what had happened.

Angela said, "We happened! We were attacked. Mike took out one of them, he might have beaten him to death. Dr. Haygood rammed another one with his car and got shot while doing it. We are being held in an interrogation room while they take three men to the hospital."

Bobby's slow response was, "Holy shit!"

Angela came back and said, "More like bloody shit! Would you go to your apartment and get Mike a change of clothes? He has blood all over him. And grab all the spare clothes that I leave over there. Jess and I could stand to get out of these dresses."

Bobby said it would be no problem. And Angela's last statement before clicking off the call was prophetic. "I have a feeling we are going to be here for a while. Thank you, sweetheart and I love you."

Listening to Angela talk to Bobby had brought Jess and Mike out of their fog. Mike was holding his left arm close to his body. His right thumb and index finger were holding his left index finger at the knuckle to stop the blood flow.

"I need to get someone to look at this finger, I'm afraid I may lose it."

Jess looked at his hands for the first time. "Oh, my God, Mike! What did you do?"

Angela got up and moved to him. He responded to Jess while Angela inspected his hand. "I heard the guy come up behind me. I turned around, saw the gun, grabbed his hand, and squeezed. He pulled the trigger and my finger blocked the hammer and kept the gun from firing."

Angela, always the steady one, looked at Mike. "You do need to get this checked right away." She went to the door, found it wasn't locked, and stepped into the hallway, closing the door behind her. She returned a few minutes later with the female officer and a paramedic.

Officer Martin asked Mike to place his hands on the table in front of him. She used her phone to take several pictures of his hands.

The paramedic took one look at Mike's finger. He said, "You need to go to the hospital, but with those three from outside ahead of you, there's going to be a long wait. So, I will see if I can clean you up and hold you over for a couple of hours."

He checked both of Mike's hands and Mike winched when he touched his left hand. He decided to focus on the finger. He opened his bag and took out cleaning swabs and said, "This is going to sting. Be as still as you can." Mike suddenly jumped. The paramedic jumped back. In fact, everyone in the room jumped.

Mike let out a groan, "Unnnhhh! I think you found a nerve."

The paramedic relaxed and said, "I'll stay away from that spot." And he continued cleaning Mike's hand.

"Officer? My name is Angela Brock, this is my brother Mike, and his girlfriend Jessica Benelli. Jess had her cell phone stolen. My boyfriend, Bobby Williams, my brother's roommate, went to the store to buy a cheap replacement phone when we came here. That's why he isn't with us. But he has gone to get us some clothes to change into. We know we are going to be here for a while. We would be much more comfortable if we weren't here in bloody clothes." She pointed at her brother. "And these little party dresses."

Officer Angela Martin didn't smile, but she did seem to relax a little. The campus police department was a fully functional police department. They weren't just security guards. The Fayetteville campus could have thirty thousand students, faculty, and staff on campus at any time. The campus police department was larger and busier than many municipal police departments in the state. Officer Martin had seen a lot of crazy things on campus, but this was a new one.

"I'll see what I can do when he gets here. And thank you for what you did for Ed. He's only been on the job for three weeks. He hasn't even gone to the academy yet. The only training he's had is what I've given him. After tonight, he may be second-guessing his career choice." She smiled and said, "We figured out who you were; the computer geeks told us who Mike and Jessica, or Jess, as they called her, were. We know you're students. What we don't know is who these men are, what's going on, and how the Professor got involved in this." She raised her eyebrows at them.

Mike had his eyes closed. He tilted his head back and grimaced from the alcohol pads the paramedic used to clean his finger. He was holding himself together as much as possible.

Jess and Angela were paying close attention to Officer Martin. Jess started to speak and Officer Martin held up her hand and said, "We will get all that information soon."

But Jess insisted on asking, "How is Dr. Haygood? Is he alive?"

"He was alive, but not coherent when he left in the ambulance," Officer Martin replied.

The paramedic had put a splint on Mike's finger and was wrapping it with gauze and tape. When he finished, he told Mike to get to his doctor or the hospital as soon as possible. Mike said he would.

When the paramedic and Officer Martin had left, Angela moved close to Mike and leaned in and hugged him.

"Always the big brother. Thank you for protecting us, Mike."

Jess reached over and touched Mike's left arm gently. He winced when that little touch sent pain all the way to his bandaged finger. She pulled her hand away, realizing what she had done.

"I'm sorry, Mike. I'm sorry I got everyone involved in this. I can't believe someone came after us with guns."

Angela reached over and pulled Jess into the hug with Mike. She whispered, "It's going to be okay. Now, when they start questioning us, we tell the truth. But we can't mention the twenty million. That would throw lots of suspicion on Jess. Remember, not a word!"

"Mike?" Jess asked.

Mike looked at her but didn't say anything.

"I found the website that had Benji's pictures this morning. I destroyed it. I traced the money and transferred it like you showed me. I think these men are here about that."

Mike snorted and reached for Jess's hand, "Jess, there's no way anyone could track you. You've taken down at least 30 to 40 of these websites. None of them had a clue how to track you. It can't be that."

Jess nodded in agreement. But she wasn't sure. She had never stolen money from anyone's account before.

It had been nearly an hour since Officer Ed had brought them to the interrogation room. Angela and Jess were fidgeting. The adrenaline rush that had helped Mike deal with the pain in his finger vanished after the paramedic had left. It took every ounce of control he had to keep from screaming. Mike was hurting and he would occasionally pound the table with his good hand and he hadn't opened his eyes or spoken in twenty minutes.

Finally, Officer Ed came in carrying three bottles of water and leading Bobby. He said, "Sorry it's taking so long, but that was a big mess to clean up out there. I brought you guys some water and your friend brought you a change of clothes."

Mike finally opened his eyes and spoke. "Do you have any Tylenol or Ibuprofen?"

Ed looked at Mike and said, "I'll see what I can find. The ladies can go change one at a time. The ladies' room on our side of the building is just large enough for one."

He stepped out of the room, leaving the four of them alone. Angela grabbed the clothes and started going through them.

"Jess, I've got some sweats here if you want to change."

Chapter 10

The next two hours were a blur. Bobby said he had talked to some of Jess and Mike's classmates who were playing computer games.

He said, "Two of them helped me set up the phones."

The police made Bobby leave since he hadn't been there during the attack. Officer Martin and Chief Jacobs, the head of the campus police department, were there to interview them. Chief Jacobs wasn't happy that he had to come back on his weekend off, but he didn't take it out on the students. They hadn't asked to be here either. He asked them to tell him everything that had happened to them. He started with Jess. When did she first notice the man following her? Why hadn't they called the police after the incident in the student union? What could they be after? He asked question after question.

When he wasn't happy with the answers he got, he pressed Jess hard until she screamed at him, "I don't know! I wish I did, then I would know what to do! That's why we wanted to meet with Dr. Haygood."

That's when he started asking about Dr. Haygood. How did she know him? How did he fit into this situation? Why was he at the police station? What had they done to make the professor threaten them with not graduating? Why would he tell her she was in danger? Again, she didn't have the answers he wanted.

He turned to Mike, leaned in, and asked, "How's your hand?"

"It hurts like hell!" Mike replied.

"Where did you learn that trick with the pistol?" the chief asked him.

Mike looked up and raised his eyebrows. "What trick?"

The chief replied, "Getting part of your hand between the firing pin and the hammer is an old close-quarters combat trick. Hurts like hell, but it can save your life. It looks like that trick and a solid right hook saved at least one life tonight if not all of you."

Mike asked quietly, "You think they wanted to kill us?"

The chief leaned back and took a deep breath. "Anytime guns are involved, someone can get hurt. Your friend, Dr. Haygood, is a prime example. You haven't given me a motive yet. Why would armed men, connected with illegal drugs, come after Miss Benelli here with guns?"

"Drugs?" Jess asked.

The chief nodded. "Now, don't get me wrong. I don't believe any of you are involved in drugs. Most students who are into drugs come to our attention very early. But there must be some reason why they would target you. Your backgrounds check out. Your school records and transcripts are too clean for you to be in anything illegal."

Jess finally sighed, "Okay!"

Angela gave her a warning look, but she continued anyway.

"My father was in the construction business. He passed away two years ago. But at one point he almost lost the business. He may or may not have borrowed some money from a questionable source. He never told me the whole story, said it was for my protection. When he died, he left me a trust fund with a little over a million dollars in it. The guidelines for the trust stipulated that I would either get access to the trust when I turned twenty-five or when I graduated from college. I graduate in two days."

She stopped and looked at the chief, waiting for him to speak. She could tell he wasn't buying her story and was playing the game of he who speaks or looks away first loses. Jess didn't speak or look away. She saw Mike watching her from the corner of his eye. She was proud of herself for telling the truth and at the same time withholding the truth.

Mike chose this as an opportunity to pound the table with his right hand again.

"Can I get some more ibuprofen, or can we leave so they can get me to the hospital?"

Everyone in the room looked at him.

They couldn't see his finger. But they could see that the gauze was turning from a bright red to brown.

Angela spoke up. "The paramedic did say that he needed to get to the hospital as soon as possible. Officer Martin was here with him."

The chief said to Mike, "Please accept my apology, we will get you there as soon as possible."

Officer Ed opened the door to the interrogation room. "Chief, you have a phone call." Chief Jacobs stepped out of the room.

Jess asked Officer Martin. "Are we in trouble?"

Officer Martin shook her head. "I don't know. Are you?"

Jess stared at her with a bewildered look. Then Officer Martin said, "Look. What happened in our parking lot tonight is obvious now. But it happened in our parking lot!" she said, slapping the table with each word to emphasize her point.

"This kind of stuff happens in a back alley or a remote parking lot. Not in front of a police station. The chief wants to know why drug thugs would be brave enough to attack someone here, at our front door, when you don't appear to be into drugs. Your attackers aren't talking. Two aren't talking for obvious reasons. The one Dr. Haygood hit with his car is still in surgery. The one your boyfriend beat up has a broken nose, a broken jaw, and a concussion that they knew about before they hauled him away. And the one the gamers tackled in the parking lot has said one word, *lawyer* since we locked him up. Yes, we have questions."

She stared straight at Jess, trying to stare her down. But Jess said, "I have those same questions."

Chief Jacobs came back into the room and heaved a heavy sigh. "Alright, kids, I think my weekend off is shot to hell now. One of your assailants has died on the operating table. And now the Feds want to get involved. They want to talk to you later today, actually, considering the time is after 1:00 a.m. And, that's not all. Miss Benelli's neighbor has called the city police to report that her duplex was broken into. The Fayetteville police are there now."

"Oh, shit!" Jess said. "Now I'm getting pissed. One day of this crap is enough! I need to know what is going on!"

She was nearly screaming when she finished.

Angela spoke up. "Chief? Bobby is still waiting outside. He can take Jess to her place, to meet the city police. Can I ask someone from the campus police department to take my brother and me to the hospital?" Mike sat with his head down. He was aware of what was going on, and yet unaware.

The chief replied, "We can do that. Officer Martin's shift ended at midnight. Can you drop them off on your way home? And be sure to tell the emergency personnel that his injury occurred four hours ago. It needs immediate attention. I will stay here a while longer in case anything else happens."

Jess looked at Mike, caressed his cheek, and said, "I will see you soon." And she kissed him gently on the lips.

Mike finally spoke. "Jess? They're after the app. They couldn't break into your phone without your fingerprint. So, they have gone after your laptop."

This caught the chief's attention. "Tell me about this app."

Mike responded first. "I'm an international finance major. Jess is a computer science major with an emphasis on internet security. We wrote an app to move money from her numbered trust fund account to her regular checking account. With a little tweaking, it could move money from one numbered account to another. Or, from regular accounts to numbered accounts using a cell phone."

He lifted his head and opened his eyes to look at the chief. "I'm sure the big money is kept in numbered accounts and cryptocurrency. But the app could be used to move money quickly and stay out of the reach of the authorities."

The Chief picked up on the thought. He added, "It could also be used by lower-level distributors, to reduce the amount of cash that has to be moved out of the country. I think you found the motive, young man. That could be worth something."

Mike added, "And they could steal Jess's money also. But I don't know how they could have found out about the app."

Jess looked at Mike with her mouth open. "I've got to go. I'll see you soon."

The chief blocked her way and said, "If you don't mind, I'll go with you. I'm beginning to believe you need an *armed* escort."

"Great, let's go," Jess replied.

Chapter 11

Officer Martin walked Mike and Angela into the emergency room and went directly to the desk. Angela liked Officer Martin because she was strictly business. Angela looked around the waiting room and saw no one. She wondered if this was normal for 2:00 a.m. on a Saturday morning. She had always assumed that emergency rooms were busy on the weekends.

"Excuse me, Chief Jacobs called ahead to let you know that we were bringing in a young man who was injured at the campus police station earlier tonight. You said you would be ready for him when we arrived."

The receptionist looked up. "Yes, ma'am. Is his name Mike Brock?"

"Yes, it is. This is his sister; she can help fill out the paperwork."

Angela shook the officer's hand and Mike nodded his thanks as she left. The receptionist handed Angela a clipboard and led them to an exam room.

* * *

Chief Jacobs took Jess to her duplex and had Bobby follow behind with his car. The city police were still there when they arrived. It felt odd for Jess to walk up to her own front door and knock. But that was what she did. The chief didn't recommend barging in on officers at work, even if it was her home and the front door was open. A plainclothes detective walked out of her kitchen and just looked at them. Chief Jacobs introduced himself and Jess. The detective was glad to see Jess once he knew she lived there.

"If the door hadn't been kicked open, we would have done a walk-through and closed the door behind us on the way out. We would have thought the door wasn't closed all the way and the wind blew it open. But the splinters on the door jamb tell a different story. Nothing seems to be missing that we can tell. So, if you would, please do a walk-through and let us know what's missing."

A city officer walked out of Jess's bedroom while the detective was talking. "The front door is the only source of entry or exit that I can find, Detective."

Jess moved toward the kitchen area and spoke while she walked. "I figure they were after my laptop. I left it on the desk in the kitchen alcove this afternoon."

Her backpack was there, but the laptop wasn't in it.

"They took my laptop," she said.

Jess gave the detective a description of the laptop and agreed to go by the city police station later to sign the report. The detective and the officer left.

The chief looked at the door and asked if she had someplace to stay the rest of the night.

Jess looked at Bobby, who immediately said, "She can stay with us; if Mike gets out of the hospital tonight, I doubt that Angela will go back to the dorm. She won't leave him."

Jess offered her hand to the chief. "Thank you, Chief Jacobs. I think we will be heading to the hospital to check on Mike."

"Okay, young lady, expect a call later this morning, and don't forget to be at the station at one o'clock to talk to the Feds."

"Yes, sir," Jess replied.

"Bobby, I need to grab a few things, would you help me, please?" She asked.

Jess went to her closet in her bedroom. She pulled out a gym bag and put some jeans and T-shirts into it. She then moved a suitcase out of the way and removed a cleverly hidden wall panel which revealed a wall safe. Bobby looked on with interest, wondering why she needed his help. Jess opened the wall safe and took out several envelopes. She didn't say what they were and Bobby didn't ask. She then opened the suitcase and Bobby realized that it wasn't a suitcase, but was more of a briefcase. It held a laptop computer, several notebooks, and several small black boxes. The boxes were a little larger than cigarette packs. "My mobile hacking lab," she said in Bobby's direction.

"No wonder Mike is so in love with you," he joked.

"Can you grab that for me, please?"

Bobby grabbed the suitcase. Jess finished grabbing undergarments and toiletries. She then scribbled a quick note to leave on her neighbor's door. They tried pulling her door closed, but it wouldn't stay shut. She propped a chair up against it and went out her back door which opened onto a small patio behind the duplex.

When she came around the duplex, Bobby already had everything loaded up in his car and they were ready to go.

When she got into the car, Bobby said, "It will take us a few minutes to get to the hospital; catch me up on what I missed."

* * *

A doctor entered the exam room. He gently removed the bandages from Mike's finger and asked Mike to explain what happened.

The doctor looked at it closely. "You were very lucky. You might have a fractured bone, a lot of torn skin, but the muscle and ligaments don't appear damaged. I'm going to give you a shot. It's a local anesthetic and it will help with the pain. It should start to take effect in about twenty minutes and should last close to twenty-four hours. I'll bring you something for the pain that will help you relax and get some sleep later. I'll be back in about twenty minutes to see how you are doing. I'll have a technician X-ray your finger in the meantime so we can see if we need to set the bone. I'll be back shortly."

Mike looked at Angela. "It might feel better if he cut it off."

"Shut up, Mike."

She stood up. "I'm going to step outside and call Bobby."

She returned a few minutes later. "They are on their way here. Which is good, because we don't have a car here."

"How's Jess doing?" Mike asked.

"Catching Bobby up on everything he missed. They busted her door in, and the chief recommended she not stay there tonight."

"No shit!" Mike said.

Angela continued, "Bobby said she could stay with us. They took her school laptop. That was the only thing she saw missing. She said they didn't find her Linux laptop."

Mike grinned. "Whoever these guys are, they still don't have anything then. Which means we aren't through with them yet."

Chapter 12

Saturday, 4:00 a.m. Fayetteville, Arkansas

The hospital discharged Mike at approximately 4:00 a.m. The bone was not broken, the doctor stopped the bleeding and put a splint on the finger to keep it immobile. He gave cleaning and care instructions to Angela because Mike didn't appear to be totally coherent at the time. The four students met in the waiting room. Jess went to Mike and hugged him tightly. He used his good hand and stroked her long blonde hair, kissed the top of her head, and said, "Let's get out of here, I have a final to take in six hours. And whatever he gave me to relax is starting to work."

Bobby wanted to talk on the way home. "Okay, I missed everything. What is going on? How is Mike doing? And how did Dr. Haygood know Jess was in danger?"

Angela shut him up when she said, "I know you have questions, but what I want to know is what is their next move? They don't have what they want, so they're not done."

Jess was sitting quietly beside Mike in the backseat with her head on his chest. She moved then, waking Mike up. "What's the saying? The best defense is a good offense? Anyway, I've been thinking all evening about who could be behind this and I still don't know if they are after the app or the money. I need to talk to my mom about my dad's friend. I also need to talk to Dr. Haygood, when he wakes up. I believe our 7:30 a.m. appointment with him has been canceled. Plus, I need to find out who put the tags on our emails."

Angela took over again, "First, we need some rest. We need to get Mike showered and in bed and up again by nine. We all need to call our families and let them know what happened last night before they hear about it on the news. After Mike finishes his exam at eleven, we will meet at the apartment to lay out a plan."

"Sounds good. I'm beat!" Jess said.

They arrived at the guys' apartment a little before 4:30 a.m. Jess walked Mike to the door, and helped him inside to the couch. The medicine was doing more than numbing the pain in his hand, it was making him loopy. She started to return for her bags, but Angela and Bobby carried them in behind her. Angela helped Jess get Mike to his bedroom. "Mike, you need a shower. You still have blood all over you. Can you make it to the shower?" Angela asked.

"I can try."

Jess winked at Angela. "I got this."

Jess's heart raced as she got Mike undressed and into the shower, then undressed herself and got into the shower with him. This was not what she imagined their first shower together would be like. He was practically asleep, and she was scrubbing dried blood off his naked body. Well, at least she could enjoy the view of broad shoulders, thick chest, flat stomach and yeah, even if he wasn't awake enough to notice her. She had to make him bend over to get his head under the shower head to wash his hair; he had blood in it, too. She laughed at him then. He was totally out of it. He had no idea her hands were all over his body. She got him cleaned up and dried both off. She had a difficult time resisting the temptation to play with a certain body part, telling herself there would be plenty of time for that later. Besides, she wanted them to both enjoy the first time together.

She got him into bed and he was asleep as soon as his head hit the pillow. She found her gym bag, went back to the bathroom, and picked up their clothes, cleaned up their mess, and brushed her teeth. She returned to Mike's room, looked at him in bed, glanced at the couch in the living room where she had planned to sleep, walked around the bed to the alarm clock, and set it for nine a.m. She then dropped the towel she had wrapped around herself and slipped into bed beside him. She took his right arm and snuggled her head into the crook of his muscular chest and shoulder. She lay on her left side, then laid her leg over his, wrapped his arm around her, and placed his hand upon her breast. As she lay there, enjoying the feel of their naked bodies against each other, she knew this was her man; she had thought about him every day for the past year. After last night, she knew she loved him, and she knew he loved her. Hadn't he defended her? He took on a man with a gun and beat him senseless to protect her, or them, as she thought of Angela. All three of them were so strong and confident. She realized as she started to drift off to sleep that they did that for each other. Just as she felt more confident and self-assured around Mike, they encouraged each other and helped each other.

* * *

Bobby and Angela had been surprised by Jess's actions, but thrilled as well. They were happy that Mike had finally found someone. They knew he would be totally embarrassed when he realized that she had given him a shower. They slipped into Bobby's bed then. It was not the first time they had slept together in his bed. As far as Mike knew, she had always slept on their couch when she stayed over at their apartment. But now, if Jess was going to sleep with Mike, then she and Bobby weren't going to hide anymore.

"Are you jealous?" Bobby asked her.

"A little," She replied quietly. "But I've also gained a sister I never had. I like her and she is crazy about Mike. Let's get some sleep. We need to make sure Mike is up in time for his final," Angela said.

"Who takes a final at ten a.m. on a Saturday?" Bobby asked.

"It was the only time the testing center had available for his online class."

She kissed him goodnight and curled up next to him and went to sleep. It had been a long day.

Chapter 13

The alarm went off in Mike's room, waking them both up. Mike reached over with his left hand to hit the snooze button. Jess rolled over on top of him and grabbed his arm before he could bang his injured finger on the snooze button. Jess reached over and hit the snooze for him. She was sitting on his stomach, and he was looking up at her. "Good morning, sleepy head," she said.

He stared at Jess groggily and asked, "What are you doing here?"

His eyes left hers and lowered to take in her naked body.

"And why are we naked?"

He didn't remember a thing, she realized. So, she decided to have a little fun.

"Mike, I'm hurt! You don't remember proposing to me? And then we came here and took a shower together? Then we had wild sex, here, in your bed, before we both passed out from exhaustion?"

He was staring at her now, wide awake. Searching her eyes to be sure. His mouth was wide open in shocked disbelief. She let him hold on to that thought for a few seconds longer, before she grinned.

She said, "I'm kidding! Sort of."

She hesitated slightly before continuing, "I did take a shower with you last night, although you were totally out of it. I'm not sure we can say we showered together; it was more like I showered with you. And, I did sleep with you last night, because I wanted to be close in case you needed anything."

"But we're naked."

"Whether you remember it or not, we saw each other naked in the shower last night."

She leaned forward and gave him a long kiss. That was when the rest of his body started to wake up.

The snooze alarm interrupted their lovemaking. And Jessica reached over and turned it off. Mike asked her, "Did I really propose last night?"

Jess laughed. "No."

"I'll have to find a way to do it properly then." He kissed her again.

Jess helped Mike get dressed. Getting a shirt on and off over the splint on his finger was a bit of a challenge. He kissed Jess and left her standing naked in his room.

* * *

Mike would have to hurry to make it to the testing center. He closed his bedroom door softly behind him, and looked up to see Angela and Bobby watching him. He blushed and grinned sheepishly, but didn't say a word. Angela and Bobby both laughed, and Angela handed him a pop tart package and a cup of coffee in a travel cup.

Bobby said, "Come on. I'll drive you to the testing center and wait for you to finish."

Angela added, "I'll have some lunch ready when you get back. Enjoy the coffee and the pop tart."

"Thanks, sis," Mike said.

As they left the apartment, he noticed that Angela seemed to be wearing nothing but one of Bobby's t-shirts. He started to say something, but quickly remembered, he had no room to talk. Especially after last night and this morning. And why should he say anything, he already knew that Bobby would be his brother-in-law someday and he was happy about that. He was still embarrassed that they knew what had happened. They had to know that Jess took a shower with him last night. And they surely heard them in his bedroom this morning. The walls weren't that thick.

* * *

Jess had been listening through the closed door, she moved away then and got dressed. She had a lot to do today. And coffee and a pop tart sounded good.

When Jess saw Angela, she blushed and smiled at her.

"Well, you are the second person to come out of that bedroom blushing and smiling this morning. Coffee?" Angela asked.

"Yes, thank you."

Jess didn't know what to say, or where to start. Angela made it easy for her by walking around the table and giving her a hug.

"Welcome to the family. I gave Mike a pop tart for breakfast, would you like one?"

Jess quickly responded, "Yes."

"How is Mike this morning? He was too embarrassed to hang around and say anything to me this morning." Angela grinned.

Jess smiled. "He is very stiff and sore, and still groggy, but not like last night! He doesn't even remember me getting into the shower with him. So, I told him that he proposed to me, then we came here, took a shower together, and had wild sex."

Jess laughed. "He just lay there in shock, his mouth wide open. He even asked me later if he had really proposed to me."

"What did he say?" Angela was laughing by now.

Jess continued after taking a bite of her pop tart, "I told him no, and he said he would have to find a way to properly ask me then."

Jess remembered her thoughts from last night about how strong and self-confident the three of them were. Jess asked Angela, "How is it that you three are so strong, so confident and positive all the time? It seems like you wouldn't hesitate to tackle anything. You seem to ask deep probing questions and then you lay out a plan and Mike and Bobby build on it from there."

Angela looked thoughtful for a moment before she replied. "I've been hanging around Mike and Bobby since I was four years old. They were six-year-old boys and I wasn't always welcome. I had to think of ways to include myself when Bobby was overplaying with Mike. By the time I was seven and they were nine, we were pretty much inseparable. When we argued as kids, our parents would make us talk about what upset us and work out a resolution, whether either of us liked it or not. We began to work out our own problems, which is what our parents wanted us to do. I played video games with them. Went exploring with them. I played football, basketball, and baseball. We were the only three kids in our neighborhood, so we played together or we played alone. By junior high, Mike and Bobby were both natural leaders. Mike was strong and reserved; he would get to know everyone on his team and he would always give them an encouraging word. Bobby was more charismatic. He has a wild streak. He would yell and scream like a cheerleader on the sidelines at football games while Mike went from player to player coaching and giving advice. They were the stars of our high school football team. Our coaches were horrible, it was Mike and Bobby that managed to give our team hope. But that is the way they are, always full of energy and excitement and ready to tackle anything. On the field, they had rules and structures to keep them in check. Off the field, they had me. When they were in the ninth grade, they took a STEM class. They were each given a little Raspberry Pi microprocessor."

Jess jumped in, "I love those and still use them."

Angela continued, "Their teacher was really good. He taught them all about using Linux operating systems, as well as Windows and Apple systems. And he taught them to program with Python. As a final project, each student was supposed to build something that used the Raspberry Pi, and that could be manufactured and sold."

"What did Mike and Bobby do?" Jess asked.

"They had a whole semester to work on the project. During the first two weeks, they tossed around robot ideas, remote-controlled projects, and Bobby even wanted to send a rocket into space. Then one day, our dad brought home a touch screen monitor from his office and he sat it on the floor under the big dry-erase calendar that our mom kept on the wall to keep up with all our activities and appointments. As we ate dinner that night, Mom asked Dad what he was going to do with that old thing. Dad wasn't sure, he thought Mike and Bobby might use it for something. Mike just kind of ignored it. It wasn't flashy enough for him and Bobby. I looked at it sitting under my mom's calendar and mentioned it was the same size as mom's calendar and it would be neat to have an electronic calendar that could be linked to everyone's phone and would automatically update when one of us added an event to the calendar. Mom loved the idea. And dad mentioned that he could use one for his office. Long story short, that's how BAM electronics was born."

Jess nearly spit out her coffee.

"You guys' own BAM? That company is talked about in every STEM class there is."

Angela looked surprised. "Mike hasn't told you?"

Jess was perplexed. "He told me last night that you guys own a small electronics company, but he didn't tell me it was BAM. It makes sense though, BAM stands for Bobby, Angela, and Mike?"

Angela laughed. "Yep, real creative! We each own twenty percent of the company and our parents own the other forty percent. Mike and Bobby were sixteen and I was fourteen at the time. Our father is an attorney, and our mother is an import/export specialist. They met in Hong Kong, twenty-five years ago. By the way, don't be shocked if you hear Mike and I speak Cantonese. Our mom taught us when we were young. Our dad speaks it a little, also.

"Wait," Jess said. "You and Mike don't look like you're Chinese."

Angela laughed. "We aren't. Our mother's parents moved to Hong Kong from England. Our father was in Hong Kong doing business with the company our mother worked for and that's how they met."

Understanding things, a little better now, Jess added, "And that's how you guys started BAM so easily. Your parents' expertise."

Angela smiled and said, "Yep."

Jess asked, "How did you and Bobby get together?"

Angela smiled and said, "We've really been boyfriend and girlfriend since I was fifteen. For some reason, we didn't think Mike and my parents would approve. So, we didn't make it official until I came to college. Bobby was afraid I'd find some other guy here. The first time we had sex was two weeks after my seventeenth birthday. We hadn't planned it; we had been washing cars in the backyard in our swimsuits. Mom had taken Mike to the dentist to get a wisdom tooth pulled and they left us there alone. I squirted Bobby with the water hose, just goofing off. He chased me down and tackled me. My bikini top got twisted and showed my boobs. He got embarrassed and apologized and I laughed and started making fun of him and told him he wouldn't know what to do with me if I were completely naked. We ended up in my bedroom. We were so scared afterward that we would be found out. Or that I may have gotten pregnant. Instead of pushing us apart, like it does with some kids, it drew us closer together. We talked about everything from sex to marriage, how many kids we wanted, everything. That's when Mike started getting suspicious that something was going on between us. So, we dated other people, nothing serious. It was just supposed to be fun dates, but one of the girls Bobby dated came to school telling everyone about the wild sex they had on their date."

"He didn't!" Jess said.

Angela laughed. "He did not! That date lasted barely an hour before he took her home and came to our house. Bobby was upset, he said the girl just wanted to have sex with the star football player. But Bobby got the reputation of a playboy after that. He would only go out with my friends after that. They knew what was going on between us and helped us out."

They laughed and chatted back and forth about Bobby and Mike. When they had finished their coffee and pop-tarts, Jess said she needed to get busy. She had a lot to do. She was about to go find her cell phone when she remembered it had been stolen.

"Angela? Did Bobby get those cheap phones last night?"

Angela shouted from Bobby's bedroom where she was getting dressed, "Yes, I'll bring them out in a minute."

Chapter 14

Jess took one of the four identical phones and programmed several phone numbers into it. Bobby had purchased the four off-brand Android smartphones the night before and had set them up while waiting on them at the campus police station. The first call she made was to her mom. She was sure the attack at the police station had made the news. Her mom had probably started calling her lost phone as soon as that news went public. The campus police never released student names for security reasons. But the media always found their names somehow.

Her mom wouldn't answer a call from an unknown number, but she might look at a text message. She sent a text that read, "Mom, this is Jess, my phone was stolen, please answer the next call." She waited about two minutes before calling. Her mom answered on the first ring.

"Is that you Jess? Are you okay? I saw you on the news with two other kids. What's going on? Talk to me, Jess."

"Mom, stop talking!" Jess yelled. "I can't answer your questions if you don't stop talking."

"I know dear, I've just been so worried about you."

"Mom, I'm fine. I spent the night with some friends."

Jess spent more time on the phone with her mom than she intended. She finally got her mom calmed down enough that she could ask her some questions.

"Mom? What was the name of Dad's friend? The one who loaned him the money for the construction company."

"That would have been Bennie Markowitz," her mom said. "They went to high school together. After high school, your dad went to work for your granddad's construction company and then took it over a few years later. Bennie went to college, but got kicked out his senior year over some cheating scandal, I think. Why do you want to know about him?"

Jess hesitated just slightly, trying to word her next sentence just right. "Did Dad ever tell you what to do with the money that he saved to pay back to Mr. Markowitz?"

"No, I thought he left all that in the hands of our attorney. I never kept up with it that much. He told you more about it than he did me. Why?"

"Yesterday was the twenty-year anniversary of the loan. And Dad said we were to keep the money for ourselves after twenty years. Thanks, Mom, I need to go. I'll call you later." They said their goodbyes and hung up.

Jess went to Mike's bedroom and got her computer bag. She rolled it back to the apartment's living room and started setting her gear up. It had been a couple of years since she had used this equipment outside of her duplex. She hoped it all still worked. She had three little black boxes that she used together. She had each one numbered one, two, and three. The boxes were small mini computers, very similar to the Raspberry Pis that BAM had used in their touchscreen calendar. Each one was set up as a private server and had its own VPN address set up to look like it was in a foreign country. They had encrypted software programs that helped her to browse the internet and not leave a trace. Well, she was almost invisible. The right people with the right software could track her easily, but they had to be looking for her to find her.

While she was setting up her hacker station, as she called it, she called her landlord about the broken door. She told him she would pay for the damages, and let her know how much it cost. She then called the hospital and asked about Dr. Haygood. They wouldn't give her much information, but they did tell her that he would be moved out of ICU and into a private room soon. He would be able to have visitors when he was moved to the private room. She still had nothing, it was almost 11:00 a.m. and they had to be at the campus police station at one.

She opened her laptop and plugged it in. Where should she start? She needed to trace the tag that she had found on her emails with Mike. She hadn't done that before, but she knew where to go to learn how to do it. Most non-computer folks knew it as the dark web, a place where criminals lurked around every website, but there were no more criminals there than there were on the regular internet. The dark web was a place that was used to communicate openly by the politically oppressed residents of many foreign countries where freedom of speech did not exist. Many tech-savvy Chinese used dark web access to get around their government's censorship of websites like Facebook. On the dark side, it also hosted trading sites like the Silk Road, where drugs, pornography, and other illicit items could be bought and sold.

If you knew where to find them, you could also find sources that told you how to hack into corporate websites, and set up security systems that couldn't be hacked, or hadn't been hacked yet. How to break through firewalls, find passwords. Whatever you wanted to know, it was out there. The trick was knowing where to find it. And Jess knew where to find the information. She had not used them much in the last two years, but she stayed current on some of the sites. You had to, to be welcome. You shared what you knew, and you learned what others knew. Information was shared freely, and no one asked how you used that information.

The laptop loaded up Windows 10 and all the usual college student programs like Microsoft Office, Facebook, and Gmail. But Jess quickly switched to the Linux partition of her one-terabyte hard drive. She started Cinnamon, her favorite Linux user interface. She asked Angela for the WIFI password and logged into Gmail to check her emails. She quickly deleted most of them without reading them. But there was one from a Tor mail account. That was highly unusual. People who used the dark web's email provider rarely sent emails to regular email accounts. She couldn't tell who the sender was from the name. She looked at the subject line and was surprised to see one word. A name actually. The name was Haygood. Her mouse pointer hovered over the Delete button. She wasn't sure why she dreaded opening this email. Her instincts told her she was about to get some answers, and things were about to change.

* * *

Angela followed Jess's lead and called her mom from her old phone. When her mom answered the phone, Angela spoke to her in Cantonese. She knew something was up, and switched the phone to speaker so her husband could hear. Angela told them about Jess and Mike getting together. They were thrilled to hear that Mike had finally found a girlfriend. Then she told them about the attack and their suspicions. She did not mention the twenty million. Her mom and dad were already driving to the college town. They would never miss an event as important as a college graduation. They had also talked Bobby's grandmother into coming with them. They would reach their hotel around 1:00 p.m., the same time their kids and Jess would be at the campus police station. Her dad spoke up and said to call him if they needed him. He wasn't a criminal lawyer, but at least his fees were negotiable. They all laughed at that. Then Angela suggested dinner at Ben's that evening; they could meet Jess and visit some before graduation on Sunday afternoon.

Angela started getting things organized for lunch. She needed to fry the bacon for BLTs, lots of bacon. Mike and Bobby could eat three or four sandwiches each when they were hungry.

Chapter 15

Bobby was sitting in his car when Mike came out of the testing center. As soon as Mike got into the car, Bobby asked, "How did you do, bro?"

"I got a seventy-eight. I needed a seventy-five to keep an A in the class," Mike smiled.

"Man, if you hadn't taken that Chinese class! You could be graduating with a 4.0."

Mike had gotten a C in the Chinese language class he had taken in his third semester. He thought it would be an easy A because he already spoke one of several dialects of the Chinese language.

"I don't know what I was thinking! Most English speakers can't make an A in English either. That's another time I should have listened to Angela."

Mike was silent for a minute. "About this morning."

"Dude, stop," Bobby replied. "Angela and I are happy you finally got together with Jess. We are even happier now that we don't have to hide that part of our relationship from you."

Mike blushed again. "You two don't have that type of relationship."

"Bullshit, bro! We've been screwing since she was seventeen and I was nineteen. We've considered ourselves a couple since she was fifteen and we were seventeen. We've known for years that as soon as she graduates, we are getting married."

Of course, Mike knew they had been having sex. The walls in their apartment really weren't that thick.

Because Bobby would have done it to him, he said, in as angry a voice as he could find, "You're screwing my sister? You're my best friend, I trusted you with my sister!"

He was thinking of what he could say next when Bobby's next statement floored him.

"Look! Angela and I are thrilled that you and Jess are together, finally. But take it slow. What happened last night is not over. Stuff like this can bring two people close that may not have that much in common. And she is the first and only girlfriend you've ever had. We don't want you to get hurt if this relationship doesn't work out."

Bobby was always joking around and making light of serious situations, but this was a serious side of Bobby that was rarely seen. Bobby being serious was like seeing a unicorn in New York City. It just didn't happen. Was he trying to gloss over the fact that he and Angela had been lying to him for years, or was this something deeper?

"What are you trying to say, Bobby?" Mike asked.

"You could have been shot last night. Or Angela and Jess, too. I would die if I lost Angela. I would grieve for the rest of my life if I lost my best friend. Jess is not safe at our place. We are not safe because we are with her. What do we do Mike? We need some help from someone more experienced than us."

Bobby took a deep breath and let it out slowly like he needed that release. Mike just stared at his friend.

"And how is your finger that stopped the gun from going off that could have killed one of you last night?" Bobby asked, with sarcasm dripping from his voice.

"I'm not sure I like you when you're serious. You're a real Donnie Downer, you know that?"

"That's Debbie Downer, dude!" Bobby replied, showing a little of his usual self.

"I'm sorry, Bobby. I haven't had time to process everything that has happened in the last few hours. The finger is fine, but starting to hurt. And the pills they gave me really played with my head. I need a little time to think."

"Well, thank goodness you have Angela and me to help you out. First, I need to ask you one more question."

"Fire away," Mike replied.

"Why are you working on a resume?"

Chapter 16

Saturday, 11:10 a.m. Fayetteville, Arkansas

Jess had just clicked on the email to open it when the doorbell rang. Angela stepped out of the kitchen and went to the front door. She looked out the peephole to see who was there, then turned to Jess and said, "It's Officer Martin."

Jess lowered her laptop screen, without closing it, so it wouldn't shut off. Angela opened the door to let the officer enter.

"Officer Martin, how can we help you this morning?" Angela asked.

"Chief Jacobs asked me to stop by and check on you on my way into work. He is worried about you. Where are the guys?" Officer Martin asked.

Angela responded first. "Mike had a final at ten, Bobby took him to the testing center, just in case he was still a little out of it."

Jess added, "He was really out of it when we left the hospital this morning. He doesn't remember coming home."

She blushed after saying that.

"Chief Jacobs wants you to come to the station about fifteen minutes before one today. He wants to go over a few things with you, and talk about how to keep you safe," she said to Jess.

* * *

Mike's cell phone rang. He still carried it with him this morning, even though it wasn't the safest thing to do. He looked at the caller ID and saw a blocked call. He wasn't sure he wanted to answer it, but he did anyway.

"Hi, this is Mike."

"Mike, this is Special Agent Carson with the FBI. You were on the news this morning; are you and your friends, ok? I got your number from your advisor. I hope you don't mind me calling."

"Yes, except for a badly bruised finger, and being scared to death, we are all okay. I'm actually glad you called. I think we are in over our heads here."

"Well, I'm still in town, I'm trying to set up another interview on Monday. Tell me what happened."

Mike gave him a quick rundown of what had happened last night. He told him about everything except Jess moving the twenty million. Agent Carson said he would make a few phone calls and get back to him shortly. Mike thanked him and hung up.

Bobby had pulled into their apartment complex and parked. He looked at Mike and asked, "Who the hell was that?"

Mike looked at his best friend, exhaled, and smiled. "That was Special Agent Carson with the FBI. My advisor scheduled an interview for me with him last week. I wasn't interested at all until we talked. They are looking for people with computer skills and knowledge of banking. And it helps that I speak two foreign languages. He saw us on the news this morning and called to see how I was doing."

"Dude, are you really thinking of joining the FBI? What about our business? We were going to be the next Microsoft or Apple. Were you really going to leave me and Angela hanging and not tell us?"

"Bobby, slow down. I didn't tell you because I had no interest at first. But he made a compelling argument. And that was before Jess came into the picture. I don't think I'm interested at all now."

"What are you trying to do Mike? Become a big-shot FBI agent? That would be cool, though."

Mike gave him a *you're crazy* look.

Bobby continued, "So why would the FBI be interested in what happened last night?"

Mike had to think for a minute before saying, "Domestic terrorism? They take the lead on domestic terrorism cases. While we think they are after Jess, the FBI may look at it as a terrorist attack against a whole college campus."

"That's cool. You're going to score some big points with the girlfriend tonight! Because you just asked your contact at the FBI for help."

Bobby laughed then. Back to his normal self again.

They got out of the car to head to the apartment and saw the campus police car leaving. They looked at each other, didn't say a word, and started running to the apartment.

Bobby made it to the door just ahead of Mike. He unlocked the door. They moved through the living room and into the kitchen, as the smell of fried bacon assaulted their senses. They found both young ladies in the kitchen, busy making bacon, lettuce, and tomato sandwiches.

"Is everything ok?" Bobby asked. "We just saw the campus police car leave."

Angela responded as Bobby moved around the table to kiss her. "Chief Jacobs wanted Officer Martin to stop by and check on us. They're worried and want us to come to the station a little early to talk it over."

Mike looked at Jess and she winked at him. "How was the test?" she asked.

"I made a seventy-eight. I needed a seventy-five to keep my A in the class." He grinned at her.

There were four plates on the table with sandwiches cut in halves from corner to corner. There were three bags of chips of different flavors.

"You guys have a seat. I have some news to share," Jess said.

Angela grabbed soft drinks out of the fridge for the guys, while she and Jess chose bottled water.

Bobby and Mike took their seats at the round dining table, and Mike said, "Do tell."

Angela and Jess sat down and Jess cleared her throat.

"After you left, I set up my laptop and checked my email. I had an email I didn't recognize that had Haygood in the description line. It was from Dr. Haygood."

She stopped long enough to take a bite of her sandwich.

She started again, "Dr. Haygood says Bennie Markowitz is still alive."

"Who is Bennie Mark A Fish?" Bobby asked, grinning at his pun.

"Markowitz," Jess corrected. "He was my father's high school friend who loaned him the ten million dollars. He disappeared after the raid. He was a witness against the drug dealers that used him to launder their drug money. His wife and daughter were supposedly found and killed by one of the drug rings that he gave evidence against."

Jess stopped long enough to take another small bite of sandwich and a quick sip of water before she started again.

"The story was that he had been killed in the raid on his business, but some official, somewhere, let one of the drug people know that he was alive and that's when they found his wife and daughter."

"Is this real?" Mike asked. "How does he know this? Can he be trusted?"

Jess looked thoughtful and answered, "I don't know. There are still a lot of unanswered questions. Like who is after me? Who informed the drug ring that he wasn't dead? Those two for starters."

"If Markowitz is alive, why hasn't he asked for his money?" Angela added.

Bobby said, "We need a quick road trip to the hospital before we go to the station."

Jess's eyes got big. "Let me go change. You guys eat fast."

She took a big bite of her sandwich then, and said as she left the kitchen, "And switch to the new phones."

Chapter 17

Mike and Bobby quickly finished their third sandwich each and looked longingly at the leftover bacon.

Angela smiled and said, "It will make a good snack when we get back."

Mike went to the living room and looked at Jess's laptop. He knew she was a hacker, but this was some setup. He would have to ask her what the black boxes were.

Bobby entered the living room carrying three phones and a small .22 caliber Midnight Special pistol that his dad had given his mom before they died years ago, and his grandmother had given to him on his sixteenth birthday.

Mike looked at it and said, "I hope you don't need that."

He remembered when his dad had taken them both out to the local shooting range and taught them how to handle it and shoot it. His dad had been adamant about guns being tools and not toys.

Bobby put a finger to his lips and whispered. "Me, too, bro! Me, too!" He put the pistol into his front pocket and handed Mike a phone.

Mike took the phone. He used his old phone for a reference and started programming the necessary numbers in. Most of the numbers he skipped, knowing he could quickly do an internet search for them and then call. He looked at his old phone and spoke aloud, more to himself than to Bobby.

"Agent Carson said he would call me back."

Bobby quickly responded, "Leave the phone here, but forward the calls from it."

"Excellent idea," he said to Bobby. "The tracker stays here, but I still get my calls."

Jess came out of Mike's bedroom wearing tight jeans and a blue t-shirt with the University logo on it. Her hair was in a ponytail and she had taken the time to apply a light amount of makeup. Angela came out of the kitchen.

"Lunch is put away, and if you guys aren't too hungry later, there might be enough for an afternoon snack."

"Sounds great!" Bobby said. "I'm ready right now."

Mike said, "I need everyone's new number."

They quickly worked their way around the group; while one gave their number, the other three programmed it into their phone.

"Jess," Mike said, "we can't leave your laptop here."

"Do you have a backpack?" she asked. "I left mine at home."

As Mike was getting up to grab his backpack and empty it, Angela told them, "Mom, Dad, and Bobby's grandmother will be in town at one. I told them we would have dinner with them tonight at Ben's."

Jess shut the laptop down and put it into the backpack that Mike handed her. She left the little boxes, but set them on the floor under the coffee table she had been working on. No one would know what they were used for anyway. Even if they did, they wouldn't have the passwords and encryption codes to log into each one.

Chapter 18

They had just gotten into Bobby's car when Mike's phone rang. It was the blocked number again.

"Hi, this is Mike."

Bobby started the car and pulled out of the parking lot.

"Mike? This is Agent Carson."

"Yes, sir," Mike replied.

"I've been on the phone with Chief Jacobs with the campus police, and he is concerned for Miss Benelli's safety. He seems to think that there is some safety in numbers, that she will be safe while she is with you and your friends. I'm not sure I agree with him. They tried to take her in front of the campus police station, for Christ's sake. I've called my office and they are getting copies of the campus police report and the city police report on the break-in at Miss Benelli's duplex. We will run our own background checks on the three known suspects involved in last night's attack. I think there were more than three. Someone broke into the duplex, and Miss Benelli's phone and laptop still haven't been found. You need to stay wherever you are and don't go running around today. Okay?"

Mike responded with, "Yes sir, but we have an interview with someone at the Campus Police Station at one. All Chief Jacobs said was that the Feds wanted to talk to us."

"The Chief didn't mention that," said Agent Carson. "I'll call him back and see who wants to talk to you. In the meantime, stay put."

"Yes, sir. Thank you, sir," Mike responded.

Bobby knew who the call was from. The young ladies did not. They both looked at him, and Angela, looking back at him from the front passenger seat, asked, "Who was that?"

"That was Special Agent Carson with the FBI," Mike replied. "My advisor set up an interview with him last week. He is trying to recruit me. He saw us on the news and called this morning to see how we were. I told him we were in over our heads and he offered to see if he could help since he was in town over the weekend."

"Will he be interviewing us this afternoon?" Jess asked.

Mike looked at her and caught a glimpse of sunlight shining on her golden hair.

"He doesn't know who is interviewing us. He doesn't want us to leave the apartment. It didn't sound like he wanted us to even leave for the interview."

"Why didn't you tell us you had talked to the FBI?" Jess asked.

Angela gave Mike a cold stare. "And while you're at it, why didn't you bother to tell us you had an interview with the FBI?"

Jess looked at Mike and leaned back away from him like she was saying, 'Yeah! That too.'

Mike sighed. "I didn't get the chance to mention it at lunch."

He looked at Jess. "We saw the campus police car leaving and you were too anxious to tell us about your email."

He looked at his sister in the front seat. "And I didn't mention the interview, because I wasn't interested in the job. I interviewed as a favor to my advisor. But he did make a compelling argument."

Angela softened a little. She knew Mike wouldn't lie to her and she knew he liked his advisor and Mike did whatever he was asked to do.

Bobby asked, as he continued driving toward the hospital, "Do we go back, or take this one chance to see Dr. Haygood while we are out?"

Jess looked at Mike anxiously. "Mike, we need to talk to Haygood. We might not get another chance."

"I agree," he said.

"Agreed," Bobby and Angela said together.

Bobby dropped them off at the front door of the hospital and went to park the car. He told them he would wait in the lobby.

Angela said she didn't know Haygood, but she would go with them. They entered the main lobby and went to the desk. The receptionist told them what room he was in, and when asked, said he was allowed two visitors at a time.

They took the elevator up two floors and asked for directions at the nurse's station. They told the nurses that they were his students. The nurses said he was awake and would be glad to see them.

They reached the door of his room and heard the TV set blaring the news. Jess rapped on the door and stuck her head in. "Dr. Haygood?"

She could have sworn that he had tears in his eyes. He jerked around when he heard her and he just stared, then looked back at the TV set, and then back at Jess and then Mike as they entered the room.

"You're alive!" he said.

"Of course, thanks to your actions," Jess replied.

"No. Mike's apartment was just blown up. It's on the news. They are saying there are four of you missing," the doctor said haltingly.

"Oh, my God! Mike!" Jess said. She tried to speak, but nothing came out.

Mike entered the room and looked at the TV. Jess couldn't believe what she was seeing. She had made love to Mike in that apartment this morning. Jess practically fell into Mike's arms, apologizing for what had happened to his apartment.

* * *

Angela entered the room as the news reporter was announcing their names and saying they were presumed missing, but a neighbor said he had seen them driving away.

She noted that Dr. Haygood looked like what many students visualized as the typical professor. He was in his fifties with black hair and a scraggly beard. But his eyes were bright and clear with just a hint of mischief in them. He wore a hospital gown and had the bed in an upright position. His right arm was in a sling and he had an IV attached to his left arm.

Angela noticed Dr. Haygood looking at her inquisitively. "Who are you?"

"I'm Mike's sister. I was with them last night at the campus police station," Angela said. "I want to thank you for protecting us against those men last night. How are you doing?"

"I will be just fine. I should thank you and Mike for protecting Jess last night. Because of an idiot's actions twenty years ago, this has all gotten out of hand. I am so sorry," he said. "The bullet went through the muscle on my shoulder. That will heal quickly. It was the stupid airbag that knocked me out, though."

Tears formed in Jess's eyes as Mike held her tightly. At the professor's apology, she pulled away slightly and asked, "What is going on Dr. Haygood? Why are people trying to kill me?"

"Angela, please come in and close the door."

"But you are only allowed two visitors at a time," Angela said.

"It will be okay. Come in, please."

He waited for the door to close before he spoke again.

"You must not repeat what I am going to tell you. It would put me in great danger as well. I knew Bennie Markowitz. I was a college buddy of his. He was a real computer maverick and the first hacker I ever knew. He almost graduated with a computer science degree but was kicked out for hacking into the university's computers and changing grades. He was brash and stupid and some of the grades he changed never were changed back."

He reached for a glass on the nightstand beside him and took a sip of water before continuing.

"After getting expelled, he moved back home. He was shamed and no one would hire him. Then he got involved in some dark online projects, hacking a few minor websites. Selling a few things on the trading sites. Then he had the opportunity to buy a pawn shop. He bought it for five thousand dollars, because the owner passed away, and the family didn't like being in that kind of business, or in that kind of neighborhood. I think they knew something dirty was going on and wanted no part of it. Bennie took over his books, figured out how to open his safe and got the shock of his life."

He took another sip. "There was another set of books and nearly a million dollars in cash in the safe. The previous owner had been laundering money for a local drug dealer. Bennie was scared shitless. He didn't touch the money in the safe. He was pretty sure he would be getting a visit. So, he waited. After a few days, someone did come to see him. They came with big bruisers and guns and they were looking for their money. He told them he had it, but he would like to carry on with what they were doing with the previous owner. They backed off a little then. Said they would have to think about it. In the meantime, they wanted their six hundred grand. He was thinking, if this guy was getting a forty percent cut, then he definitely wanted in."

He sipped some more water before continuing.

"They came back and made a deal with him. They started slow at first. He made twenty percent off everything he laundered. But they had more money than one little business could justify. So, he opened another pawn shop, and then another. And then he got into the check cashing and short loan business. The hard work was creating and faking the loans to justify the cash flow. The IRS finally came calling. Everything they looked at was on the up and up. But Bennie started moving money. In five years, he told me he'd made over twelve million dollars. Before the IRS and the DEA raided him, he had made another five million. He told me he had several numbered accounts in another country. And nearly seven million in cash scattered across twenty-one businesses, which the IRS confiscated."

He appeared to be thinking for a few seconds before continuing. "The DEA had an informant inside the drug ring, so they thought they had him cold. He had loan papers drawn up that showed he had borrowed money from the leader of the drug ring. The business looked legitimate in the eyes of the DEA and the IRS. It just looked like he had used poor judgment with whom he did business. But then they offered him a deal. The second time they raided him was when he supposedly died.

"He knew they were going to raid him again but he didn't know the time or the day. The Feds didn't want him to change his routine because he knew what was going to happen. Some of the thugs that worked for the drug dealer got to his home before the Feds did. They knew what was happening ahead of time. By the time the FBI arrived, all they found were the bodies of his wife and daughter.

Angela had been watching the professor closely. "How do you know so much about Markowitz? What does he have to do with this? And why are these drug people after Jess?"

Dr. Haygood looked up at them. They could see him starting to get tired.

"Bennie and I were friends in college. He was a talented programmer. I learned a lot of tricks from him. He confided in me what he was doing. He wanted me to look after his wife and daughter if something happened. It's not the original drug dealers. They are long gone. The only people who possibly knew about the money were the government agents and Bennie Markowitz. I think he is behind your attacks. The government didn't know about the money he hid, but they suspected he had hidden some. They couldn't even search for it until they were able to use laws passed to hunt down terrorists to find their money. I've been carefully looking for Bennie and watching the government for years. There are two agents from different agencies who know as much as I do. One is John Carson with the FBI."

Angela originally had doubts about Dr. Haygood, but the story was just too good and fit too well. At the name of Agent Carson, Mike stiffened and Dr. Haygood noticed.

"Do you know the name, Mike?"

"Yes sir, I had an interview with him this week for the FBI."

Dr. Haygood looked at him. "And I presume that he has offered to help with the investigation into the attack on you?"

"I kind of told him that we were in over our heads," Mike said.

Dr. Haygood just looked at him without saying anything. It was the kind of look that said *You're in deep shit.*

Dr. Haygood continued, "The other one was a DEA agent named Matthew West."

This time Angela and Jess both stiffened. It was Jess who spoke up. "That's who Officer Martin said is to interview us at one today."

Dr. Haygood took a deep breath and started to speak, but Angela spoke before he could. She could tell Mike and Jess had believed everything he said. And to be honest, she believed him also.

"Dr. Haygood? If you were such close friends with Bennie Markowitz? How do we know you are telling us the truth?" Angela asked.

"You don't."

Chapter 19

Saturday, 12:30 p.m. Fayetteville, Arkansas

Bobby had stayed in his car for a few minutes listening to a song on the radio. Then he left his car and entered the lobby. He found the waiting area and took a seat. A breaking news story scrolled across the bottom of the screen. He had seen the last part of the scrolling message. Something about students presumed dead or missing in an apartment explosion.

That's when a live report came on. "Oh, God!" Bobby said to himself. "This is bad! This is really bad. What have you gotten us into, Mike?"

He reached for his hip pocket to get his phone and realized he still had his old phone. The new one was in his front pants pocket.

His brain raced. He was graduating tomorrow with a degree in electrical engineering. He didn't have the grade point average that Mike and Angela had, but he was getting his degree. His engineering classes had taught him to analyze a problem, break it into pieces, and solve one piece at a time.

They were in danger. That was obvious from the attack last night, and now the destruction of his and Mike's apartment. It was Jess they were after. Whoever *they* were.

It was possible that if they walked away from Jess, they could walk away from the danger. Bobby knew Mike wasn't walking away from Jess, and he knew that he and Angela weren't walking away from Mike, therefore they were in danger.

Was the attack and the apartment fire supposed to kill them or scare them? Scare them most likely, Bobby thought. No, he realized, it was meant to scare Jess. He realized that Mike, Angela, and himself were probably expendable, and in their way. They had to be very careful.

Bobby figured they were after the money. Whoever, they were. That was yet another problem he figured Mike and Jess were talking to Haygood about.

He had told Mike earlier that he was lucky to have him and Angela on his side. Was that true? What had he done so far? He, the engineer, had been the gopher. Go for phones. Go for clothes. Go take Mike to his exam. That was not good. He needed to break it down, and analyze the problem and he needed to be proactive.

He thought of the old football saying. The best defense is a good offense. How do you attack someone you don't know? The goons, as he called them, had not talked. He was wasting his time on that line of thinking because he didn't know who the enemy was. All right. Okay, he thought, we are in defense right now. They have scored twice so far, they still have the ball, we have to play defense and keep them from scoring again. If they got Jess, they would win the game.

What could he do to help? He wasn't just a gopher. He was an engineer, he told himself. They had been followed. They had tracked their phones, which meant they could track his phone, too. Why did he still have it? He should have left it in the apartment. He took it out of his pocket and turned it off. If they were tracking it, it would come back on in ten minutes, like Mike and Jess's phones had done last night.

What's next? he thought. He wasn't making much progress. He felt useless so far. He looked up, and looked around the hospital waiting room hoping for inspiration. He searched the waiting room. He could see furniture, magazines, a television, a reception desk, and telephones. They already had the phones, and he had taken care of that.

He looked outside through the waiting room window at the parking lot. He saw cars. Cars! They needed to find a different car. He assumed all their cars were known, especially Jess's and Mike's. But Mike had not driven his lately, and Angela didn't have one. They had left Jess's car in the M lot last night. His car might have a tracker on it because the attackers had found them at Ben's last night. They needed a different car and they needed to leave town as soon as possible. Then they needed to find out who was behind this mess and put an end to it. Easier said than done. He pulled out the new phone and sent a text to Angela asking how much longer.

Angela texted him back. She was not sure, but they were learning a few things. That left Bobby feeling like an outsider again. He reminded himself that he had picked this spot.

* * *

Angela replied to Dr. Haygood, "Then what do you recommend we do? It's technically Markowitz's money that Jess was trying to protect and these people are after. What should she do?"

"I would keep it and move where he can't get it. If Bennie wanted it, he would have gotten it by now. The Man is a monster. I have come to believe that he is the one responsible for the death of his wife and daughter. The money should be used to bring him down."

Angela raised her eyebrows and asked, "Why do you call him a Monster?"

Dr. Haygood sighed deeply before answering. "The court sealed the autopsy reports. But a friend told me what was in them. Bennie's daughter was abused. Sexually abused, before she was murdered. Her mother wasn't touched."

"Oh, my God!" Jess gasped. "And you think it was Markowitz?"

"DNA proves it was him."

The room was silent, except for the television news, which was now on the weather forecast. Jess was pale. Mike was stroking her hair and staring blankly at the opposite wall.

"I don't really care about the money either, I just didn't want someone stealing it," Jess whispered. "But he's not getting it now."

"How do we do that?" Mike asked. "We stopped the attack last night."

"I believe that was supposed to be a kidnapping. He needs Jess to get the money," Dr. Haygood said.

"But they tried to kill us by blowing up Mike's apartment," Angela countered.

"They knew you weren't there," Dr. Haygood said. "That was to frighten you into running. When you run, you make mistakes."

"You tried to warn us," Jess said. "How did you know what was going on?"

"I still have many friends who deal on the other side of the law. I made it known to several of those friends a couple of months ago that you might be in trouble and that I was watching over you. They let me know that you were in danger," Dr. Haygood answered.

"How did you know to watch her and what do we do?" Mike asked.

Dr. Haygood looked at Jess instead of Mike, but he answered Mike's questions.

"I have friends in a lot of places. I know Jess has been tracking down child porn websites and turning the information over to the National Center for Missing and Exploited Children. I've known that for a while, and I couldn't be prouder of one of my students. But you did something yesterday that set off alarms in several government agencies. I don't know what you did, and I don't want to know. You are in danger. I fear for your life. No one is telling me anything right now."

While he took another sip of water, Mike looked at Jess and repeated the second part of his question, "What do we do now?"

"You prepare to run," Dr. Haygood said. "But you disappear instead."

All three of them looked confused, and he saw it in their faces. He was getting tired. The nurses would be coming soon. But he felt like he was the one who let Jess get into this mess.

"I will help you. I have many contacts that I made from my years of programming and hacking. But I need my laptop and my phone. I think my phone is still in my car," Dr. Haygood said.

"Right now, you do what you are scheduled to do. Go to your interview, and make it last as long as possible. Go buy some clothes to replace what you lost in the fire, get a room for the night, and go out to eat. Stay in the public eye around lots of people. In the meantime, you need a new car, you need new names, and new IDs and passports. I need headshot photos of the three of you. Front and side photos."

"Four. Bobby, too," Jess said.

"Ok, four," Dr. Haygood said. "You need cash, no credit or debit cards after tonight."

"Got it," Jess said.

Jess took the backpack off her shoulder. She handed three envelopes to Mike and then pulled her laptop out, opened it up, and handed it to Dr. Haygood. She took a notebook out and handed it to him.

"Use my laptop. Do we have an extra phone?" Jess asked, looking from Mike to Angela.

"There are passwords and encryption codes in the notebook. While I'm thinking about it, did you send an email to my Tor mail account?"

Dr. Haygood smiled and said, "Yes."

Jess looked puzzled and asked, "How did you get my Tor mail address?"

He just continued to smile and said, "I'm a pretty good hacker myself. I wouldn't be a very good internet security teacher if I didn't know how to do lots of illegal things. I'll teach you how I found it one day."

Angela spoke then and said, "He can have mine. Bobby and I can share one."

Dr. Haygood looked at Jess and Mike. "Listen, I'm sorry you got into this mess. You need to go to your interview. Tell them nothing. I will get to work on a plan and we will talk again later."

Jess had moved the hospital table over to set the laptop on. She pulled the charger out and plugged it in just in case he needed it. She then showed him how she had her laptop set up. He found the Linux partition and started the Cinnamon operating system, and smiled when he saw the Tor browser.

Angela handed her phone to Dr. Haygood. "Mike's, Jess's, and Bobby's numbers are already saved on the phone. You can call or text us now."

"Good, good," Dr. Haygood said. "Now get out of here. I have work to do."

Chapter 20

Mike called his dad as they were taking the elevator down to the lobby. Jess called the campus police station to tell them they were running late. Chief Jacobs blustered that they had better have a good excuse for being late. He was having to babysit an upset DEA agent.

Jess just told him, "Someone blew up the apartment we were staying in last night. Turn on the news, Chief." And she hung up on him.

"The chief and the DEA agent are upset that we are running late," she said. "I told him to turn on the news."

Mike said as they stepped off the elevator, "Dad said he would meet us there. He wanted to know why we thought we needed an attorney. I told him about the apartment and he started cussing."

"Dad doesn't cuss," Angela said.

"I know, but he did this time," Mike answered. "Where's Bobby?"

Angela pointed out the door. "Waiting on us."

Bobby had the car running and waiting for them just outside the front door. He let everyone get in and get buckled in before saying, "Talk to me, what did you learn? And where are we going?"

Jess recapped the story, part of which he had heard earlier from the email. Mike talked about Haygood's friendship with Markowitz. Angela finished with Haygood saying they needed to disappear, not run, and he was going to help them with that. Bobby replied that he had put in a little groundwork looking for another vehicle while waiting in the lobby. He had found a used four-wheel-drive Grand Cherokee Jeep in good condition for four thousand dollars in cash. It belonged to a fellow engineering student who was going into the Air Force right after graduation and didn't need a vehicle for a while.

Jess reached for the backpack on Mike's lap and pulled out one of the envelopes. She counted out four thousand dollars, put it back in the envelope, and handed it to Angela. She told Bobby to go buy it after he dropped them off at the campus police station. They discussed plans for picking it up and decided to let Bobby work it out. Jess saw Mike looking at the envelopes, but she ignored his look.

"The next thing," Bobby said, "is where are we staying tonight? Our place is a little crispy."

Angela said, "I'll call Mom, and see if she can get a couple more rooms for us tonight. We can ask Chief Jacobs if he will talk to the city police about providing the hotel some extra security, too."

Jess said, "I don't want to go back to my place. We need to get some clothes and toiletries for all of us."

"You do realize that we cannot walk in our graduation tomorrow, right? We need to disappear before then. We cannot let our parents know we are planning to disappear. They must be totally shocked that we went missing," Mike said.

Everyone was silent, realizing for the first time that tonight's dinner might be the last time they ever saw their parents.

"I hadn't planned on walking tomorrow," Jess said. "And Mom isn't coming. I was planning to start grad school this summer, and I was going to walk when I got my Master's."

They were all silent for a few minutes. Finally, Bobby broke the silence. "Can we disappear in the tropics? I never did care for cold weather much."

Angela hit him on the shoulder. "You just want to get me out of my bikini again."

Jess grinned at Angela's joke and spoke up. "We have to get Dr. Haygood individual photos of each of us."

* * *

Dr. Haygood sat in his hospital room in quiet contemplation. Was his plan going to work? He hated using Jess and her friends, but he had been unable to discover where Bennie Markowitz had disappeared to. He was an FBI consultant and he was working on two cases. The first was the Markowitz case. The wife and daughter had been killed. They had been unable to find Markowitz and everyone assumed he was still alive. The theory that Markowitz had killed his own wife and daughter was not conclusive, but other evidence was conclusive and it made sense. It took his breath away to think about them. The FBI had intel that Markowitz was still alive, but they couldn't track him down. They figured he would come after the money he had loaned Jess's father. When Jess and her mother had talked to Agent Carson about someone checking on the account, it was the first good lead they had received on Markowitz in years. Agent Carson had insisted on keeping tabs on Jess while she was in college and Markowitz had been an obvious choice to help.

The second case was the credit card and identity thefts. At first, they believed it was an organized group. But now it was looking more like several unassociated individuals were responsible for the thefts.

Whoever was behind the attacks on Jess must know about the money. The pawn shops and quick loan businesses had each used a separate bank. The bank where the money was deposited in Belize was the only location where the money had come together. Multiple attorneys had been used to set up the businesses. It had taken a lot of effort, but the payoff had been fast. Markowitz had used the same accountant that the drug ring used for some of their businesses. He used different ones for the other businesses. All the practices appeared above-board and had paid income taxes every year. The catch had been that most of the loans had been fake. Monthly payments were made to pay off a thirty- or forty-thousand-dollar car loan, except, no money had been loaned and the cars didn't exist. He took his interest payment off the top and the rest went back to the drug ring. It was easy money. Too easy, and when people started to notice, he just opened another pawn shop or quick loan store. He had planned very well.

Haygood logged into the computer and the VPN, then logged onto the hospital WIFI and finally opened the Tor browser. He went directly to Tor-mail and sent an email to get new identification for the kids. He would need four passports and four driver's licenses. He needed names for them and decided to make it easier on himself and the forger, and a little harder for whoever might be following. He sent another email and added two marriage licenses and the names. He was worried that Markowitz was after his money and that Jess was getting in the way.

He sent two more emails to contacts, letting them know the new number he had and that he would be calling them soon. He logged out of everything. You never wanted to use those sites for very long, you might leave a trail. He closed the computer and pushed the table away. He leaned back and closed his eyes. A nurse looked in the door to check on him. He looked like he was sleeping, so she left him alone.

He lay there thinking. His mind ran through many different possibilities and found few answers. He sat up a little in his hospital bed and Jess's notebook slid down beside his hand.

He picked it up and looked at the page where Jess had written her passwords and encryption codes. He flipped the page and read her notes, and then flipped another page. He spoke out loud. "Jess! You little hacker! Had I known these tricks, there's no telling how much trouble I could have gotten into."

Chapter 21

DEA Agent Matthew West was pacing the floor. There was only supposed to be one girl involved, Jessica Benelli, and now she suddenly had a boyfriend and the boyfriend's sister involved. He had learned that four guys had been sent to watch her and they were to steal her computer and her phone if necessary. She must have put so many passwords on the laptop and her phone that the guys decided to kidnap her. Thankfully, they had really botched that up. One was dead, another was in an induced coma with a fractured jaw and a cracked skull, and a third was in jail and not talking. Others had set fire to an apartment where the kids lived. Thank goodness they hadn't been there. They would get the death penalty if she were dead.

And now, before the kids even showed up at the police station, an FBI agent and a lawyer showed up asking for them. This was fucked up, really fucked up. The smartest thing for him to do would be to ask a few simple questions and leave, but he couldn't do that. Markowitz's wife had told him about the numbered account with ten million dollars in it nearly twenty years ago. It had taken him a long time to track it down. Especially since he found that it had nearly twenty million in it. If that girl hadn't transferred the money to a different account, this might all be over. Well, he let that thought go.

He was even angrier now because the lawyer and the FBI agent had been talking to a young Black female officer and the campus police Chief. They would have the full details of the story before he could even interview that girl. And to top it off, both guys were a good eight inches taller than him. He didn't like big guys, especially when he had to look up at them.

The campus police had been better at their job than he expected. He was used to campus police being little more than security guards with little training. But this department sent their officers to a police academy and required them to take extra training courses each year after that. They had physical fitness standards that exceeded the local police departments. When asked why they did that, the chief replied, "We deal with college students, they are smarter than the average person, younger, and usually in better shape. We are, in a way, policing an elite population that loves to drink, try drugs, have sex, and party a lot. That can be a dangerous combination."

DEA Agent West had to admit the chief was correct.

He was starting to get angry again when two tall girls and a very tall and muscular young man came through the police station doors. He watched as the dark-haired boy and girl went to the lawyer and gave him a hug. Then he watched as the boy introduced the blonde girl to the lawyer and then he introduced them to the FBI agent. What the hell was going on, he wondered. How could college students be this connected? Then they all turned toward him.

The campus police chief said, "Agent West? Are you ready to get started?"

The young man stepped toward the DEA agent and said, "Please accept our apologies for running late. Someone decided to torch our apartment and we weren't sure we should even show our faces in public. I'm Mike Brock and this is my sister Angela, and this is Jessica Benelli."

DEA Agent West was surprised. This was a very confident young man. And one look at Mike told him how he had managed to take out one of the attackers last nights. He must be six foot three inches tall and about two hundred and twenty pounds of muscle. And handsome, too, the agent thought. He hated him immediately, but he smiled and shook his hand. He noticed the bandage on his left hand and remembered the report saying something about stopping a shooting by grabbing the handgun and blocking the hammer fall with his finger.

Agent West replied, "Apology accepted. This shouldn't take too long. I just need a few minutes with Miss Benelli."

Jess looked at the lawyer and asked. "Mr. Brock? Would you be my legal counsel?"

Mr. Brock smiled at Jess and said, "Why, of course, Jess."

Agent West was angry all over again. Nothing was going his way. "Chief Jacobs, may we use one of your interview rooms?"

Chief Jacobs led Agent West, Mr. Brock, and Jess down a hallway to an interview room. He opened the door to one of two interview rooms in the station. Mr. Brock held out a chair for Jess and she took a seat, thanking him.

As Mr. Brock took his seat, he pulled his cell phone out of his pocket and found the record button. Agent West also seated himself across from them.

"I just have a few questions for you, Miss Benelli. Because your attackers from last night all have criminal records involving drugs, my department is trying to figure out why they were interested in you."

He hesitated for just a minute to let that sink in.

"Do you have any idea why men who have *criminal* records for trafficking in *drugs* would be interested in you, Miss Benelli?"

Jess was suddenly frightened. She said, "No."

Mr. Brock asked, "Are you accusing my client of something, Agent West? If you are, then this interview is over."

"No, no, Mr. Brock!" It suddenly dawned on him that this lawyer, Brock, was related to the two kids outside. Why did he keep thinking of them as kids? Two of them were graduating from college tomorrow. He, himself, had considered himself a full-grown adult and extremely intelligent at twenty-two. If only he felt that way now.

"I'm just trying to find a motive for why drug traffickers are interested in this young lady. Now, Miss Benelli, do you remember a man named Bennie Markowitz?"

"I know the name because my father told me about him. But I was two years old when he died," Jess answered.

Agent West knew he was getting nowhere. "Tell the story as you remember it."

Jess hesitated. "He was a high school friend of my father, my father borrowed money from him when the banks would not loan his construction company money for his projects. That's all I know, except that he died in some kind of accident shortly after the loan was made."

"Did your father tell you where Markowitz made his money?"

"No," replied Jess.

Agent West sighed and said, "I think we are done here. But to tell you a little more of the story. Markowitz may still be alive. He used a chain of pawn shops, check cashing, and small loan businesses to launder drug money. The money he loaned your father was probably drug money. I don't believe your father knew that. But Markowitz may be after the money now.

"I'm sorry to have bothered you, Miss Benelli. I knew it was a long shot to follow up on a twenty-year-old case. Now, before I go, I have to give you a message from Malachi Smith. Do you know him?"

"Yes sir. That is my friend's father."

Jess knew Benji's dad better than she would ever tell anyone. He had found her nearly a year ago and laid out a plan for her to find Benji's abductor. He had given her the information on the first ten child pornographers she had helped to take down. He had shown her how to follow the leads to the next website and he had predicted that she would find the one they wanted somewhere around number forty. He had been very accurate. Jess remembered asking him why he couldn't do it. His response had chilled her to the bone, as it did now.

Agent West looked at Mr. Brock. "What I'm about to say falls under attorney-client privilege and should not be discussed with any law enforcement agency without you present. And the person I just mentioned and the letters DEA should never be mentioned in the same sentence." He looked at Jess. "Am I clear?"

Jess swallowed and nodded.

"He thanks you for taking down the website. But you should not have touched the money. He said you would understand. Now, if you will excuse me, have a good day, Miss Benelli. Mr. Brock."

* * *

Jess watched as Agent West suddenly left the room.

"That was strange," Mr. Brock said. "What was he talking about, Jess?"

"Very strange," Jess agreed. "I search the internet for child pornography. A friend of mine was abducted years ago and I found his pictures and videos yesterday. If the sites sold pictures or videos, I also took their money. I provide all the information and money to the FBI so they can prosecute the perverts. I've found over forty sites in the last year."

"Wow. Why don't we go back out there and catch up with Mike and Angela, hmm?" Mr. Brock said. He looked at the phone he held in his hand and hit the button to stop recording.

They had just stood up when the door opened and Mike stepped in.

He looked at Jess. "Agent Carson and the Chief want to talk to us."

Mike moved to Jess's side, but kind of held himself back from her. Angela came in, followed by Chief Jacobs and Agent Carson. There wasn't enough room for six people to sit at the small table so they all stood.

Chief Jacobs observed, "Agent West left very quickly. What happened here?"

Mr. Brock spoke up first. "He asked Jess some questions about someone her father knew twenty years ago. She knew a few things because her father had told her about it, but it all happened when she was two years old. He was frustrated, but then he apologized and left."

"Jess? Anything to add?" the chief asked.

Jess looked at the chief. "I couldn't shake the feeling that things would have been very different if Mr. Brock hadn't been here. I think he knew more than he wanted to let me know. He told us that the attackers were either from Bennie Markowitz, or the drug dealers that Mr. Markowitz had worked for."

"At least part of that is not true," Agent Carson said. "There is not a single member of that drug ring left alive or out of prison. The interesting part is that Bennie Markowitz was reported dead. The DEA reported that his wife and child were found dead during an attempt to take them into protective custody. And Bennie Markowitz just vanished."

Agent Carson looked like he wanted to say something else, but he didn't.

He finally looked at Jess. "Jess, I think it's time we explained a few things to your friends and the chief here, don't you think?"

Jess exhaled deeply. "Yes, I don't like keeping secrets."

"Five and a half years ago, I went to Jess's home looking for a computer hacker. She came to our attention because she kept hacking into the ACT testing website," Carson said.

"I only wanted to know my score. And they emailed me the notice that the score was posted before I even hacked back in and saw it," Jess replied.

"The FBI talked the ACT out of filing charges because we recognize and recruit good talent whenever we find it. Jess has helped us with several cases by using her computer skills. We have never, intentionally, put her in harm's way. But now things have gotten out of control, I'm afraid."

Angela spoke up first. "So how does Dr. Haygood fit into all this?"

Agent Carson looked at Angela. "That's a very good question. I'm afraid I don't know." The Agent looked at Jess. "Do you have any ideas, Jess?"

Jess looked at everyone, except Agent Carson.

"I need to clarify a few things. Bennie Markowitz loaned my dad ten million dollars. The money in that account, that my family has watched, was money that we put back to repay the loan. So, in one way it is our money, in another way, it's Markowitz's money. We always intended to repay it, if we ever found him or his family."

Jess looked at Agent Carson, and he said, "Continue, please."

Jess swallowed and said, "When my father passed away, my mother and I had a lot of business issues to finalize before we sold my father's construction business. My father had left detailed instructions on what to do with everything. Even the loan money. Because the money had been paid to an offshore account, United States laws do not apply. My father's instructions were for us to take the money out of the account after twenty years and invest it as we saw fit. The twenty-year anniversary was Friday, and I moved the money. We knew someone else had called the bank and asked about the account several times in the past year. But the banks are very protective of their account information. The second time, the bank called my mom about an inquiry, we called Agent Carson. With our permission, he contacted the bank and we decided to set up a sting operation. They have tried four times to contact the bank and gain access to the account. They knew the account number, but not the access requirements. We thought it might be Markowitz, but he should have known about the other requirements and what they were. Once I moved the money, all hell broke loose and I still have no idea who is after it."

Agent Carson continued, "And neither does the FBI."

"Something is fishy about Haygood," Mike said. "He knew Jess was in danger. He wanted Jess and me to be in his office at 7:30 this morning. But last night, he blew up my phone to warn us that she was in danger. And he somehow knew that Jess and I were together. We didn't even know we were going to be together last night until after 6:30 so how did he know we were together? And how did he know Jess was in danger? His story and his concern sound good, but it's too good. And yet, he took a bullet and killed a man to protect Jess last night. It doesn't make sense."

"We might know something soon," Jess replied. "I left my laptop at the hospital with Dr. Haygood. I have a tracking program installed on it that allows me to see all the activity that has happened on my computer. It's like antivirus software. It will allow me to see what programs he ran and what websites he has been to. It backs itself up to the cloud so I can access it remotely."

She looked at Mike. "I'm sorry I couldn't tell you the whole truth before. I told you more than I was supposed to tell anyone. I am the reason Agent Carson interviewed you. I recommended you. I didn't know that your family owned BAM until Angela told me this morning.

Jess looked Mike in the eyes.

"It seems we've learned a lot about each other in the last few hours," Mike said.

Angela interrupted the moment. "Before you two start making out, we need more information and a plan. Chief Jacobs?"

He had been standing quietly by the door and looked at Angela now. "You need to know that Jess was not planning to walk during her graduation ceremony, and Mike and Bobby's caps and gowns were destroyed in the apartment fire, so they have decided not to walk either. That should ease some safety concerns at the graduation ceremonies for you."

Chief Jacobs nodded. "That was my primary reason for being here. Don't get me wrong, I'm concerned for you four, but I have a whole campus to look after. Now, if you will excuse me, I need to make a few calls. I'll have the registrar send your diplomas to your home addresses. I've also contacted the Fayetteville Police about your apartment to let them know your location and that you are okay."

Jess looked at Mike and Angela. She didn't trust Agent Carson right now. Something was off and she wasn't sure what it was.

Mike spoke then. "Agent Carson? How do we protect Jess and ourselves now?"

"I think the best thing is to get you settled someplace out of town and out of the public eye. We need to get your computer back or get you a replacement and get you out of town. Stick to your planned routine for the next few hours. Let me make a few calls, and I'll call Mike when I have a plan."

Mr. Brock spoke up then. "Agent Carson, thank you for looking out for my children and their friends. May I have a few minutes alone with them please?"

"Absolutely, Mr. Brock. It was a pleasure meeting you sir. I think I will head to the hospital and visit Dr. Haygood."

After Agent Carson left the room, Mr. Brock moved around the table and looked at his children and Jess.

"I agree that we need to get you someplace safe. But I don't know where that would be right now. You still don't know who is after Jess. The most suspicious person I've met today is that DEA agent. He was acting strange."

Mike moved to the table. "Take a seat, everyone." He met Jess's gaze and put his hand on her shoulder. "I'll tell you what we are saying shortly."

He turned to Angela and his dad and started speaking in Cantonese.

Chapter 22

Bobby had called the student with the Jeep and said he wanted to look at it and drove to the address he was given. He talked the seller into taking thirty-five hundred for the Jeep since he was paying cash. He also talked the seller into driving the Jeep to the hotel where the Brocks and his grandmother were staying. Then he gave him a ride back home. He had taken most of an hour to complete the deal.

Since he had not heard anything from the others, he went to Angela's dormitory. He explained the situation to the resident assistant on duty who had seen the news and recognized her immediately as one of their residents. She recognized Bobby and called Angela's roommate for him. Angela's roommate escorted him to her and Angela's room. He gathered most of her clothes, shoes, her laptop, and iPad and packed them into the luggage she had stored in her closet. He told the roommate that Angela's parents would be by later to get the rest of her stuff.

Bobby loaded the clothes and other stuff into the trunk and headed to the campus police station. He was pulling into the parking lot when he got the text from Angela. They were done at the station.

Bobby got out of his car and gave Mr. Brock a hug. He had been more of a father to Bobby than any man he had known. He loved the Brocks as much as he did his own grandmother. That was to be expected, as he had spent most of his waking hours with Angela and Mike for as long as he could remember.

They said their goodbyes to Mr. Brock. Mike and Bobby opened the car doors for Jess and Angela.

When they had seated themselves in the car and closed the doors, Bobby said, "Talk to me. What did I miss this time?"

Jess added, "Yes. Talk to me, too."

Bobby looked at Jess in the rear-view mirror and grinned. "I see that they just had a conversation with their father in Chinese. Don't worry! It's happened to me more times than I can count."

Mike looked at Jess and said, "Dad was being a dad. He was asking me how well I knew you. If I really believed you and trusted you."

It was Angela's turn. "I told him about the two of you meeting in a class last semester, and about you having lunch with all of us and how we all knew you and trusted you."

Mike added, "She shut him down. Told him to focus on the problem at hand. So, he said he would."

Angela looked at Bobby then. "We didn't learn much. The DEA agent's interview was very short. Jess said he asked questions about Bennie Markowitz. Was there anything else, Jess?"

Jess replied, "Not really, but he seemed very upset the whole time. I think he knew some of the men who attacked us."

"We need to talk to Dr. Haygood again," Mike said. "We need to know more about them and why he doesn't like them."

Bobby leaned forward and started his car. "So, are we heading back to the hospital then?" he asked.

"Not yet," Mike answered. "Let's head to Walmart and pick up some clothes and toiletries."

Angela asked, "Can you run me by the dorm? I'll pack some things really quick."

"Your things are already in the trunk," Bobby said.

"You went through my underwear?" Angela asked.

"Darling, I was admiring them, that's all," Bobby said, as Angela hit him on the shoulder.

"Shh, not in front of the kids," she joked.

Chapter 23

They spent over an hour in Walmart. They were trying to think of everything they needed so they wouldn't have to come back and get something they had forgotten. After picking up two or three sets of clothes, undergarments, toothbrushes, toothpaste, shampoo and, a few other odds and ends, they checked out and drove to the hotel.

Angela called her mother. She had managed to get them adjoining rooms. One for the boys and one for girls, she had said. Angela didn't argue. They were in adjoining rooms; how they used them would be up to them.

Jess called the cell phone she had given Dr. Haygood. He didn't answer, so she left a message.

Angela went to her parent's room, picked up their room key cards, and met the others at their room. They had carried their Walmart bags and some of Angela's things to their rooms. They opened the connecting door and discussed the sleeping arrangements. They all leaned toward the boyfriend and girlfriend arrangement, but they respected their parents' ideology also.

Finally, Mike said, "Let's just go with the boy's room and the girl's room. I have a feeling we aren't going to sleep much tonight anyway. We can change our minds later. I feel like this is the calm before the storm."

They all turned to Mike. Hoping that he wasn't right.

Bobby asked Angela, "Did your mom mention what room my grandmother was in?"

"I think Mom said she's next door to them. Let's go see her before dinner. We haven't been home since spring break. And Mike, Mom would like to see you and meet Jess."

Mike replied, "Okay, I need a quick shower. I can't remember the last time I took a shower." Then he remembered and blushed.

Everyone laughed and Jess, holding her hand over her mouth, looked at Angela and Bobby.

"He sure doesn't!" she said.

Angela went with Bobby to visit his grandmother. Jess helped Mike take his shower. This time, she knew he would remember it.

When Bobby and Angela were back in their room, Mike and Jess went to see his mom and dad. They had decided it would be safer for two of them to be in the rooms at all times. When they weren't in the room, they would take their clothes, phones, and Angela's laptop with them.

Mike knew that they were bordering on paranoia. But there was a thin line between caution and phobia. They had been followed, attacked, Jess's apartment broken into, and his and Bobby's apartment blown up. To expect something else to happen wasn't delusional, it was reality.

Jess said she was nervous about meeting Mike's mother. He assured her she didn't need to worry. To keep her mind off the meeting, Mike suggested she try calling Haygood again.

Jess did as he suggested. Haygood still didn't answer and Mike could tell she was beginning to worry. He wondered if something had happened to him. The four of them had taken pictures of themselves in the hotel room earlier and Jess had sent them to Dr. Haygood. She didn't have time to worry about it much more, they were now at the elder Brocks' hotel room. Mike took her hand in his, smiled, and mouthed, "It's going to be fine."

Five minutes after they entered the room, Jess was in total awe of Mike and Angela's mother. Mrs. Brock was beautiful, intelligent, and so intuitive and kind that Jess felt she could tell her anything. And she answered all of Mrs. Brock's questions without realizing that she and Mike were being quizzed.

Eventually, though, it dawned on Jess that she and Mike were being interrogated. And occasionally Mr. or Mrs. Brock would add an observation that helped Mike and Jess understand the situation a little better.

Mike said to his mother, "I don't know if Dad told you, because of everything that has happened the last two days, we've decided it would not be safe to walk during commencement. We don't want to put anyone in danger."

Mr. Brock replied, "I know we drove here to watch you and Bobby graduate, but we understand your decision not to walk. We are very proud of all three of you. Your mom and I think the four of you need to take a few weeks off and take a road trip. Lay low for a few weeks. See if this will blow over and be forgotten."

Mrs. Brock added, "We know you have some pretty smart people on your side. Listen to them, but decide for yourselves."

Jess smiled at the Brocks. "Thank you for your encouragement and understanding. I'm not sure where I would be right now if it weren't for Mike, Angela, and Bobby. They have treated me like family since Mike and I met last semester."

Mrs. Brock laughed. "Sweetheart, you're still getting to know Mike; we've always expected him to stick with the first young lady he introduced to us. So welcome to the family."

They said their goodbyes, even though they would be meeting them at Ben's in a few minutes.

They left the elder Brocks' hotel room and turned down the hallway back to their rooms. Jess's phone pinged indicating she had a text message. She checked her phone, shot Mike a glance, and said, "It's Haygood."

As Jess unlocked her phone to read the rest of the message, Mike asked, "What does he have to say?"

"He says we need to meet with him and Agent Carson. He wants to know where we are and what we're doing in one hour."

Mike said. "Tell him we're having dinner with my parents at Ben's at 6:30, we'll go by the hospital when we leave Ben's."

Mike took her arm as she typed the text message. He didn't want her walking into a wall while she was looking at her phone.

Jess stopped walking. Mike turned to her. "He said they will meet us at Ben's. They have an idea who is behind this and they have a plan."

"Okay," Mike replied. "Suddenly, he's buddies with Agent Carson? Something is fishy. Let's see if Angela and Bobby are ready to go to dinner."

They took the elevator up two floors to get to their rooms. As they exited the elevator, Mike caught a movement from his left and turned just in time to see a man duck into the stairwell. It could have been a hotel guest, but Mike's senses were on alert for anything unusual. They went to their room and Mike took the card key out of the pocket of his jeans and slid it into the lock. Their room door swung open and Mike found a pistol pointed at his chest.

Chapter 24

Bobby quickly dropped his hand and pointed his pistol at the floor, and heaved a breath of relief. Angela and Bobby explained that they had heard someone trying the room door as they were getting dressed for dinner. They were tired of being the victims and decided to fight back if they heard someone try the door again.

Jess told them about Dr. Haygood's message. "And he and Agent Carson will be joining us at Ben's for dinner."

"Good!" Angela said. "I'm ready for a vacation."

Mike added, "Mom and Dad suggested we take a few weeks off and lay low. Where do we want to go?"

The mountains," Bobby answered.

"The beach," Angela said as she hit Bobby on the shoulder.

"Why not both?" Jess replied.

"Belize?" Mike asked.

"Yep," Jess replied.

"Sounds like the beginning of a plan," Bobby added. "Let's grab our stuff and go eat. I'm starving since someone decided to refry the bacon we had left over from lunch."

"You're always starving!" Angela laughed.

"I'm a growing boy," he replied.

They packed their clothes up and slipped out of the hotel room. They took the stairs on the opposite end of the hotel from which they had seen the man leave. It could have been a coincidence, but they weren't taking any chances.

Bobby left the hotel ahead of the others and went to get his car. He drove his car to the door and stopped. The others left the hotel and hurried to the car, threw their clothes in the trunk, and before the doors were all closed, Bobby pulled away from the curb.

Bobby said, "There was a silver Kia parked two rows behind me; there was a young white male watching every move I made."

"Look at you, spymaster," Angela said.

Mike asked, "Where's the Jeep, Bobby?"

As they drove around the hotel, Bobby pointed and said, "Right there."

He pointed to an older model Jeep Cherokee. "Don't look too closely, or the guy following us might realize that Cherokee belongs to us," Bobby added.

Jess asked, "When and how do we swap cars if someone is watching us this close?"

No one answered. There was no easy answer.

Jess spoke up then. "Angela, call the campus police. Bobby, take a slow straight route to campus. Let's see if the campus police will pull our friend over for us."

Mike smiled. "I like how you are thinking, gorgeous."

Angela hung up the phone. "Officer Martin said to drive past the Engineering building, an officer is parked there. She said to drive twenty miles per hour through the crosswalk. Someone knocked down the ten-mile-per-hour speed limit sign."

Mike said, "Remind me to add her to my Christmas card list."

"Correction!" Jess said. "We need to add the entire campus police department to our Christmas list."

A few minutes later, the campus police pulled over a silver Kia for speeding through a pedestrian crosswalk. And because he had been doing twice the posted speed limit, they had the driver take a field sobriety test while they ran his license for a background check.

Bobby slowed down after he saw the Kia get pulled over. He turned down a side street, circled the block, and drove by the traffic stop on his way to Ben's. They all stared at the man as they drove by so they could identify him later. If he knew they were there, he never acknowledged them.

They arrived at Ben's right on time. Ben Jr. wasn't working as the host, but he was there and playfully harassed them about leaving without paying the night before. He then said to Jess, "Are you still hanging around with this guy?"

Jess smiled at Ben. "He's stuck with me now."

Ben showed them upstairs to the Train room. It was decorated with pictures of steam engines, a wall-size picture of the local train station, and a full-size railroad crossing sign hanging by a window.

The elder Brocks and Grandmother Williams were already there. Mike told Ben they were expecting two more and who they were. Ben said he would show them up as soon as they arrived. Right before he left them, he leaned toward Mike and lowered his voice. "I saw the news, are you guys, okay?"

Mike held his finger up. "The only injury so far, but I could have been shot if that finger hadn't gotten in the way. Dr. Haygood was shot once." Mike hesitated before continuing, "You've been good to us Ben, but this will probably be the last time you see us for a while." Mike and Ben said their goodbyes and Mike entered the Train room. A waiter was already taking orders.

Chapter 25

Mike looked around the table. There were seven people at the table where normally only six sat. Mike looked at Jess and smiled. She was talking to his mother and Bobby's grandmother. It felt right that she was there with him and his family. If things had happened differently in the last twenty-four hours, one or both might be dead now. That was something he could not allow to happen. He knew that he loved her. He had fallen for her last semester, and even though they had stopped dating to focus on classes, they had not stopped talking to each other or having lunch once or twice a week. He listened to Grandma Williams tell Jess a story about meeting her husband. She said she knew the first time they met that he was the one she would marry.

He found himself hoping that Dr. Haygood had more answers this time. He wanted to take a few weeks off and enjoy being with Jess.

"Mike?" Mr. Brock turned to his son. "I think I have a place for you to lay low for a few days."

He had Mike's full attention.

"Do you remember where I took you and Bobby deer hunting when you were fifteen?"

Mike nodded, and Bobby said, "I remember that place, you called it Uncle John's cabin."

Mr. Brock nodded and said, "Yes. I talked to John last week, he said he was having some trouble with someone driving through his property or something. He was asking me questions about how he could legally close a road that went across his property. I called him earlier; he would be happy to have you stay there for a few days and watch the place. He said you would need to bring food and cleaning supplies, though."

Bobby looked at Mike. "That might be perfect."

"It might be," Mike replied. "But let's keep it to ourselves, I'm not sure I trust anyone outside this room right now."

Their waiter brought their meals and they ate without talking. As they were finishing their food, Ben Jr. showed Dr. Haygood and Special Agent Carson into their private room and closed the door behind him.

Mr. Brock looked at Mike, and Mike took the cue his dad was giving him. He stood and introduced everyone. Agent Carson now wore his tailored black suit with a white button-down shirt and a red tie. That meant he was working, and no longer off duty. Dr. Haygood had apparently been home, because he was also wearing a suit, no tie, and had his arm in a sling.

Mike told them to sit and asked if they wanted anything to eat or drink. They both asked for water but didn't order anything to eat.

"So? What can you tell us?" Mike asked, looking from Agent Carson to Dr. Haygood.

Agent Carson said, "Why don't you start, Dr. Haygood."

"Very well. After you left my room at the hospital, I sent a few emails, and made a couple of phone calls." He looked at Jess. "I found something in your notebook that was very useful."

"What was that?" Jess asked.

"The login and password for the federal employee database," Haygood replied.

"Which no longer works," Carson added.

"I only used it to check you out," Jess added, looking at Agent Carson. "How did that help you?" she asked Dr. Haygood.

"I, too, was checking out Agent Carson and DEA Agent West. I decided to call Special Agent Carson."

He stopped and took a drink of water.

"Through some of my contacts, I discovered that Agent West's daughter is married to a guy who calls himself an IT consultant and has his own business. The business appears to be a front for internet scams, and identity thefts, but mainly credit card skimmers and anything that can bring in illegal and easy money. I believe he is behind the attacks on you Jess."

Agent Carson chimed in, "Which now makes it a federal cyber-crimes case. And the FBI has already started investigating."

"Who is he?" Jess asked.

"And, what does he look like?" Mike added, a hunch forming in his mind.

"His name is Charles Anderson. And this is the latest picture we can find," Agent Carson said, turning his smartphone to show Mike and Jess the photo.

"He's here," Mike said. "He followed us from the hotel to campus. We called campus police and they stopped him from following us right before we came here."

"Excuse me, I need to make a call," Agent Carson said as he got up from his chair and left the room.

"Dr. Haygood, do you have any idea what's happening?" Jess asked.

"I can only guess," he replied. "Agent West's daughter married a petty thief; he must have learned of the money somehow and started looking for it. People will do crazy things for money. Trust me, I know. But money is not as important as the people you love. Unfortunately, most don't learn that until it's too late."

"How does Agent West fit into this?" Mike asked.

"Agent Carson and I don't know. Unless he's trying to stop his son-in-law from making a big mistake. He's been unable to reach Agent West since your interview this afternoon."

Agent Carson entered the room. "The Campus police issued him a ticket and let him go about five minutes after they stopped him. I've asked them to notify the local police departments to be on the lookout for him. I told them he was wanted for questioning in a federal case. Now we wait and see."

Mike started to ask Dr. Haygood how he knew that he and Jess were together last night. Something told him not to ask. Something was bothering him about Haygood. He knew too much about some things and not enough about other things. Mike knew he was becoming paranoid. But paranoia just might keep them alive.

"Dr. Haygood?" Mike asked. "Did you bring Jess's laptop and notebook with you?"

"Yes, they are in Agent Carson's car. He was kind enough to pick me up at the hospital and take me home to change before coming here since I do not have a car now," he replied.

"Other than Angela's laptop and iPad, that's the only computer we have between the four of us at the moment," Mike said.

Before anyone else could say anything, he looked at Agent Carson. "What's the plan? What do we do now?"

He knew Jess didn't trust Agent Carson. He had forgotten to ask her why and he would have to remember to ask her later.

Agent Carson responded with, "I think you'll be safe. They have shown themselves, made their mistakes, and with Dr. Haygood's information, I think we are onto the leader."

"So, you're saying we should go home and let you do your job?" Jess asked.

"That's pretty much it. Yes," he answered her. "I think we will have this wrapped up very soon. But, if you decide to take a vacation, let me know where you're going."

Mike raised an eyebrow at his dad. Mr. Brock stood up and turned to their two visitors. "Dr. Haygood, Agent Carson, thank you for everything you have done. You have been very helpful. Since they won't be going through commencement tomorrow, we will be heading home in the morning."

Mike and Jess stood and shook their hands and thanked them both for their help. Mike said, "I'll walk down with you to get Jess's computer."

* * *

When they had left, everyone looked at Jess. Mr. Brock asked the question, "What's going on, Jess? Mike thinks something stinks, doesn't he?"

Jess nodded. "I think so, too. I just followed his lead. He knows I don't trust Agent Carson. I don't know why I don't trust him, I just don't. And Mike has huge questions about Dr. Haygood. Now that I think about it, I do too."

Angela spoke up then. "I feel like someone botched the job, and this is the clean-up. They will let things calm down and then try again." She asked Jess, "What are your plans for the next few weeks?"

"I was planning to go home for the summer and see Mom," Jess answered.

Angela spoke carefully. "I hesitate to plan too much without Mike. But he won't mind if we discuss some possible plans."

Angela turned to her mom and dad. "What are your thoughts?"

Mr. Brock looked at his wife, and she smiled sadly at him. "We have an idea," she said. "We will share it with you when Mike gets back."

Angela didn't question her mom anymore. She knew she wouldn't get anything out of her parents until Mike got back. They were professionals at keeping secrets. Being an attorney and international trade consultant required it.

Angela asked Jess, "What was it that Haygood said to us today? That we didn't need to run, we needed to disappear?"

Jess thought for a few seconds. "He said we prepare to run, but we disappear instead. He said he would explain later, that he had to come up with a plan."

"He didn't mention anything about that before he left," Angela pointed out.

Jess raised her eyebrows. "He and Agent Carson think this will all be over if they find Charles Anderson."

Mrs. Brock broke in then. "Mike is obviously nervous about this, I can tell he doesn't believe this is over. What do you think, Jess? It's your money they are after."

Jess stared at Mrs. Brock, disturbed by the question. She looked down at the table, remembering Agent West's warning, before speaking. "It's not over," she said. "It probably would have been, if not for Mike, Angela, Bobby, and Dr. Haygood. They kept me from being kidnapped. Everything felt like it was amateur gangster hour. I think they expected me to be alone, but I wasn't."

Jess hesitated for a moment, then said, "I'm sorry I got everyone involved in this. Mike and I stopped dating last semester because we were committed to finishing our degrees without distractions. We have texted each other back and forth every day since last semester though. When Angela asked me about the party, I was hoping Mike and I could get back together and see how we felt about each other. I'm crazy about him. I didn't have any idea someone was going to do all of this. I'm sorry."

She was almost in tears when she finished. Angela reached over and put a hand on her arm. "If you're going to be my sister, don't be apologizing for something you have no control over. That's time better spent planning and figuring out who is behind this and why. If you have no ideas, then we have our work cut for us."

Jess was shocked. Not that Angela would suggest they would become sisters, but that she would suggest that she shouldn't apologize. Jess started to protest, but Angela stopped her cold by saying, "If you and Mike had continued dating last semester, and for all practical purposes you did, you would probably still be dealing with this. Mike, Bobby, and I have had many discussions about football. What's more important, offense or defense? You need both. One cannot win without the other. We have been on defense for the last twenty-four hours, it's time for us to start playing offense."

Bobby said. "Do I get to hit someone this time? Put me in, coach!"

Everyone laughed. Bobby got serious suddenly. "Jess, we need your hacker skills. Angela told me the FBI was recruiting you, which means you have some impressive skills. How can you use them to fight back?"

Jess was about to answer when Mike came back into their dining room. Everyone turned to watch him enter the room. He carried a campus bookstore bag, which held Jess's notebook and laptop. He frowned when he sat down by Jess.

Mr. Brock looked at him. "What's wrong, son?"

Mike just said, "Man plans and God laughs."

They all remained silent, watching Mike, and waiting for him to explain.

When Mike finally spoke, he used a slow, serious voice. "I spoke to Ben. We have the room for as long as we need it. I get the feeling we are being used. I feel like we are being herded in a certain direction."

They could tell Mike was working his way toward a specific thought and they remained quiet. Waiting for what was coming. He swallowed before continuing, "We are being used as bait."

Mike looked around the table. "Mom, Dad, Grandma Williams, I think we need to disappear for a couple of weeks and see what happens."

Mr. Brock replied, "Your mom and I agree. Where do you plan to go?"

Mike's response was slow in coming. "I think we will flip a coin and decide after we hit the road." He winked at his father as he said it though. And his father nodded.

Mike reached into the bag with Jess's laptop in it. He pulled out a brown legal-sized envelope. He didn't say a word but gestured to his father to take pictures. Mike reached into the envelope and pulled out several legal documents and driver's licenses. Mr. and Mrs. Brock started to say something, but Mike put a finger to his lips.

Mr. Brock used his smartphone and took photos of four sets of driver's licenses, four birth certificates, four passports, and two marriage licenses.

"What's your plan, Dad?" Mike asked as he put papers and licenses back into the envelope.

"Well, your mother and I thought you could take a few weeks off and lay low. Maybe, stay at Uncle John's and let this cool off some," Mr. Brock replied as he watched Mike writing furiously on a piece of notebook paper from Jess's notebook.

Mike said, "That sounds good to me. What do you guys think?" He passed the notebook to his mom and dad.

Right on cue, Bobby said, "We'll need plenty of bug spray if we are going to Uncle John's."

Mike held a finger to his lips, moved his finger to his ear and then pointed at the bag. Then he said, "If everyone has finished, why don't we go back to the hotel so we can head out early tomorrow morning."

Everyone was a little confused, but they trusted Mike. He took the brown envelope out of the bag and took the notebook from his parents. He handed the notebook to Bobby and Angela. They read it and handed it to Jess. Jess closed the notebook. She had seen Mike write it and knew what it said. *The bag is bugged.*

Everyone stood up and Mr. Brock said, "I'll go down and settle the bill."

Mike handed the bag with Jess's laptop in it to his mother. He mouthed the words, "Take this back with you."

When Jess started to object, he leaned over and whispered in her ear and reminded her, "The bag is bugged and there is no telling what's on your computer now."

Jess was disappointed, but she nodded.

Bobby said, "I'll drop y'all off at the hotel. I need to fill my car up before we head out in the morning."

"That's a good idea. One less thing to worry about in the morning," Angela responded.

Mike indicated that Bobby should stay, and that Mrs. Brock, Angela, and Jess to go. He and Bobby had some explaining to do to Grandma Williams.

She looked at them and said, "I have an idea what you are going to do. Don't explain anything to me. Just take care of yourselves and those two beautiful girls. Clear this up and come home soon."

With their, "Yes ma'am!", and "Yes Grandma!" said, they both hugged her and helped her out of the restaurant and into the Brocks' SUV.

As they walked to Bobby's car, Mike whispered to Bobby, "Follow Mom and Dad back to the hotel. Let us out, and we will walk through the hotel to the Jeep and meet you at the Seven-Eleven. I'll fill you guys in on the plan then. And I'll need the keys to the Jeep, too."

"You don't plan on staying the night?" Bobby whispered back. Then reached into his pants pocket and retrieved the Jeep's keys.

"No way!" Mike replied and nodded to the silver Kia parked at the end of the restaurant's parking lot.

"Geez!" Bobby said. "Can I go beat the shit out of this guy?"

"No!" Mike replied, barely over a whisper. "He probably has a gun, and I'll bet it's bigger than yours."

Chapter 26

Saturday, 8:00 p.m. Fayetteville, Arkansas

They arrived at the hotel and drove around the parking lot. The lot was nearly full and there were very few parking spots. The guy in the Kia made no attempt to stay out of sight. Whether or not he was who Agent Carson claimed didn't matter, if Mike's plan worked.

Bobby pulled under the canopy at the entrance to the hotel. Mike watched the Kia find a parking spot in the back of the lot, away from the hotel, but with a good view of the front door. Mike and the women got out of the car and walked toward the hotel. Bobby drove around the lot again before pulling back out onto the street and slowly driving away.

Mike watched a black SUV follow Bobby from an adjoining parking lot. He had stopped just inside the hotel door and held it open for some other guests who were entering with their luggage. Mike was watching the entire area for movement, using his peripheral vision, as he did as a quarterback in high school; he saw the vehicle pull out behind Bobby. Mike's mind was immediately working. Were they working together? Was one handing off to the other? Was he being too suspicious? Was it a coincidence?

He realized he was holding the door open for no one when Jess softly called his name from inside the door.

"Sorry."

He looked around the lobby, hoping to see his parents before leaving. His sister saw him looking and said, "They have gone to their room, Mike."

He nodded. "Okay, let's go."

They headed down a hallway, past the lobby desk, and turned beside the hotel manager's office. Mike led them out the back door to the parking lot behind the hotel.

He stopped immediately and grinned at a tall, skinny, Asian young man. He was leaning against their Jeep. As soon as he realized that no one was supposed to know about the Jeep, he frowned. "Hey, Steven, what are you doing here? And how did you know what vehicle was ours?"

Mike and Jess knew Steven from their programming class. Where Mike considered Jess a near-genius programmer, he and Jess considered Steven a true genius. They figured Steven knew more about computers and programming than most professors. Outside of playing computer games, Steven was pretty much a loner. Steven's Parents were of Vietnamese descent, but he was born and raised in Fort Smith, Arkansas.

Steven grinned back and said, "Hi, Mike. Hi, Jess. I figured you guys needed some help after last night. I'm friends with Officer Martin. She helped me out of a little trouble last year. I talked to her and she filled me in on the details that she could. Do you guys have a few minutes to talk? I think I have some information you may need."

"Not really, man," Mike replied. "We were just about to leave town."

"You don't want to leave yet," Steven said.

Jess asked him why.

He looked around. "You guys were going to follow your roommate to the gas station. I'll ride with you if that's okay."

Mike moved to the Jeep Cherokee and unlocked the door. "Come on. We need some answers," Mike said.

Angela and Jess got into the back seats, while Mike and Steven got into the front. Before Mike started the Jeep, he looked at Steven. "What the fuck is going on man? Why do you know what we are going to do before we do it?"

Before Steven could answer, Mike started the Jeep and backed out of the parking spot.

Steven started talking. "I was at the police station Friday night and saw most of the show. Me and some of the other guys got together and we started talking. A couple of us have been watching you guys since then. What we've learned has raised some serious questions. We started doing some deep internet dives also. We checked out Haygood, and that FBI agent. What we found raises more questions than answers."

"What do you mean?" Jess asked.

He said, "What I mean is that Haygood didn't exist anywhere before coming to teach at our fair university. He is undercover FBI, his name is Green, I think."

Angela said, "He told us he was a friend of Bennie Markowitz. Who is he? Really."

"We're working on that," Steven said.

Mike had been driving slowly down the street to the Seven-Eleven. He reached across the console with his right hand and grabbed the front of Steven's shirt with a backhand grab. He stopped the Jeep in the street, pulled Steven toward him across the console, and stared into his frightened eyes.

Mike asked, "Who do you mean by 'we' and how do you know so much about what we're doing?"

Steven grabbed Mike's arm with both of his hands. "Okay! Okay! *We* are your friends from computer classes. We helped Bobby set up your phones at the police station, and we've been listening to y'all through your phones. I'm sorry. We're sorry. We're only trying to help, man."

A car horn sounded behind them. Mike let him go and started down the street. Jess and Angela sat with their mouths open in the back seat. They looked at each other in the dim glow of the passing street lights, shocked at Mike's actions as much as Steven's confession.

"You hacked our phones? Why didn't you tell us sooner?" Mike asked.

Steven sighed. "We didn't start listening until your apartment got firebombed today. We knew you guys were in serious trouble then. We've been listening for less than eight hours." Angela jumped in as soon as Steven took a breath. "We left one of the phones with Haygood, or whoever he is. What did you hear on that phone?"

"That's how we know his name is Green," Steven said. "He called about new IDs. Then he called an Agent Carson and they talked for twenty minutes. They are using Jess as bait to try and catch a dangerous thief or something. After that, the phone must have been turned off, because we haven't heard anything."

Mike pulled into the Seven-Eleven and parked beside Bobby. Bobby got out of his car and walked to Mike's window. Mike rolled the window down.

Bobby looked at Steven and back at Mike. "What's up?"

Mike explained what Steven had told them. Then he turned to Steven and asked, "Why should we not leave tonight?"

"Because they want you to run. By running, you make people start looking for you. When these people start looking for you, they start to draw attention to themselves and they make it easier for the FBI to track them down. They figured they would have had it wrapped up last night, but things didn't go as planned. There are at least six FBI agents in town, and several are watching you. Jess was supposed to be kidnapped from her duplex last night and the FBI was going to swoop in and take them there. But Jess changed her plans, and you got involved."

Mike said to Jess, "That explains how Haygood knew we were together."

Then he looked at Steven. "You got all this from listening to our phones? Why didn't you call or text us and let us know?"

Steven grinned. "As smart as we are, we forgot to write down any of the new phone numbers."

When Steven continued, he said, "I missed you at the hotel this afternoon. We didn't know where you were staying, and you never mentioned the name of the hotel, just room numbers. I lost you on the way to dinner with your parents, so I went back to Bets' duplex. When you talked to Bobby about the Jeep, I put it together since this was the only Jeep in the parking lot. This is the first time we've been able to catch up with you."

"I still don't understand why we shouldn't run?" Jess asked.

Steven looked at Jess. "Because we want to help, but we need your laptop."

"Why do you need my laptop?" Jess asked. "We're pretty sure the FBI, or Haygood, has hacked it by now."

Steven smiled. "Exactly! But, one of you said it earlier. It's time to play offense, and running away is defense."

Chapter 27

Saturday, 9:00 p.m. Fayetteville, Arkansas

Jess said, "He's right Mike. It's time to fight back. We've been talking about it, but we've only been trying to run away. Bobby challenged me at dinner. And I've been thinking about ways to fight back, but I need a computer and internet access."

"Now we're talking," Steven said. "What do we do?"

Angela spoke up then. "Bobby, let Steven take your car back to the hotel. Steven, you will need to go to my parent's room and get Jess's laptop. I'll let them know you're coming. Then you and your friends need to meet us at Jess's duplex."

Bobby handed Steven the keys and said, "Leave the keys in the ashtray, I have a door key hidden on the car."

"Steven?" Jess asked. He looked at her over his shoulder. "Bring Benji, he's the best hacker I know."

Mike looked at Steven. "You heard the ladies. Let's go."

They grabbed all their clothes and luggage out of Bobby's car and put it into the back of the Jeep Cherokee. As soon as Steven had driven away, Mike looked in the rearview mirror at Jess and his sister.

"You've lost me. What are we planning? We've been followed, attacked, and almost burned alive, and now we are bringing more people into this? I don't understand. Jess? Tell me you have a plan."

Angela spoke first. "Mike, we need someone on our side. They can be a base of operations when we decide to hit the road. Where we are going, there may not be internet, WIFI, and probably not a cell phone signal. Right?"

Mike sighed. "Right!" His sister was always right.

Jess added, "And my laptop has all the information they need to track the tag on the email. They can see what websites Dr. Haygood accessed with it. And once I sweep it for foreign software, it's the most secure laptop around."

"Alright," Mike said. He turned the ignition and started the Jeep, put the vehicle into gear, and backed out of the parking spot. He headed down a side street leaving the neon lights behind for the darkness of an older neighborhood.

Mike looked at Bobby and whispered, "Watch behind us for a black Chevy Tahoe."

Mike noticed Bobby watching him closely. "You okay, bro?" he whispered.

Mike shook his head from side to side just enough for Bobby to see. He had a feeling that their opportunity to run had just closed. But he didn't feel like spending his life running either. He reached into his shirt pocket and handed Bobby a page of folded paper. It said, *Leave town tonight. Your lives are in danger. Haygood*

Bobby turned and looked out the rearview mirror on the passenger side of the Cherokee SUV and adjusted the mirror to look behind them.

"We have a tail," he said.

Mike cursed their luck. It probably didn't matter. If Steven was right, and there were six FBI agents in town; they wouldn't have gotten away without being followed anyway. Mike cursed again and said as much.

"If Steven was right, we never would have made it out of town without the FBI knowing. So, we fight back. What's our plan?"

Jess answered, "One. We need to dig into Dr. Haygood, aka FBI Special Agent Green. Is he one and the same? Or is he lying? Two. We need to check the tracer I put on the tag that I found. Three. We need to research Agent West and the Markowitz family. We need to see if we can find death certificates for any of them. And four, get Steven, Bets, and Benji working on this stuff and we spend our time figuring out who is behind this."

Bobby added, "Like who is Charles Anderson? Is he really the one behind this? Or is there someone behind him?"

"Exactly," Angela said. "Why is someone trying to get the money after twenty years?"

"What if it's not after twenty years?" Mike asked. "What if they just found out about the money recently? Any thoughts, Jess?"

Jess hesitated, "The only people we have talked to about the money is the bank."

Angela asked, "Your bank here, or the one in Belize?"

"The one in Belize. The bank we use here doesn't have a clue about the bank in Belize. And besides, emails could have been snooped anywhere. I email the account manager in Belize most of the time. It's cheaper than an international phone call."

"Why Belize?" Bobby asked.

"A lot of the Caribbean nations are considered international tax havens, or tax shelters. They allow businesses and rich people to keep their money out of countries with high corporate income tax rates, like the US. They will also protect the owner's identity from other foreign countries. Plus, you can drive to Belize. You don't have to fly or take a ship. Two things my father was afraid to do," Jess replied.

"I bet Uncle Sam doesn't like that," Bobby said.

Mike answered this time. "The US can get the information by working with the Caribbean governments and getting a court order from their Supreme Courts. But that takes time, and money can be wired quickly if accounts are already set up. Most accounts must be set up in person, but that is often done by a registered representative, like a corporate attorney. So, the real owner is never seen."

Mike went on to explain how these corporations hid their money. By using their names and existing Caribbean islands.

He said, "Let's say Mike Corporation, registered in the Cayman Islands, owned Jess Corporation, registered in Bermuda. Then, Jess Corporation, which is owned by Bobby Corporation, is registered in Antigua. Bobby Corporation is owned by Angela Corporation, which is registered in Belize. And finally, the shareholders of Angela Corporation could be other shell corporations. Unlike in the books and the movies, you can't just Google who owns these companies. Someone usually must go to each country, to their respective government office, and find the paperwork and track down the owners the hard way. And shares can be sold or transferred privately so that no one knows who the owner is."

Angela asked, "Is that what you learned in international finance? How to hide money?"

Mike laughed. "A little. We spent a lot of time learning the financial laws of different countries, and how to deal with exchange rates."

As they were pulling down the street where Jess lived, Mike said, "I don't feel comfortable coming here, Jess. Is there anywhere else we can go?"

Mike was looking out his side view mirror and Bobby was looking out the other side view mirror. He looked at the road ahead and caught Jess's stare in the rearview mirror.

Jess asked, "What's wrong, Mike?"

Mike didn't know any other way to answer. The truth was always best.

"We're being followed," he said.

"We have two tails," Bobby added.

"Going back to your place, Jess, was not a good idea," Mike said. "Do you know anyone who lives behind you?"

Jess said, "Sure. Bets lives in the duplex right behind me. She will probably come to my back door to meet us."

"Change of plans," Mike said. "Call her and Steven, and have them meet you at her place. When we get to your duplex, you and Angela walk right through and out the back door. Go straight to her duplex. Bobby and I will stay behind to make it look like we're all there."

Jess started to protest. "Why can't we—"

"Call them!" Mike yelled.

"Okay," she said, pulling out her phone. "Please don't yell at me."

Mike apologized as he drove past her street. He wanted to give her time to make the calls. And he hoped to try to lose the followers. He knew the chances weren't good, but he wanted to try.

He made three left-hand turns. The vehicles behind them had backed off. The first one behind him went straight at the first turn. He assumed it was trying to avoid being too conspicuous. It was a little late for that. The second car followed him then. By the time he was ready to turn right to head back to Jess's street, the first SUV had caught back up and was the last one in their little caravan.

"Jess, do you have any kind of weapon at your place? A baseball bat? Anything?" Bobby asked.

"No," she said. "You can't stay behind; you have to come with us. Both of you."

Mike glanced at her in the rearview mirror. He thought he could see tears in her eyes.

"Jess, we need to stop this now. Or else they will keep coming."

Bobby showed her the pistol he had been carrying. "We aren't exactly unarmed. We know they are coming. We just need something else to fight with."

Angela reached behind her seat. "Will this do?" she asked, as she handed Bobby a tire iron.

"That will have to do," Bobby said.

Chapter 28

Mike parked the Jeep Cherokee in front of Jess's duplex. Like most college housing, parking was limited and Mike took the last parking spot. Their tails drove on by. But Mike felt they would be back.

"Come on. Let's go," Bobby said. "Hurry!"

Bobby handed Mike the pistol.

"I'll take the tire iron, you're handicapped by your finger splint, bro," Bobby said.

Mike wanted to protest, but he knew Bobby was right. Bobby held the tire iron so that it laid against his forearm and wasn't easily seen.

They all got out of the Jeep and followed Jess to her front door. It had already been repaired from the previous night's break-in. As Jess unlocked the door, she said, "It seems like a week since I was here."

As they entered her home, Jess turned on Mike, grabbed his shirt, and looked him directly in the eyes. "If we're going to be together, you do not tell me what to do."

Mike leaned down and kissed her hard. "Yes, dear. Now, please, please get out of here," he said to her.

She frowned at him and shoved him hard on his shoulder, then turned and headed to the door that led out onto her patio. Angela followed her and told both her brother and Bobby to be safe.

Angela asked, "Jess, which duplex is Bets's?"

But the question wasn't necessary as she saw the patio door of one of the duplexes open wide and a short Black girl with curly black hair stepped out and waved to them. Angela started to jog and Jess followed her.

Mike and Bobby didn't have long to get ready. Mike turned the lights off and peeked out the window. He saw the car pull up behind the Jeep, blocking it, and two men got out. They had taken about ten steps toward the duplex when the black SUV raced up and jumped the curb, cutting the men off. Someone yelled, "DEA, get down on the ground."

A city police car pulled up with blue lights flashing. Bobby peeked out of the other side of the window and said, "What the hell? Does everyone know what we're going to do before we do it?"

DEA Agent West walked towards the duplex. Mike moved to the front door to open it. Bobby grabbed his arm and took the pistol out of his hand and stuck it back into his pocket.

Mike looked at Bobby. "Thanks, man. That would not be good."

There was a loud knock on the door. "DEA, open up."

Mike opened the door. "Agent West. Come in."

Mike reached for the light switch and turned the light on. Agent West entered the duplex and looked around. He looked at Bobby who was still holding the tire iron and grinned. "Where's Miss Benelli and your sister?"

"Next street over, at a friend's house. We got here and they went straight out the back door," Mike said.

"Smart. But it was stupid for you guys to stay behind. Why didn't you call the police? You knew you were being followed," Agent West said.

Mike just stared at him. "We don't know who to trust. Dr. Haygood has lied to us, and apparently, he is working with Agent Carson. We don't know why any of this is happening. You didn't exactly impress Jess and my father today. So, what were we supposed to do?"

Agent West looked up at Mike and nodded. "Fair enough. We don't have much time. Sit down, please."

Mike and Bobby took a seat on Jess's sofa.

Agent West took out his phone and showed Mike and Bobby a picture of Charles Anderson. "Have you seen this man?"

Bobby answered, "He's driving a silver Kia, and is parked in the hotel parking lot where our family is staying. What do you want with Charles Anderson?"

Agent West stared at Bobby. "How do you know his name?"

"Agent Carson," Mike said. "He claimed that Charles Anderson was behind all this and if they caught him, it would all be over."

Agent West sighed and said, "Bennie Markowitz is assumed dead, his wife and daughter are dead. I was there when it all happened. It's my belief that he killed his wife and daughter, faked his death, and disappeared. Charles Anderson is my son-in-law. He got involved in some internet scams and told his partner the story about Markowitz. Somehow they tracked down Jess and the money her father borrowed."

Mike asked, "Who is his partner?"

"I don't know, to answer your question, but I believe the FBI does know and is using Miss Benelli as bait," Agent West said.

Another DEA agent stuck his head into the duplex. "We're clear out here, Matt."

Agent West waved his hand over his shoulder at the other agent who turned and walked out. He pulled a card out of his pocket and handed it to Mike.

"I know you have no reason to trust me, but you're good guys who are being hunted. I know you've ditched your old phones. Get rid of the ones you have now and replace them. Don't use your old emails or log into any existing accounts. Email me a single contact email as soon as you can create a new one. Call me on my cell number tomorrow afternoon. I hope to have some information by then," Agent West said. "You need to leave town immediately. Get as far away as possible and see if the FBI can straighten this out."

He looked at Bobby. "I need your car keys; by this time tomorrow morning, it will be reported that all of you died in a car crash. It will take a few hours before the local authorities realize there are no bodies to be found and that you are probably still alive. But it should give you some time to get away."

"The keys are in the ashtray in the car at the hotel. There's a hidden door key under the back bumper. Do I get paid for my car?" Bobby asked.

Agent West laughed. "We're doing you a favor getting rid of that rust bucket. Now get the girls and leave town. Drive through the night and don't stop. Tell no one where you're going, not even me. Now go."

Bobby asked, "Why are you and the DEA involved in this?"

"Fair question," Agent West said. "I believe the guy Charles is working with is involved in a lot of things, financing and money laundering for drug cartels are just part of it. If we can shut down the flow of money, we can slow down the drug flow. And maybe I can save my son-in-law, and my granddaughter can have her daddy back."

Without another word, Agent West walked out and closed the door behind him. Mike wanted to ask him about the FBI involvement, and where they were, but he never got the chance.

Bobby said, "Wow!"

Mike was already calling Jess.

Chapter 29

Before Jess and Angela came back, Mike and Bobby were hesitant to tell them everything that Agent West had said. Particularly, the part about being reported dead by the next morning.

The back door of the duplex slammed open and Jess and Angela ran to their guys, hugged them, and started asking questions.

"What happened?"

"Were you hurt?"

Bets and Steven came in after them. They were out of breath and stood with their hands on their knees.

Mike had already moved Jess to his side and had his right arm around her.

"Okay, okay, let us tell the story," Mike said. "We watched through the curtains as two men stopped behind the Jeep, got out, and started walking toward the door. The black SUV raced into the yard in front of them and the DEA jumped out and arrested them. It was Agent West. He came in and asked where you were. I told him that y'all went straight out the back door to a friend's place."

Bobby jumped in. "He said that was smart, but Mike and I were stupid for staying behind."

"You were," echoed Jess and Angela in unison.

Mike continued, "He asked why we didn't call the police when we knew we were being followed. I told him we weren't sure who to trust. Carson and Haygood hadn't left us with good feelings, and he hadn't impressed my father or Jess."

"I think that got his attention," Bobby said, "because he told us to sit down. And he started talking."

"What did he say?" Jess asked.

Mike answered, "That the Markowitz family are all dead and Bennie Markowitz is assumed dead. West said he was there when they all died. He doesn't know who is after you. He does know that whoever is after you, is his son-in-law's, Charles Anderson's, partner. He also said the guy finances drug cartels and launders money for them."

"Whoa," Jess said. "Why is he after me?"

"He said the guy is also into a lot of internet scams. Anything for easy money it sounds like," Bobby added. "He figures his son-in-law told the guy the Markowitz story and they tracked you down somehow."

"Think about it," Angela said. "I'm sure it takes a lot of work putting out credit card skimmers, and running online scams. And the payoff is probably pretty low. Getting your money would look like a huge return for the money invested."

"Oh, my God!" Jess said. "I never thought of it like that."

Mike said, "He doesn't think they will stop coming after you. He told us to leave now and keep driving until we are far away. He said to throw away our phones again, not to tell anyone where we're going."

Everyone was silent. Mike knew they needed to go, but Jess wanted to fight back. Steven broke the silence when he looked at Jess and said, "Are you rich, or something?"

Jess laughed a nervous laugh. She said, "Or something. No time for the story now. If what Agent West said is true, I just became a multimillionaire."

Bobby said, "We need to hit the road. We can stay in contact with you by email and text. Jess, do you need to grab any more clothes or anything while we're here?"

Bets said, "Why run away? We can help."

Jess turned to her. "You are helping. You'll have to do the deep searches that we can't do while we're on the move. I'll keep in touch. Thank you so much, Bets. I owe you." And then they hugged each other.

"Bets, help me grab a few things, please," Jess said. And she headed to the bedroom.

Steven looked at Mike. "What's going on, Mike?"

Mike met his gaze." A man named Markowitz loaned her dad ten million dollars for construction loans. He and his family were apparently killed right after the loan was made. She now has about twenty million dollars that these people are trying to steal. They're not going to give up easily. We have to run. And we need you guys to help us find them. Cover your tracks and do not get caught."

Jess and Bets came back into the living room carrying a couple of bags of clothes.

"I'm ready," Jess said.

Mike threw his phone on the table.

"Our phones stay here," he said.

Everyone put their phone on the table. Steven grabbed the phones. "We'll take care of those."

Jess looked at Bets and Steven. "Thank you, guys, we'll get together when this is all over, okay?"

Bets and Steven nodded their okays and headed out the back door as Mike led the others out the front door. Thunder rumbled in the distance and the smell of rain was in the wind. The yellow glow of the street light attracted hundreds of bugs creating pulsating shadows on the street as they drove away.

Chapter 30

Mr. Brock awoke to the sound of knocking on his hotel room door. Then he heard the distant sound of knocking from the room next door. He thought it might have been thunder again. But the knocking was coming from Mrs. Williams's room. He got out of bed and said, "Who is it?" He looked over to see his wife getting dressed. He grabbed his pants when he heard, "State Police. We need to speak to Mr. and Mrs. Brock please." He could hear a similar conversation from next door.

When they were dressed, he opened the door to see two uniformed troopers standing in the hallway. Mrs. Williams had just opened her door. They knew something was up; the troopers stood with their hats in their hands in front of them. The only time a trooper was allowed to take their hat off was when they were in their car or off duty.

"May we speak to all of you privately in one room please?" one of the troopers asked.

"Of course," Mr. Brock said. "Let's go to Mrs. Williams's room." He grabbed the room key card as he closed the door behind his wife.

As the second trooper closed the door behind him, the first trooper said, "I apologize for the early intrusion, but there has been an accident."

Mrs. Williams gasped and put her hand to her mouth. Mrs. Brock grabbed her and they sat on the bed hugging each other.

"Go on," Mr. Brock said.

"We are in the process of recovering a vehicle from the White River, east of Elkins. It was registered to Bobby Williams," he said. "When we arrived at the scene, the DEA had a man in custody. They said he had been stalking Mr. Williams and three others and ran them off the road. In addition to Bobby, who we understand is Mrs. Williams's grandson, they named Angela and

Mike Brock, and Jessica Benelli as passengers in the car. Last we heard; they have not found their bodies. The DEA agent in charge at the scene told us we could find you here."

Mrs. Williams and Mrs. Brock were sobbing and holding onto each other. Mr. Brock was shaking his head. He had tears streaming down his face when he asked, "Where did it happen?"

The troopers gave him as much information as they could and promised to keep him up to date. They took his phone number and quietly left the room, putting their hats on as soon as they stepped into the hallway.

Mr. Brock knelt in front of both women. "Let's have hope," he said. "They haven't found their bodies."

Chapter 31

Michael and Jessica Bennett, along with their best friends, Robert and Angela Parker, were driving their Jeep Cherokee into the suburbs of Houston when their gas light came on. Robert, or Bobby as they called him, took the first exit to find a gas station. They had taken turns, driving eight hours straight, sleeping in shifts, and only stopping for fuel, food, and bathroom breaks. Michael and Jessica had taken the first two shifts.

An hour out of Fayetteville, they had stopped at a Walmart and bought two cheap smartphones and a one-month unlimited text, calling, and data plan for each. The plan could be renewed online monthly if needed. They had talked about a laptop, but decided against it; they would rely on their friends for now. They then decided to put some of Jess's cash onto prepaid credit cards. Putting two thousand dollars each onto two new cards seemed like a lot. But it felt safer than carrying that much cash. And she still had almost six thousand dollars cash in her envelopes.

They discussed their options as they drove south. They could drive to Belize. But that meant driving through Mexico. An option none of them were thrilled about. They could fly out of Houston, or they could take a cruise ship out of Galveston. The cruise ship sounded like a little more fun and some time to relax and put together a plan. None of them had ever been on a cruise before, and since their new identities showed them to be newlyweds, what was better than taking a cruise for a honeymoon?

Using the two phones, Jessica and Angela started searching for a cruise out of Galveston that would stop in Belize. They found a seven-day cruise that had a stop in Belize. All the booking companies were showing that the next cruise was sold out. But one travel agency told Jessica that sometimes the cruise lines had last-minute cancellations. They should call the cruise line directly and ask about last-minute openings.

They had stopped at a Murphy station, in front of another Wal-Mart, to get gas when Jessica made the call to the cruise line. They had just had a cancellation on two ocean-view rooms and for one thousand dollars, they could have both rooms. Jessica made the deal using one of their prepaid cards. She and Angela had to spend several minutes taking pictures of their new documents, including their marriage licenses, which they discovered needed their signatures.

A few minutes after sending the documents, the sales clerk for the cruise line called back. She wanted to let them know that she had received everything and that she had emailed them boarding passes and last-minute information. She let them know that they might want to arrive early, since they did not have printed confirmations and their check-in would take a little longer.

It was a little after one in the morning when Jess started driving. The local painkiller in Mike's finger had finally worn off, but with several ibuprofen pills and a large coffee, he was prepared to stay awake for two more hours and help Jess navigate.

They were feeling very tired, but confident when they reached Houston. They were sure they had not been followed. Their last-minute purchases of a cruise should not show up at all since they had used a prepaid credit card.

It was during this stop that Jess checked their new email account. It was an old habit and she only expected to see the two emails from the cruise line. But a new email popped up when she opened it. It was from Agent West. They had texted him their new number and email address when they got their new phones. They weren't sure they could trust him, but he had promised to keep them informed.

It was short and she read it twice before reading it to everyone else.

"The four of you have been reported missing and presumed dead from a car crash caused by Charles Anderson. Anderson is in custody but is not talking. Find somewhere to hide. I will send more info when we can make sense of it."

"What do you make of that?" Bobby asked.

"I don't know," Jess replied.

"I think," Mike started and hesitated, "that Jess was being used as bait by the FBI. But we already knew that."

They stared at him, waiting for him to continue.

"Where were they last night, when we went to Jess's duplex? We told Agent Carson about Anderson. You couldn't miss him in the restaurant or the hotel parking lot. They wanted Anderson free to lead them to his partner. They were prepared for us to be collateral damage. And the DEA is only in it because of Agent West's son-in-law," Mike finished.

Jess replied, "I think you're right. We need his phone."

"Whose phone?" Angela asked.

"Anderson's phone," she said.

"I'm not driving back to get it," Bobby said. "You just booked us on a honeymoon cruise, remember?"

Mike said, "Let's disappear for the next few days and catch up on our sleep. Then we can reach out to Agent West and see if they have found the bad guy."

Jess sighed deeply. "Okay," she said. Then she hit send on the phone and turned it off.

Chapter 32

FBI Consultant Green, also known as Dr. Haygood, cursed himself. He had overplayed his hand. Now, he may have gotten four innocent students killed. He and Agent Carson had decided to back off on the surveillance the night before. They could tell Mike was getting suspicious. With the help of the bug in the bookstore bag, they also knew their plans. Or so they thought.

Besides, Charles Anderson was their paid informant. He was working both sides and following them closely. Somehow, they had slipped away. And Charles Anderson had been arrested for running them off the road.

He and Special Agent Carson had been tracking this criminal activity for two years, and this was the closest they had ever gotten to a lead on the main person behind all these online financial thefts. They had traced the thefts to someone associated with the University. Green had gone undercover and ruled out all the staff. That meant it had to be a student. Their primary suspect had been Jess, but they had ruled her out after she started taking Dr. Haygood's class. He had been able to rule out all the students who had taken his class. They had been making progress with other sources until the DEA agent stuck his nose into his son-in-law's business. Now it had been blown all to pieces.

The knock on his apartment door brought him back to reality. He opened his door to find Special Agent Carson standing there. He stepped aside to let the younger agent come in.

"What have you heard?" asked Green.

"No more than we already knew," Carson said. "West isn't saying anything to anyone. And the state police can only tell us what's on the report."

"How the hell did Charles get charged with running them off the road?" Green asked. "You and I know he couldn't have done that."

Carson nodded. "We blew it," he said. "And those kids are in real trouble if they're still alive. We should have had additional surveillance besides Charles.

"That's my fault," Green said. "We were warned about the problems with using people without their knowledge. I warned Mike to get out of town and hide. I didn't think they could do it without us knowing."

Chapter 33

DEA Agent West was pissed at his supposed tech guy. He couldn't get into Charles Anderson's phone. Then he got the email from Jess. He got mad again because he had told them when they were supposed to contact him. But, when he finally read her message, he had to smile. The girl had an idea of who was behind the attacks and was thinking ahead.

Agent West grabbed the phone from his tech guy and said, "Let's go for a ride."

Fifteen minutes later, Agent West and his tech guy, Daniel, stopped in front of Bet's duplex.

"Let's crack this phone open and get you educated."

Daniel protested, "I know what I'm doing. It just takes some time."

"Time is something we don't have," replied Agent West.

Fifteen minutes later, they were walking out of Bets's duplex. Agent West sported a rare smile, while Daniel walked with his head down, fuming.

Daniel said, "You do realize that everything they did in there was illegal. Without a search warrant, everything we got off of that phone cannot be used in court."

Agent West was still smiling as he replied, "Yes."

"Then why are you so smug right now?" Daniel asked.

Agent West waited until they had gotten into the black SUV before he replied.

"This phone belongs to my son-in-law. He's in over his head on two counts. One, he has no idea who he is working with on the criminal side. Those kids, as you called them, can probably tell us more in a few hours from now than

Charles will ever find out. Two, they told us within two minutes of looking at his call log that he has had extensive contact with the FBI. Which means he's working with them. The information that we get will just be had sooner than we would get it through an interagency cooperation agreement with the FBI. And third, this information will never be used in court."

"What do you mean?" Daniel asked.

"They didn't break into Charles's phone. They copied his sim card and added a program to the sim card that reports back to them all communication that's made on that phone," Agent West said.

Daniel started to speak but Agent West held his hand up to the young man. He said, "I know you are going to say something about illegal wiretapping. Don't. We're going to release Charles. They'll monitor his contacts. Not us. They'll provide us with tips from concerned citizens. Then we follow up on an anonymous tip. Understand?"

"Yes, sir," Daniel replied. But he didn't look too happy.

"Now, did you make note of the equipment that they were using?" asked West.

"I know what they were using. But we can't do what they just did," Daniel said.

"That's not what I'm thinking," Agent West said. "What can we add to our agency phones that will help us do our job better? Remote trackers, remote recorders, anything that our agents can use that will help us keep them safe."

The young agent smiled for the first time. "I think I see what you are getting at," he said. "And as long our agents know they're there, most of the options would be legal. And some of these options are already on the phone. We just have to teach them how to use them."

Agent West gave him a wink. "Now, let's start with how can I record a phone call that comes to my phone?"

"Oh, that's easy," the tech said.

Chapter 34

Bobby caught himself closing his eyes; he was getting sleepy. Even though it was early Sunday morning, they were still in the middle of five lanes on I-45 near downtown Houston.

He was white-knuckling the steering wheel. Angela had told him the population of Houston was around 2.4 million, about half a million people less than the entire state of Arkansas. She had assured him that at least two million of them were still asleep or at home this early on Sunday morning.

"Relax," Angela told Bobby. "Houston covers six-hundred-fifty-five square miles. Out of the half million people that are awake, that puts just seven-hundred-sixty people in the square mile we are in. I'm sure most of them are at home."

"And at least a million more will wake up shortly, and get ready to go to work and to church," Bobby replied. "How can this many people live together in one spot on this planet? Where does all the sewage go? And trash? The landfill must be larger than most towns."

Angela grinned at him. "Are you awake now?"

"Not exactly the kind of trashy thoughts I like to have this early in the morning. Some coffee wouldn't hurt," he replied.

"There's a mall up ahead. Maybe we can find a restaurant and get some breakfast. We have about five hours before we need to check-in. We need to figure out where to park for the cruise. And we need to buy you and Mike some more clothes," Angela said.

"Sounds like a plan. Can we get out of Houston before the other two million people wake up?"

Angela turned to look back at her brother and Jess. They had pulled some luggage between the seats and Jess was lying across it with her head in Mike's lap. Mike was leaning his head back against the headrest, his eyes closed. He opened his eyes as if he felt his sister looking at him.

"Sounds good," he said to her. "I need to take some more ibuprofen. My finger is swelling."

His talking woke Jess up. She opened her eyes and sat up.

"Are we there yet?" she asked.

"We're stopping to get some breakfast. And do a little shopping in the mall before we head onto the ship," Angela said.

"Okay," she said, yawning. "Do I hear sirens?"

"Shit! Coming up fast from behind us," Bobby said while looking in the rearview mirror.

"Get your seatbelts on!" He shouted as he started reducing his speed and changing lanes to get to the shoulder.

The Cadillac clipped the back driver-side corner of the Jeep Cherokee. The Cherokee spun around in a complete circle three times. Bobby tried to steer and bring the Jeep to a stop, while screaming something about flying turd heads. They could hear the sounds of their screeching tires and the crashing of the car that had lost control, flipped on its side, and started rolling after hitting them. That, mixed with the sirens of approaching police cars and their own screaming, created a cacophony of sounds that reached down into their very being, found their primal fears, and brought them to the surface. Just as quickly as it happened, it was over. The Jeep came to a skidding halt after snapping a universal joint and losing its rear axle. The radio was still playing, the engine still running and windshield wipers were slapping at the non-existent rain.

Angela moaned because her head had slammed into the passenger door window. Jess had never gotten her seat belt buckled and Mike had grabbed her and held her tightly. Their heads had banged together several times. Mike groaned and held his head. Jess was not moving. Bobby still had two hands on the steering wheel and was looking straight ahead through the windshield.

"Ladies and gentlemen, thank you for flying Air Bobby. It appears we have experienced a little turbulence upon our landing," Bobby quipped, his voice shaky.

They were staring in the direction they had just come from and were watching the police cars arrive on the scene of their wreck. There must have been twenty police cars chasing the car that crashed. He asked, "Is everyone okay?"

When no one answered, he turned to check on Angela first. Seeing that she was moving, he turned and looked at Mike and Jess. He saw Mike holding his head but saw no movement from Jess.

Several police cars passed them and surrounded the remains of the Cadillac. Two police cars surrounded their Jeep and the officers rushed to them, assessing their injuries, and calling for ambulances. The officers made them stay in the Jeep until an ambulance arrived and paramedics could check them over. Jess woke up right before the ambulance arrived.

"What happened?" she asked. "My head is killing me."

Mike was still holding his head. He started to speak, but nothing came out.

Bobby, watching them both in the rearview mirror, said, "We were in an accident. We got clipped by a Cadillac doing at least a hundred. You two stay still, the ambulance is here."

A police officer appeared at Bobby's window. "Are y'all okay? Might want to turn that Jeep off. Ah don't think you're going too far without them rear wheels," he drawled.

Bobby turned the ignition off. The radio and the windshield wiper stopped.

"Yes, sir. Just in shock, it happened so fast," said Bobby.

"You did a nice piece of driving, son. How fast were you going when he hit you?"

Bobby said, "I was slowing down to get on the shoulder. I was doing around forty-five, I think."

"Slowing down probably saved your lives. Allowed the Jeep to spin and not flip," the officer said. "Where y'all headed? The beach?"

"A cruise," Bobby replied. "We just graduated from college and got married. Honeymoon cruise."

"Congratulations," the officer drawled. "I'll be close by. I'll step back and let these good paramedics do their job."

The paramedics were quick and thorough. After checking all four, they spent the most time talking to Mike and Jess. They had given the three with head injuries ice packs to hold against their heads. Bobby was okay. Angela had hit her head on the window. Mike and Jess had somehow head-butted each other during the spin-out. They were told that they were lucky to not have concussions.

As the paramedics were preparing to leave, Bobby asked about the driver of the other car. The officer who had talked to him earlier answered for the paramedics.

"He didn't make it. They're still trying to cut his body out of the car. Some of the officers chasing him said he had reached speeds of a hundred and fifty miles per hour," he said. "Now," he drawled. "We got a tow truck coming for the Jeep. I'm trying to find you a cab to take y'all to Galveston, so y'all can take that honeymoon cruise. Never been on a cruise myself. Is this your first time?"

Before Bobby could answer, the officer excused himself to answer a radio call. The officer came back to Bobby and asked, "How long have you owned the Jeep?"

"I just bought it yesterday from a college buddy. I have a bill of sale in the glove box."

Bobby was suddenly worried that he might have to reveal who he really was. Trying to explain the different IDs was going to be difficult.

The officer relayed Bobby's answer to his dispatcher. That seemed to be all he needed.

The officer said, "We finally found a cab company with a minivan that will take y'all all the way to the cruise ship in Galveston. He will be here in twenty minutes. Now, I need to get y'all's names and addresses for the accident report."

Chapter 35

Benji had volunteered for the graveyard shift because he was usually up all night anyway. He had encouraged Bets and Steven to get some sleep. None of them had slept very much that weekend. Besides, he needed them out of the way so he could find Jess. He was tired of hacking cell phones, creating credit card skimmers and copiers, running email scams, and stealing credit card info over unsecured WIFI. You never made much money from those scams. His biggest scam had been the fake income tax returns he had done two years before. But that one had almost gotten him caught. He had already realized that he could make more with his degree in a year than he could make scamming people in three years. Why not go clean? He had asked himself that a hundred times. But he had bills to pay, that's why he didn't go clean. There was something about the adrenaline rush, too, like a video game high, that kept him doing it.

Then the DEA guys showed up, asking for help with a cell phone. Steven and Bets had let them in and seemed to know the older one by name. Benji explained that it was illegal to break into someone's phone. That was odd. Imagine him explaining the law to the law. When the older agent explained what he wanted and that it meant protecting Jess and her friends, Benji didn't hesitate. It might be his last chance to find Jess. He had taken out the sim card and copied it, put the copied sim card into another phone, and got the information they wanted. He didn't know whose phone it was and didn't care. What the DEA didn't know was that he had made a third copy at the same time.

He had an internet search running in the background. If there was any mention of Jess or Mike, it would notify him immediately. He had checked it several times to make sure it was running correctly. It had found nothing since midnight and what it found then were updates on yesterday's events.

When it finally found their names, he read the screen with disbelief. Presumed dead from a car crash? They ran off the road. How could that have happened?

He finally said to Steven and Bets, "Shit! It's over guys. They're dead." He left the report up on the screen for Steven and Bets to read. He started packing his other gear, getting ready to leave. Then he received a text message from his dad. It simply said *RUN*.

Bets was crying. Steven was trying to console her, but he was crying, too. By then Benji was packing up his laptop into an old backpack. Steven looked at Benji and asked him where he was going. He had to help them find out who did this.

"I'm going home. If the police don't know by now, they'll never know." And Benji walked out the door.

He loaded his gear into his old Volkswagen Jetta and headed to his apartment.

About halfway to his apartment, it dawned on him who owned the phone the DEA had brought to him that morning. Right then Benji decided his dad was right, it was time to leave town.

He parked the Jetta in the apartment complex parking lot, unloaded his computer gear, and went to his apartment. Twenty minutes later, he had showered, shaved, and dressed.

He took a few extra minutes to put on the blonde wig, and apply some lipstick and eyeliner. He checked himself in the mirror. Approved the look and smiled to himself.

He grabbed a duffle bag from his closet and threw in some clothes. Then he went to his desk, opened the bottom drawer, and opened a small lock box hidden under several notebooks. He took out all the cash, threw the lockbox back into the drawer, and closed it. He grabbed the old backpack and stuffed the money into it. He then picked up the duffle and walked to his door.

He listened for sounds from the walkway. Hearing nothing, he opened the door carefully and peeked out. Seeing no one, he assumed the identity of a blond woman and walked away from the apartment for good.

She walked straight past the VW Jetta to a white minivan with 'Internet and Computer Repair' written on the side. Got in and drove away.

Chapter 36

Steven and Bets looked at each other after Benji left.

Bets said, "You think he bought it?"

"He believes we believe they're dead. I think he believes they're dead."

"Did the DEA agent get what he needed?" Bets asked Steven.

"I'm not sure what they were after. I think they really wanted the information Benji gave them. Plus, I think they wanted to know how much Benji knew about hacking," Steven said.

"I got the IP address off his laptop when he went to the bathroom last night. And for good measure, I added a little data mining file. We should know soon what he's up to."

"Let's get busy then," Bets said. "Jess gave us a lot of work to do."

Chapter 37

Agent West pulled into an apartment complex. This one was a little more upscale and a little further from campus. He drove around looking at the numbers on the buildings until he found the building he wanted.

He found a parking space and said to Daniel, "Come on. Let's go practice a little interagency cooperation."

"What do you mean?" asked Daniel.

"Watch and learn," West said.

West knocked. He was relieved when the FBI consultant opened his door. He wasn't sure he would be home. Green appeared surprised to see the DEA agent.

"Agent West, what a surprise."

"Hello, Green. Or should I call you Haygood?"

"I think Green is good. Come in. I'm sure this is not a social call."

Once they were in the apartment and introductions were made, Green invited them to sit down and offered them coffee. West accepted, saying it had been a long night. Daniel declined. FBI Special Agent Carson was still there and already had a cup. Green struggled a little with one arm still in a sling.

"So, what can I do for you this morning, West?"

"We're just doing a little interagency cooperation, unlike you. You could have let me know that my son-in-law was working for you," West growled.

"I'm sorry," Green said. "That was need-to-know only."

West nodded. He didn't like it, but he understood. There were a lot of things about his job he didn't like. But you had to do a lot of little things you didn't like, or were a little on the unethical side, to catch the criminals who weren't bound by the same rules of ethics you were.

"We came by to give you an update. I think you lost the trust of your girl and her friends. I'm pretty sure they know you were using her for bait."

Green looked down at the floor, admitting nothing.

"Go on," Green said.

"She and her friends are alive," West said and leaned forward. "They went back to her duplex last night. We took down two more guys at her place. She had gotten some of her hacker friends together to help them trace who was after her. I didn't talk to her. She and her boyfriend's sister ran straight through her duplex to her friend's duplex. There she helped one of the hackers set up his computer and she saw something that bothered her. I left my card with her boyfriend. She sent me an email this morning. She is pretty certain that a young man named Benji Smith is involved. I did a little checking, and his father is suspected of a lot of credit card scams and funding some start-up drug operations. I'm fairly sure that Benji is Charles's local contact. We're thinking about releasing Charles in a little while. We have nothing on him. The charges are bogus. But we needed to give the kids some time to disappear."

Agent West leaned back and studied Green and Carson. They exchanged glances.

Green sighed. "I'm glad they're okay."

Carson said, "We originally suspected Jess of the credit card scams and other crimes. We tracked them to Fayetteville, and then to someone at the University. But they were very good at hiding their tracks. Every time we got close, they changed tactics. Green, here, who really does have a Ph.D. in computer science, went undercover as a professor. This gave him access to most of the students' records and we could access the faculty and students' computers to see who was doing what. We quickly ruled out many of our prime suspects, including Miss Benelli."

Green picked up the story then.

"Benji was on our radar, but we couldn't access any of his personal data. He rarely used the University computers, and then it was only for classwork. We couldn't access his personal computer because we couldn't get through his firewalls before he shut it down. He seems to get online, do what he needs to do, and get off, leaving very little evidence."

Agent West added, "Jess believes he is using multiple cell phones. He has the hardware to copy SIM cards and he may have found a way to counterfeit SIM cards as well. He probably has the equipment to copy and make fake credit cards also."

"Not all carriers use SIM cards," Daniel said. "But some phones can hold two sim cards, usually one for a nationwide plan and the other for international calling."

Green said, "By using an international sim card, he can call a computer outside the U.S. and control it remotely. By using different VPNs, he can hack from anywhere in the world. We need to bring him in now for questioning. West, do you want the honors?"

"No. I think you need to clean up your own mess. You have been following this for two years. But I did have an agent follow him." He looked at his phone. "He just went to his apartment. You can catch him there."

Green said to Carson, "Let's finish this."

Chapter 38

The tow truck showed up. They had unloaded their luggage from the Jeep and set it on the side of the freeway. Bobby gave his new name and one of their cell phone numbers to the tow truck driver. He got a business card from the driver and told him they were going on a one-week honeymoon cruise.

He said he would call the tow company in a couple of days to decide what to do with the Jeep. He paid the driver in cash and shook his hand. He walked back to the others and their luggage. "At least we don't have to pay for cruise ship parking now."

Mike laughed. "Leave it to Bobby to find the bright side of a wreck."

Suddenly they were all laughing. Bobby knew his comment wasn't very funny. But they needed the release from the exhaustion and tension. They had been holding everything back the last few hours and it needed to be broken, if only for a few minutes.

When they had finished laughing, Mike observed, "At least we survived this one, we didn't do as well in the first one this morning."

"It's a damn good thing we weren't there for it," Bobby said.

The officer with the drawl was walking toward them. As he got closer, he said, "I hope one of y'all can speak some Spanish, because your taxi driver doesn't speak much English."

"We get by," Angela said, speaking for the first time since the wreck. "Our housekeeper taught us to speak Spanish when we were growing up."

"Well, you're going to need it. I'm sorry y'all had this happen in our city. I hope y'all enjoy your cruise."

As he walked back to his patrol car, a minivan with taxi stickers on it pulled up. A rather plump man with a dark round face got out of the van and walked around to the group, and asked in Spanish if they were looking for a ride. Mike responded, "Si, and I bet you speak English also."

Javier, that's what the driver said his name was, smiled sheepishly, and explained he was ashamed of his English-speaking ability. Mike made a deal with him; they would help him with his English if he would help them with their Spanish.

"Deal?" Mike asked.

"Deal!" Javier grinned.

They had a few hiccups in their conversations, but they laughed them off. Jess, who had taken high school French, was even picking up a little Spanish along the way.

Javier was from El Salvador. It chafed him that Americans thought of everyone from Central America as Mexican. Mike and Angela told him they understood, their housekeeper had been born in Guatemala, and she had the same experience. Javier smiled happily at this. At least some Americans understood that all Spanish-speaking people did not come from Mexico.

By the time they reached the port in Galveston, Javier was speaking decent English. He knew the words from watching television, but not how to shape his mouth and tongue to make them sound right. Mike, Angela, and Bobby had a refresher course in Spanish, and Jess had picked up a few phrases also.

It was twelve-thirty p.m. when they reached Galveston. They had talked Javier into a quick stop at a FedEx store to print their boarding passes and luggage tags. They had even bought him breakfast at a fast-food restaurant.

Chapter 39

The on-call FBI agents responded within ten minutes of Agent Green's call. They confirmed with the DEA agent that Benji had not left the apartment complex. The DEA agent pointed to the Jetta and said his car was still there.

They contacted the apartment manager just in case they needed to be let in. When the apartment manager showed up five minutes later, the FBI team of four agents, three men and a woman, moved to the apartment. They had no reason to believe he was armed, so they didn't draw their weapons.

The lead agent knocked on the door. "FBI, open up!"

There was no sound from the apartment. After two minutes, they had the apartment manager unlock the door. This time they drew their side arms and moved carefully into the apartment, clearing each room as they went.

It didn't take long to clear a one-bedroom apartment. There was no one there. And very little in the apartment.

The lead agent called Green to let him know. Then he told one of the other agents to go get the DEA agent.

The DEA agent entered the apartment, looked at the lead FBI agent, and shook his head.

"The only person who left this apartment complex was a tall blond woman. She got into a white minivan with internet and computer repair signs on the side of it and left."

"Shit!" the female agent said.

All eyes turned to her. She quickly related her story from Friday morning of her seeing a blonde woman get into a white minivan and then seeing a young man drive it away.

"He's wearing a disguise and driving a different vehicle," the female agent said.

The lead FBI agent looked at the DEA agent. He knew the answer before he asked. "Did you get a plate number?"

The DEA agent shook his head.

The female FBI agent said, "I did."

When it was determined that the suspect had left just five minutes before the FBI arrived, all agents quickly left and started searching for the white minivan. An APB had been issued to the local police. But Benji had left over twenty minutes before.

* * *

Benji stopped at a secluded car wash and took the magnetic signs off the sides of the van and disposed of them in an overflowing dumpster. He opened the back hatch of the minivan, found a box, and changed the license plate. He had kept the original plate from the previous owner. It was expired, but it would serve as a distraction.

He then put four quarters into the box and washed the dust lines off that showed where the magnetic signs had been. In less than five minutes, he was heading out of town on back roads that took him past cattle farms and the occasional grape farm. The small community of Highfill was his destination. That's where Northwest Arkansas National Airport was located.

Chapter 40

Mr. and Mrs. Brock and Mrs. Williams had talked for over an hour after the state troopers had left. They finally decided that the police finding no bodies was a good thing. They had, in fact, decided their kids weren't dead. They speculated that their kids had decided to disappear. They needed to help them by carrying on as if they were dead. Doing the things that grieving parents and grandparents do when they lose their children. And the truth was that they acted as if they had lost them. There was still that slim possibility that they were really gone. But it was possible the kids didn't tell them what was going on because they needed their parents' reactions to be real. Or the kids' plan changed so quickly that hat they didn't have time to tell them.

They decided to shower, get dressed, and start making phone calls. Mrs. Brock was in the shower when she suddenly thought of Mrs. Benelli, Jess's mother. After finishing her shower, she searched the white pages app on her phone, found Mrs. Benelli's phone number, and called her.

She could tell Mrs. Benelli had been crying. She explained who she was and why she was calling. She told Mrs. Benelli that they needed to talk in private and in person. There were things she needed to know. There were things that had recently happened which the police probably would not tell her.

Mrs. Benelli was hesitant to leave home, afraid she might miss some notification about her only daughter. Mrs. Brock assured her she had lost three kids that morning. Mike and Angela as well as Bobby, who had been Mike's best friend since they were four years old and whom she was sure would have become her son-in-law soon. She also told her that Jess was the first and only girlfriend that Mike had ever had, she felt that Jess would have become her daughter-in-law eventually.

Mrs. Brock promised Mrs. Benelli that if the police notified her of anything, Mrs. Benelli would be the first person she called. Then she told Mrs. Benelli that they believed the longer the search went without finding any bodies, the greater the chance their kids were alive.

* * *

Mrs. Benelli decided that she would drive to Fayetteville. It would take her a few hours to get there. First, she had to get a grip on herself. She had sobbed uncontrollably after the phone call telling her about the wreck. She would call Mrs. Brock as soon as she arrived. Her husband passed away two years ago. She couldn't survive losing Jess this soon after losing her husband. Parents weren't supposed to outlive their children, she thought. She wanted to believe Mrs. Brock. She really did.

Chapter 41

Bets and Steven were in shock from what they had uncovered. In fact, they were in shock from several things. The first shock was Jess's laptop and her three notebooks full of notes. They had discovered software on her laptop they had never seen before. Her notebooks were full of logins and passwords for many websites. She could access her high school's records, the college registrar's database, and some government and law enforcement sites.

The third notebook listed websites and chat rooms where she could go to get information and help from other hackers. This was the one that helped them the most.

They found Jess's notes about a dark chat room called emailjailbreaker. Her notes mentioned her username as wonderwoman415 and a contact's name of #1HackerGod. Bets pecked at the keyboard of the laptop, and Steven watched over her shoulder.

Bets logged into the chat room and saw that #1HackerGod had just commented on someone's post. Bets typed into the comment box, "#1HackerGod, I need some help."

He responded, "Hello wonderwoman415, where have you been?"

Bets was about to type, "Busy with finals," when a guy's face appeared on the screen. He had a chubby face with a full black beard and thick eyeglasses.

"You're not wonderwoman415! You have two minutes to explain why you're using her login and password in this chatroom," he said.

This was the second shock of their morning. Steven said, "We're friends of wonderwoman415. She has been attacked by attempted kidnappers. Her place was broken into, her phone and one of her laptops were stolen. Her boyfriend's apartment was firebombed. And there was a second attempted attack at her duplex last night."

"Prove it!" the round face of #1HackerGod said.

Steven grabbed the second of three laptops they had open on Bets's dining room table. He held out the screen beside Bets's head and adjusted Jess's laptop camera to see the screen. He said, "This is the attack at the police station. The blonde in the picture is Jess, I mean wonderwoman415."

Steven could see the guy's head and eyes darting back and forth between computer monitors. He looked directly back at them.

"That's enough!" the face on the screen said. He seemed a little deflated. "I'm way ahead of you. I see a police report from this morning that says she died in a car crash. But they haven't found any bodies yet. Is that right?"

"That's right," Bets said. "We have reason to believe that they may still be alive. Either way, we want to find who is behind this. We are computer science majors, but whoever is doing this is a good hacker. I mean a really good hacker."

"Not as good as me!" an irritated #1HackerGod said. "Alright, I'm in. Wonderwoman415 helped me out one time and I repay debts. Don't change this screen, I need to close a few things out and I will be right back."

Two minutes later he was back on the screen.

"Talk to me. Tell me everything from the beginning." This time they picked up on a British accent.

Bets and Steven told the story, as they knew it, starting with the attack Friday evening. They finished with the story they heard in Jess's duplex last night. #1HackerGod seemed to be processing the information when Steven remembered to mention Jess's suspicion of Benji and his reaction this morning.

"Okay, Jess, as you called her, and I have chatted before. My real name is Harvey. That's why I was able to see you and pop up on her screen. It's easier to talk this way than to type back and forth. What do you have to work with and what have you done so far?" he asked.

They told him that Jess had traced a tag on an email between her and her boyfriend. The trace came back to an unknown IP address. It appeared that when they tried to use GPS functions to locate it, it showed Jess's address.

Harvey was quick to respond. He said, "That's simple. Someone has placed a microcomputer in or near her place that can eavesdrop and piggyback on her or her neighbor's WIFI. Finding it won't tell us who it belongs to though."

"It might have fingerprints," Bets said.

"Who's going to check for those?" Harvey asked.

"Well, the DEA was here this morning asking for help breaking into a phone. Maybe we can get them to help," Steven said.

Harvey nearly choked, "The cops were there asking for help breaking into a phone?"

"Weird, huh?" Bets said while looking at Steven.

Steven said, "Hey, we're in the clear. The DEA and the FBI are really after this person. We have done nothing wrong."

"Really?" Harvey asked. "Listen, call your pal, the cop. Tell him to look for a microcomputer about the size of a pack of cigarettes in or around wonderwoman's apartment. Tell him to check for fingerprints. Tell him to check out your friend Benji. I'm betting they are one and the same. Write down my email address and keep me posted. I want to be long gone before your cop friend shows up."

Bets wrote down the email address and they said bye to Harvey. She then pulled out the business card that Agent West had given her that morning. She grabbed her phone, sighed, and dialed the number. She hated talking on her phone.

Agent West answered on the first ring. Bets turned her phone on speaker and explained what they had learned. And that they suspected Benji was behind it.

Agent West sighed and said, "I've turned this back over to the FBI. They raided Benji's apartment an hour ago. He's disappeared. Did you know he would dress up as a girl to hide his identity?" This was the third shock of the day for Bets and Steven.

"Whoa! What?" Steven responded.

West said he would relay their information to the FBI. But they were pretty busy looking for Benji, whom he believed had skipped town.

Chapter 42

Even though they had their Jeep wrecked, they would arrive in Galveston with two hours to spare. They needed to make a few clothing purchases before the cruise. They convinced Javier to take them to a mall. They told him to keep the meter running. They would be back as soon as possible.

The few dress clothes they had with them at college had burned in the apartment. They would need them for the formal dinner on the second night. They divided the two phones they had and the guys went one direction and the girls went the other.

After thirty minutes, the guys had found sports coats, shirts, and khaki slacks. But they were having trouble finding shoes. The girls were having better luck. They had both found semi-formal dresses that fit them. They already had shoes that would match. They spent a few more minutes finding sandals and looking at sundresses for the cruise. They decided not to splurge and to shop at the ports.

They found the guys trying on shoes in a Dillard's. The women looked at their jackets and approved. They asked about ties and belts. The guys said they had not found any yet. They told the guys to keep trying on shoes and they would find ties and belts.

After ten more minutes, they checked out and called Javier. He would pick them up at the main entrance.

It had taken them an hour in the mall. They still had an hour to get to the cruise terminal. "Plenty of time," Javier assured them.

Mike rubbed his head. "Can we make one more stop at a pharmacy?"

Javier found a Walgreens and, armed with a list, Bobby went in to find Tylenol, Ibuprofen, bandages, and tape for Mike's finger. Another ten minutes, and they were on the final leg of their trip to Galveston.

The cruise terminal was alive with people arriving. The smell of the salt water was in the air and the sound of reggae music came from the overhead speakers. A crowd of people were chatting and laughing and carrying luggage toward the terminal.

They had taken Javier's advice and checked their luggage with the pursers. It would be waiting outside their room when they got on the ship. They needed to check in early because of the last-minute purchases of their tickets. They were only thirty minutes early, but as it turned out, they were not allowed to check in before 2:30.

Mike and Jess were standing in the queue with Bobby and Angela behind them. If they could get checked in, they might have time to check out a few shops and get something to drink before heading to their rooms.

Now that they had finally arrived and slowed down, they were all feeling that slow crash from total exhaustion. The lack of sleep over the last forty-eight hours was beginning to catch up with them.

Mike turned to Bobby and asked softly, "Do you still have the pistol?"

Bobby smiled. "No, bro, I gifted it to Javier."

"What do you mean?" Jess asked, looking confused.

Bobby smiled again. "I told him every cab driver needed some protection, and I couldn't take it with me."

Jess looked at Mike. "My poor mom thinks I'm dead by now." She leaned her head against his chest and hugged him tightly.

Mike hugged her back but looked at his sister. "I've been thinking the same thing about our parents. Angela? Do you still have Mom's email password?"

"Yes," she replied. "What are you thinking Mike?"

"Log in. Write an email and save it as a draft. She will find it when she checks her email. Can you write it in Cantonese?" Mike asked.

"The email I can do. The Cantonese, I cannot. I'm like you, Mike, I can speak it, but I can't write it."

"Tell her we're okay. And ask her to reach out to Jess's mother and let her know, too."

Angela took out her phone. It took her a couple of minutes to find the online login and get into the email account.

"She hasn't checked her email all weekend," Angela said.

She talked out loud as she composed the email. "Mom, we are okay. Just laying low for a while. Please contact Jess's mom and let her know the truth. But please continue to act like we are gone. We need some time. Love." She hesitated and asked, "How do I sign it?"

Jess smiled and said, "Sign it JAMB."

Angela smiled back, "I like that. She will know exactly what it means, too."

She saved the email as a draft. Because a draft is never sent, it leaves no trail to follow.

"Are we ready to trash another phone?" Angela asked.

"Not yet," Mike responded. "We need to call Agent West. And we probably need to contact Steven and Bets. Then we trash the phone."

"Okay, I'm sending Mom a text to check her email drafts. Then I'll give you the phone to call Agent West, and Jess can call Bets."

Chapter 43

Sunday, 2:00 p.m. Fayetteville, Arkansas

Mrs. Benelli called the phone number Mrs. Brock had given her. Mrs. Brock answered on the first ring.

"I'm in your hotel parking lot," said Mrs. Benelli.

"I'll meet you in the lobby. We can come back to my room and talk in private," Mrs. Brock responded.

"Okay," Mrs. Benelli answered with a sniffle.

She had cried most of the way there. The only reason she hadn't had a complete breakdown was the hope that Mrs. Brock was correct. Sometimes it only takes a little hope. A slight chance will hold a strong spirit together, and keep it from shattering into a thousand pieces.

They met in the lobby. Mrs. Brock recognized the grieving mother immediately. She stepped forward and enveloped Mrs. Benelli in a big hug. Mrs. Benelli let loose the emotions she had been controlling and the tears flowed freely then. Mrs. Brock held her tight and let her own tears flow.

Sitting in the corner of the lobby hiding behind a newspaper, Charles Anderson watched the two women. His father-in-law had arrested him and charged him with killing their kids. Then he was released this morning. He knew he hadn't killed them. He had been sitting in his car at the hotel at the time the wreck occurred. He was here now out of curiosity more than anything else. His internet contact had not responded to him since he was released. He had not reached out to the FBI or his father-in-law. He knew he was done here. It was time to go home. He snapped a picture with his phone. He sent three messages. All included the picture and said the same thing. "The parents are convinced the kids are dead, I'm done."

Mrs. Brock loosened her hug and guided Mrs. Benelli to the elevators. Mrs. Brock noticed the man in the corner. She saw him put down the paper and walk out of the hotel. She had not seen the picture the FBI had shown the kids last night, but her instincts told her that this was the man who had been following her children.

As the two ladies took the elevator to the Brocks' hotel room, they made idle chit-chat. How was the drive? How are you holding up?

Mrs. Brock opened the hotel room and entered, then introduced her husband and Mrs. Williams.

Mr. Brock was holding his wife's cell phone. His eyes were wide when he interrupted his wife and said, "You have a text message."

"Not now, dear," she replied.

He held the phone out to her and said, "Yes, dear. Now! It's from J. A. M. B."

She looked him in the eyes about to protest, when she realized what J. A. M. B. must stand for. She grabbed the phone from him and read the message aloud.

"Please check your draft email messages. Do not respond to this message. J. A. M. B."

Mrs. Williams and Mrs. Benelli were looking back and forth at the Brocks. Mrs. Brock worked frantically to open her email account. She found the draft message box and opened the draft. She skimmed it quickly before reading it aloud.

"They're okay," she whispered and slowly sat on the bed. Then she read the message.

"Mom, we are okay. Just laying low for a while. Please contact Jess's mom and let her know the truth. But please continue to act like we are gone. We need some time. Love JAMB."

Mrs. Williams and Mrs. Benelli still looked confused.

"Who is JAMB?" Mrs. Benelli asked.

"That would be Jessica, Angela, Mike, and Bobby," Mr. Brock said. "You see, Bobby, Angela, and Mike started a small electronics business in high school and they named it BAM, after Bobby, Angela, and Mike. That would be their way of sending us a message in a message, letting us know it's real."

"So, Jessica is alive? And your kids, too?" she asked, still in shock.

Mrs. Williams reached over and grabbed her hand. "Yes, dear. Those kids are smart, resilient and they are survivors. But we can't celebrate right now. We have to act like they are gone, so they can come back to us."

Mrs. Williams nodded. "But why? What is happening?"

"What has Jess told you?" asked Mrs. Brock.

Mrs. Benelli told them about seeing the Friday night attack on the news. Then Jess called her Saturday morning. That was the last time she talked to her.

Mrs. Brock sighed. "We have a lot to tell you, and I'm sure we don't know everything."

Mrs. Brock looked at her husband. "You need to tell this part, dear. You were there for some of it."

Mr. Brock nodded and told her about the fire at the apartment. He relayed what he knew about the kids meeting with Dr. Haygood and telling them about his friendship with Bennie Markowitz. He told her about meeting Jess and his children at the campus police station and the interview with the DEA agent, and about dinner and one of Jess's friends picking up her laptop on Saturday night.

He finished his story by saying, "Something else must have happened after dinner last night. And we don't know those details."

"Oh, my God," said Mrs. Benelli. "Have you heard anything else from the police?"

Mrs. Brock shook her head. "Nothing," she said.

Mr. Brock remembered something he hadn't mentioned. He said, "The FBI did give them new documents and IDs with new names. Mike had me take pictures of them last night. They had new driver's licenses, passports, birth certificates, and even marriage licenses."

"Why would they need marriage licenses?" asked Mrs. Benelli.

"Whoever is tracking them would be looking for four young single college students, not two married couples," replied Mrs. Williams.

"Why did they fake a car accident?" asked Mrs. Benelli, still not grasping what was happening.

"We don't know that. Maybe they needed to create a diversion to get away," said Mr. Brock.

Mrs. Williams was looking at Mrs. Benelli. She knew the pain the other woman was feeling. Bobby was her only grandchild. Jess was Mrs. Benelli's only child. But she knew Mike and Angela, and she had started treating them like family years ago. She looked up and finally broke the short silence.

"At dinner last night, I got the feeling that our kids didn't know who was doing all this or why they were doing it. The FBI agent showed them a picture of a guy and said he was behind it. But Mike did not believe them."

Mr. Brock nodded at this.

Mrs. Williams continued, "I've raised Bobby since he was four. I've known Mike and Angela for nearly as long. They spent all their time together. I only talked to Jess for a few minutes last night, and she's a very intelligent young woman. I know you are proud of her. If anyone can figure out what's happening, those four can. We have to trust them."

Chapter 44

As their line started to move to check in, they temporarily forgot about making the calls to Agent West, and to their friends back home. They pulled out their identification papers and their reservations and moved slowly through the line.

Jess was nervous about their IDs. Mike told her not to worry. They were from the FBI, they were perfect. Jess was still worried.

Five minutes later, they stepped up to the clerk. The clerk took their papers, typed some things into her computer terminal, and stepped away. Mike and Jess got lumps in their throats. But the clerk came back holding some papers. She gave them a map of the ship, and their room numbers, then explained that she needed to take their pictures so they could identify them in case they lost their sail and sign card which doubled as their room key. She then explained that their room keys would be available outside their room in about an hour and wished them a pleasant cruise experience.

Bobby and Angela had watched Mike and Jess and had relaxed tremendously when it was their turn. They went through the same process and caught up to Mike and Jess, who had waited on them.

Bobby was prepared to say something sarcastic, but took one look at Mike and Jess and realized they were barely hanging on. They were exhausted, bruises were starting to show on their heads, and they could barely keep their eyes open.

Bobby said, "Hey, guys! Let's get on board before they discover these IDs are fake and throw us off."

He got a small smile from Mike, nothing from Jess, and an elbow from Angela for his efforts.

"Come on," Bobby said. "Let's make these last two calls and head to our rooms for some sleep."

They worked their way through the roped-off aisles and headed to the ramp. "This thing is huge," marveled Jess as she walked across the ramp, holding Mike's hand, to the ship.

There was upbeat music coming from all the speakers. An occasional announcement would be made over them looking for a lost party and asking them to report to a certain location.

Once they were on board, they found a quiet place on the channel side of the ship, away from the other boarding passengers. Mike put the phone on speaker and called Agent West. He didn't answer with a hello, or how are you?

"You should really avoid nationally televised high-speed car chases when you're trying to disappear," said Agent West.

"Shit!" Mike replied.

"Y'all did a good job of trying to get out of the way. But there was little you could do to get out of the way of someone who had already lost control at one hundred and twenty miles an hour," West said. "Fortunately, the TV cameras only caught one face from a long distance. If you're lucky, no one will recognize you."

"Shit!" Mike said again. "We couldn't avoid the crash. It happened so fast I think we're lucky to be alive."

"You are," West replied. "Listen. I've turned this over to the FBI. My son-in-law is out of the picture now and so am I. You can still call me, though, if you're hesitant to talk to Special Agent Green."

"Thank you," Mike said. "We plan to drop out of sight for a week. Then we'll check back in with you. If that's okay?"

"Sure. You need to know that the lead suspect now is Benji Smith. One of your fellow students."

Mike looked at Jess and said, "Benji is the lead suspect?"

Jess grabbed the phone from Mike and put it to her ear. She was so tired she didn't realize what she was doing.

"Agent West?"

The phone was still on speaker so everyone could hear Agent West.

"Tell me what happened," Jess said.

"He caught the story we planted about the car accident this morning. Told your friends it was over, you were dead. He packed his gear up and headed to his apartment. One of my agents followed him back to his apartment and never saw him leave. The only person my agent saw leave was a tall girl with blonde hair. She got into a white van with 'Internet and Computer Repair' written on the side."

It was Jess's turn. "Shit!" she said.

"You got that right," Agent West said. "An FBI agent followed the girl out of a Starbucks on Friday morning. She watched her get into the van, and then watched a guy matching Benji's description drive away."

Jess said, "So he's using the software programs that I saw on his laptop to steal credit card info wherever he can find free WIFI spots."

"That and the FBI found a microcomputer at your place with his fingerprints on it. He was monitoring your WIFI also."

"Son of a bitch! I'll kill him," Mike said.

Jess looked at him and realized the phone was on speaker. She blushed and pulled the phone away from her ear.

"What else do you know?" Jess asked.

Agent West said, "He drove out of the parking lot this morning and disappeared. No one has seen him, or her, since then."

Jess whispered, "I'm going to track his ass down and destroy him!"

Agent West heard the comment. "You just track him down. Let's let the FBI destroy him. I have your new email address. I'll email you if we catch him. You kids stay safe."

Agent West hung up, leaving them all speechless. Jess still had the phone in her hand and started dialing. Mike touched her face and got her attention.

"I'm calling Bets," she said.

Mike nodded. Angela and Bobby were looking on. Both had open mouths and shocked looks on their faces.

It was cliche but Bobby said it anyway. "With friends like that, who needs enemies?"

As the phone rang on the other end, Jess replied, "Worse than that, he's an ex-boyfriend."

This time, it was Mike's turn to have a shocked look.

Jess caught Mike's expression and said, "We were freshmen in high school. He started teaching me how to program and how to hack. It lasted six weeks and I broke up with him. There was never anything physical."

"Bets? It's Jess. Catch me up on what's going on," Jess said.

"Steven, it's Jess. I'm going to put you on speakerphone," Bets said.

Jess interrupted. "We just talked to Agent West. He just told us that the primary suspect is Benji. What do you know?"

Steven responded first. "It is Benji. He's a crossdresser and disguised himself as a girl and got away."

Bets chimed in, "You were right about the software on his laptop. Steven put a snooper file on his laptop. When he connects to WIFI it reports back to Steven his latitude and longitude. He was in Dallas an hour ago."

"That's good," Jess said. "He won't dump his laptop. He will dump every cell phone he has, but he won't dump that laptop."

"The FBI found a Raspberry Pi at your place. It was set up to spy on your WIFI," Steven said.

Jess wasn't surprised. Agent West had just told them about it. "Where did they find it? And why did they search my place?"

Bets answered, "Your friend Harvey, or #1HackerGod, suggested we look for it. They found it in the utility closet between your duplexes where the hot water tanks and the heating unit are stored. The FBI took it and are analyzing it now."

Jess switched back to talking to Steven. "Steven? Where did you install the snooper file?"

"Don't worry," Steven replied. "It's added onto the bootup file. His scans skip that part of the computer files."

"Thank goodness," Jess said. "Listen, email us anything new. We are going to stay off the phones for a few days."

They said their goodbyes and hung up. Jess said to Mike, "This may be worse than I thought."

Mike looked at her, confused.

"We can handle Benji," he said.

"It's not Benji I'm worried about. It's his father," Jess replied. "Let's find our rooms and get some sleep. I'll explain later."

"That's the second-best idea I've heard all day," Bobby said.

"What was the best idea?" Angela asked.

"It's a tie," Bobby replied. "Between 'let's take a cruise' and 'never get in the middle of a high-speed police chase.'"

There were groans from them all. But at least they were smiling when they entered the ship to search for their rooms.

Chapter 45

Sunday, 4:00 p.m. Fayetteville, Arkansas

The FBI had assumed full responsibility for their actions and were playing catch up. They made arrangements for military support for the local search and rescue team.

The local sheriff had to be convinced that it was best to let the feds get involved. But the promise of extra equipment and funding for special training for his deputies went a long way in convincing him to let the feds help.

It didn't hurt that the White River was flooded from heavy rains the week before. The searching had been difficult and his teams were exhausted. By the time the military team arrived, they would be welcomed with open arms.

Special Agents Green and Carson had gone to the hotel to explain the situation to some very upset and angry parents and an even angrier grandmother. Mrs. Williams may have been in her seventies, but she cursed the FBI agents in a way that would have made dead sailors sit up and cheer.

Once everyone had kind of settled down, Green tried telling them that they thought the kids were alive. But Mrs. Williams would have none of it. She told the agent to shut the hell up and quit lying. Then she looked at Special Agent Carson, told him they knew the kids were alive, and asked him how they intended to protect the kids this time.

Mrs. Benelli and the Brocks were silent on the outside, but they were cheering for Grandma Williams on the inside. No one, not even the FBI, tells an angry Black grandmother to be quiet. Especially, when she was right and they botched their job.

After a half hour of abuse from Grandma Williams, Green excused himself. Mrs. Williams had asked him three times what his real name was. Was it Haygood or was it Green?

Special Agent Carson held his hands up after Green left and proclaimed that they deserved the ass-chewing and he would tell them the truth regardless of how harsh it was.

Mrs. Benelli spoke softly for the first time and asked him to start from the beginning, and he did. He told them about the credit card thefts, internet scams, and income tax return thefts and about tracing them to the University. They initially thought it was Jess, but they quickly ruled her out. That's when they brought in Green to be a professor, so he could check out students and faculty.

He told them about the attacks, about Charles Anderson working for them, and that that was how they knew Jess was going to be attacked.

He explained the involvement of the DEA, and how they had stopped another attack last night. He also told them that it was the DEA's idea to crash Bobby's car while the kids disappeared in another one. So far, it had worked. He also told them that they now knew who was behind the attacks. He would not tell them now, for fear the information might change the way they should act the next few days.

Thirty minutes later, when Special Agent Carson left, they knew everything the FBI knew, and they were fully on board with the FBI's plan to help the kids hide.

With the help of Bets and Steven, the FBI knew that Benji Smith was at the DFW International Airport. It was an easy assumption that he got there by flying out of NWA International Airport. After searching NWA International they found the white minivan, without the internet and computer repair signs and different license plates, in a long-term parking lot. They had obtained a search warrant while other agents searched for the van.

When they opened the van, they found equipment that could be used to skim credit cards, copy credit cards, and make new credit cards. They found a box of white credit card blanks. He could make new cards out of the credit information he stole. They were still the old magnetic strip cards, not the ones with chips. But so much could be purchased online, that he wouldn't need to show the credit card.

Chapter 46

Benji used the computer equipment in the van and made a credit card with the information he had stolen from the FBI agent on Friday morning. The bank was supposed to notify them as soon as a charge was made on the account. Unfortunately, there was a glitch somewhere. By the time the FBI had the information, Benji was already on the flight to Belize City, Belize.

By accessing the account, they were able to track his next steps because he used the stolen debit card information to book a flight to Houston and then on to Belize.

The FBI would have to contact the Belize police force or ask if they could enter the country. Entering the country to enforce U.S. laws on U.S. citizens probably wasn't going to happen without approval from higher levels of the FBI.

They were following him. But they were still far behind him. Immediately after using the stolen card to buy the tickets, he had trashed the card. It would not be used again. That was okay though, he had twenty more stolen credit cards in his pocket. Many would be useless, because flags went up quickly, and the cards may not work outside the U.S. because that was a red flag for credit card companies. Most U.S. citizens never left the country, or even the city or state where they lived. Benji still had nearly two thousand dollars in cash. He could survive for a little while.

Benji would use most cards once or twice and then throw them away. Sometimes he would leave them lying around for other thieves to pick up and use. That way, they might get caught and blamed for the theft.

The key was to never take too much. Never get greedy. If you thought the authorities were getting close, then you moved on quickly.

Benji was tired and depressed. The police report was real. He had checked it several times in disbelief. His best friend from high school was dead. Who would do that? Had she really hacked someone that powerful? Jess was a better hacker than she gave herself credit for being. She would never believe it, but he considered her a better hacker than himself. The only person he knew who was a better hacker than Jess was his dad.

His dad lost it though when his mom died. He barely held himself together during her funeral. Then he disappeared for several weeks before coming back home and making sure Benji was alive. It was Jess who had helped him deal with his mom's death and his dad's strange behavior. Jess had talked Benji out of suicide and helped him find a counselor.

He missed the counselor and wished many times he could pick up the phone and call her. She had helped him to understand he was bi-gender. She explained that he needed to understand and come to grips with how he felt at different times. But most importantly, she had explained that society couldn't grasp the concept of a man having feminine feelings, they would simply call him gay and other names. He needed to understand his feelings and discipline himself to act the sex of the genitalia he was born with. He wasn't gay. He felt no sexual attraction toward men or women, in fact, he was disgusted with the thought of sex. His sexual experiences as a child were brutal and physically painful.

His counselor passed away from AIDS just a couple of months after he started seeing her. She left a letter for him. He'd read it so many times he was forced to make a copy of it before the original fell apart. She had understood his pain. She believed in him and the letter often comforted him.

Jess was the only person he trusted enough to share his story. They had grown apart since coming to college, but they still talked weekly. Staci was part of the reason they had grown apart. He promised her he would find Staci and make sure she was okay. He hadn't expected to find her addicted to meth and so near death. He didn't abandon Staci the first time when they escaped their abuser, he couldn't abandon her when he found her the second time. Having to find a way to pay for Staci's rehab had forced him to find alternative ways to get money and that's what pulled him away from Jess. He couldn't tell her how he was getting the money to pay for Staci's rehab because he hadn't told Jess he'd found Staci. He was embarrassed for Staci and Jess would have insisted on loaning him the money to pay for rehab. He couldn't do that. Staci was his responsibility.

Now he was planning to avenge Jess. Did she find his abductor? Was he the one who killed Jess and Mike? He knew about the money in Belize. If he was going to get revenge for Jess, he needed money. Since Jess was dead, the money was there for the taking.

Tomorrow, he would have it. He would put on the blond wig, a dress with built-in-n padding to make him look more feminine, the makeup, and he would walk into the Caribbean Bank as Miss Jessica Benelli and transfer the money to another bank. He had worked on his female impersonation for two years. He even had the voice down pretty close. It would be simple and easy, or so he thought.

Chapter 47

The parents huddled in the Brocks hotel room. They were starving, but they did not want to go out to eat. They were afraid they would forget to look like grieving parents if someone were watching them. That was part of the FBI's plan. They needed to be mourning the loss of their children.

They weren't mourning though, they were visiting and telling stories. They were making lists of things they needed to do first thing Monday morning. Pack up and move things from Angela's dormitory, and Jess's duplex. Find their cars and arrange to get them home.

Mrs. Benelli had the longest list. They all offered and agreed to pitch in and help her out. She felt overwhelmed with gratitude.

They ordered pizza delivery to the room and bought sodas and water from the vending machines down the hall. Mrs. Benelli started telling a story about Jess and one of her high school boyfriends, she had no clue that it might be this boyfriend who was behind all the trouble.

They shared stories until after midnight. Mrs. Benelli realized she had neglected to get a room. The Brocks realized they had neglected to tell the front desk they didn't need the two rooms for the kids. They urged Mrs. Benelli to use one of the rooms and she readily agreed.

Chapter 48

Sunday, 10:00 p.m. Elkins, Arkansas

The White River had its origins in the Boston mountains of northwest Arkansas. It was the source of several man-made lakes, most built and operated by the U.S. Army Corps of Engineers. It meandered northward into Missouri and then back into Arkansas before making its way south to converge with the Arkansas River and dump millions of gallons of water into the Mighty Mississippi River in southeast Arkansas.

The upper reaches of the White were fairly mundane most of the year. But it could become dangerous during flash floods. The riverbed was the size of a large creek most of the year, but when flooded it would overflow the banks and spread across pastures and forest land, pushing water and debris wherever the water could reach.

A helicopter flew low and slow over the river from North to South. At this point, the river flowed north for a mile or two into Lake Sequoia. There was a powerful search light on the front enabling the pilot and copilot to see below and ahead of them. Special Agent Carson and the sheriff had parked their cars in a hay field beside the river. Their headlights made a cross that marked a landing spot for the helicopter.

The sheriff and Special Agent Carson had been discussing the search. The rescue team did not see how survivors or bodies could have made it this far. There were too many low-hanging limbs and rocks for someone to grab onto. The rescue team did not believe anyone ever made it to the river. If they didn't, someone picked them up and they disappeared.

The co-pilot exited the helicopter and headed toward the growing group of rescuers around the sheriff. After brief introductions, the sheriff explained their thoughts about the victims. He also expressed concern over one of their rescuers who hadn't shown up yet. Agent Carson spoke up then and told the officer to have his team focus on finding the one person they knew was still out there.

The helicopter took off flying low over the river. They flew north because several rescuers had said the missing kayaker had been ahead of them and they had not seen him. It was possible he had missed the stopping point. In five minutes, they could still hear the helicopter, but they could no longer see the lights.

After twenty minutes, they could see and hear the helicopter coming back upriver. They were still flying low with searchlights shining on three sides. As soon as it reached the hay field it turned off and landed.

Two men exited the helicopter, ducked under the rotor wash, and ran to the small group of men. One was the co-pilot and the other was an embarrassed rescuer. The rescuer explained he had missed the stopping point. And when he tried to turn around and paddle back, he had been swept under a limb and gotten tangled up in the branches and the tow rope he had tied to his kayak. The rescue team had to cut him loose. They had tied his kayak to the limb; he would go back and get it when the water went down in a few days.

The sheriff and the rescuer thanked the co-pilot for what his team had done. Special Agent Carson told the officer they had decided to call off the search, but asked if they could do a flyover of the river to the south to the first bridge. A second look wouldn't hurt.

The helicopter took off just before the news crews found them. Special Agent Carson excused himself and left the sheriff to handle the media. As he left the hay field and found the farm road, he called Green. They had to make the rescue look real. Whoever was after Jess needed to think they had succeeded.

Green sounded frustrated, but they now knew where Benji was and they were about eighty percent certain Jess and her friends were now on a cruise ship.

Knowing who was involved, and where the parties were, was half the battle. Now to contact the Belize Police force and warn them about Benji Smith. But that would have to wait until morning.

Chapter 49

Jess woke up to the phone alarm she had set. She was trying to remember why they had set the alarm for midnight, then her stomach reminded her. She was starving.

She looked at Mike, lying in bed beside her. How many times had she thought about doing this very thing, then forced it out of her mind to do classwork? They were together now, and she had no intention of letting him go. She sat up and shook his shoulder. He mumbled and rolled onto his back, but did not open his eyes.

There was a small stream of light coming through the window curtains. She could vaguely make out his face and the bruise forming on his forehead. She touched her own head and jerked her hand away immediately. It was definitely bruised with some slight swelling and hurt now that she had touched it.

She leaned over and kissed him on the lips. His response was slow. She kissed him harder and he responded a little more aggressively that time. When he finally opened his eyes, he blinked several times and stared at her. He raised his hand to her face and smiled.

"Wake up, sleepy head," she said. "Let's go find something to eat. I'm starving."

He sat up and kissed her. "As long as dessert is in bed."

She kissed him back and said, "Sounds like a plan."

They quickly dressed and Jess brushed her long wavy hair. They stepped into the hallway and knocked on Bobby and Angela's door. There was no answer. Jess looked back at their own room and saw a note. It said, "Pizza, Lido deck."

The Lido deck was the same deck their rooms were on, so they walked down the hallway to an area that housed various cafes and a buffet. They found

Angela and Bobby at the Pizza Pirate. They were sitting at a table between the pizza place and a bar. With a quick hello to Angela and Bobby, they grabbed several slices of pizza, and then bought a couple of beers from the bar.

"Ah, yes," Bobby said. "Pizza and beer, are we in heaven?"

"How was your nap?" Angela asked.

Jess laughed, "That wasn't a nap. That was a self-induced coma. I think hunger woke me up. Mike didn't want to wake up."

Mike took a gulp of beer and said, "All true and I'm still hungry." He bit off another piece of pizza.

Bobby grinned and said, "I think Mike has the right idea. A little less talk and a lot more pizza." And he picked up another piece himself.

They spoke very little until they had consumed at least three large pizzas and had three rounds of beer. They were full from pizza, relaxed from the beer, and sleepy again. For the first time, since Friday evening, they were starting to relax a little.

Mike said to Jess, "I have two questions. Why do you carry so much cash? And tell us about Benji and why his father is the problem."

Jess frowned. "My father believed in keeping cash on hand in case of emergencies. But not as much as I have. I had fifteen thousand in my wall safe because I thought I could live off that for a few months if someone compromised my bank account. I had started taking one to two thousand out each month, several months ago. I have withdrawal limits on how much I can take out."

Mike looked relieved. "So, you don't carry that kind of money around all the time?"

Jess screwed up her face, offended. "No! I rarely have more than fifty in cash on me. Usually, less than twenty."

Bobby and Angela were leaning back in their chairs holding hands. They glanced at each other, realizing they might be watching the first argument between Mike and Jess.

Mike looked Jess in the eyes. "I'm sorry, I didn't mean to imply you were being foolish. That was actually good planning. Something we need to remember and continue to do, I believe."

Bobby and Angela smiled at each other. They knew what was coming next.

Jess frowned and said, "Wait! What? I thought we were about to have a fight."

Mike said, "No. The fact that you had that much cash saved our asses. I saw you take those three envelopes out of your backpack; I was afraid you were nonchalantly carrying it around."

Bobby said, "She took them out of a well-hidden wall safe in her bedroom. Her laptop was hidden in what looked like empty suitcases. She hid it well, bro."

Mike nodded at Bobby and then turned back to Jess. "I'm just trying to fill in the gaps. To understand why Benji is attacking you."

Jess sighed heavily. "Benji was never much of a boyfriend. The cross-dressing explains a lot of the quirks about him."

"What do you mean?" Angela asked.

"I think I was his first friend, honestly," Jess replied. "I mentioned something to one of the computer geeks at school one day in the ninth grade about a computer problem I was having. He didn't know how to fix it, but told me to ask Benji. So, I did."

"Benji was antisocial. He had very few friends, if any. He asked me to bring my laptop to him so he could check it out. I surprised him by taking it to his house. His mother forced him to invite me in. He was an only child. He and his mom lived in a small two-bedroom house. His room was full of computers and gadgets."

Jess hesitated and collected her thoughts. "He was a hacker even then. He had my computer running in just a few minutes. I had gotten some kind of worm that my antivirus program didn't protect against. Anyway, I started asking questions about computers and for six weeks, he introduced me to computer hacking."

"Six weeks?" Mike asked.

"Yeah," Jess said. "Just when I thought he was trying to get me out of my clothes, I realized he wanted to wear my clothes. I think he felt like a girl trapped in a guy's body. That was kind of weird at first, but I got over it and we became friends. He considers himself bi-gender. Sometimes he feels like a man, sometimes he feels like a woman. He finds it hard to explain. He is not bi-sexual, or even interested in sex."

"That explains the cross-dressing," Angela said.

Mike shook his head. "Okay, I think I regret asking that question. I'm not judging him. I just can't bring myself to understand the conflict that's going on in his mind. How long has he known about the money?"

"That, I don't know," Jess answered. "I don't remember telling him anything about the Markowitz money. He must have found out by eavesdropping on my WIFI

. Probably from my emails. That must be how he tagged our email," she said, looking at Mike.

"I wonder who else he's eavesdropping on," Bobby said.

"Shit!" Jess replied. "I need to tell Bets and Steven to check their places."

"That's not going to happen, our phones stay turned off and in the room safes," Mike said.

"Besides, I'll bet the FBI, or Bets and Steven have already thought of that," Angela added.

Jess would worry about it until she was able to call them though. Mike leaned forward and kissed her gently, avoiding bumping their heads together.

"They know who is responsible for all this. Bets and Steven know how good a hacker he is. He's not after their money. He's after yours and it's safe now. Tomorrow, we can figure out how to contact your banker in Belize and let him know you are coming. Then he will know to only deal with you in person."

"Okay," Jess said. "I must still be exhausted because I'm not thinking very clearly right now. I don't believe Benji did any of this."

Bobby quipped, "Who can think clearly after all the beer and pizza we had?"

They chuckled at Bobby's comment. It was true. They were still exhausted, but they were full of pizza and buzzed from the beer.

"Jess," Mike said. "If Benji didn't do this, then who did? We can fight back. We are your team now. There is nothing I wouldn't tackle with Bobby and Angela. You are smart, and beautiful, too. With you as the fourth person on this team, we can be unstoppable."

"Preach it, bro! I love it when you get on your soapbox," Bobby said.

"In the end, it's just money. It can be replaced. Our lives can't. But you aren't going to lose the money, because tomorrow. No, it's one a.m. Later today, we are going to come up with a plan to stop this."

"Where did you take your motivational speaking class?" Jess asked, laughing.

"YouTube!" Mike said, without missing a beat.

"What are you going to do with twenty million dollars?" Angela asked.

Jess looked at her and frowned.

"I'm not sure."

"You could use some of it to become a partner in BAM, with us," Mike said.

"That's your business. Yours, Bobby's, and Angela's," Jess replied.

Bobby said, "If you two are going to be together, that's not a bad idea. Mike and I were going home to take over the business from his mom and dad. They want to retire from the day-to-day management, buy an RV, and travel around the country. Mike was going to be the manager and do a little computer programming if needed. As chief engineer, I was going to design new products. And when Angela finishes her psychology degree next semester, she is headed to law school. You could be our computer programmer."

Angela added, "It's just a thought. There's no pressure. BAM is valued at about two million dollars. We had planned to buy Mom and Dad out after a couple of years so they could retire completely."

"It's something to think about," Mike said. "Right now, let's relax and enjoy the next few days."

"Wait," Angela said. "Jess never told us why Benji's father was the problem."

Jess sighed and said, "Benji's father was in the Air Force. He was dishonorably discharged for smuggling and dealing drugs. He disappeared before they could put him in jail. He's the one who taught Benji how to hack, and supplied him with computers and gear, I believe. He's still out there. And Benji said he is ruthless. He knows who is doing this, but he can't stop them."

"Do you think his father is involved also?" Mike asked.

"I don't know, but with all the guys that have attacked us, it makes sense," she replied. "I don't believe Benji has those kinds of connections with drug dealers." She knew she should tell them about Agent West's warning. But she was tired and needed some more time to think.

Chapter 50

Mike and Jess had returned to their cabin earlier that morning and opened the curtains to the window of their cabin. Out their window, they had discovered a half-moon glimmering streaks of light across the endless water of the Gulf of Mexico. They sat on the bed, mesmerized by the moonlight on the water. Then Jess put her arms around Mike. That led to a kiss, which led to cuddling, which led to undressing, and the discovery of more aches and bruises from the previous morning's wreck. And finally, they had slow and careful sex, slow because they had plenty of time, and careful not to touch the new bruises they were finding.

Jess awoke and found her left arm numb and lifeless. Her arm was under Mike's head and the circulation had been cut off when they fell asleep. She tried to roll over but found that they were rolled up in the sheets like a tightly wrapped burrito. Totally naked and wrapped up tight.

"Mike, Mike! Wake up!" she whispered.

Mike groaned and tried to roll over. The sheets kept him from going anywhere. After a second attempt failed, he opened his eyes and raised his head, which caused the blood to start flowing back into Jess's arm. The sudden shock of tingling sensations down her arm caused Jess to gasp.

"What? What? What's the matter?" Mike asked.

"My arm's asleep," Jess replied. "I need to go pee, but we're wrapped up in the sheets and I can't move."

Mike thought for a moment and he started laughing. His arms had been around her waist. He grabbed her and rolled onto his back and then onto their other side. He was able to get the sheets off then and helped Jess to stand up. Her left arm hung limply at her side as she hurried to the bathroom.

"What is so funny?" Jess asked.

"You and me. We fell asleep so tangled up we couldn't move," he said.

"Well, my arm sure didn't move," she groaned.

She flushed the toilet and stepped out of the restroom shaking her arm. Mike ran past her and said, "My turn."

Jess was sitting on the bed when Mike stepped out of the restroom. She had the sheet pulled up around her and was holding the cell phone in her hand.

She looked up at Mike. "Did you know we have WIFI on board?"

"No, why? I thought we were going to relax for a couple of days."

"Well, if this morning is any indication, we haven't relaxed much yet," she replied. "I need to email the banker and let him know that I'm going to be there in person on Tuesday."

"Tell him *we* will be there," Mike said. "Also, tell him your husband is coming with you and that you have a new identification."

"That means I have to use my old email account. If Benji was getting my information, someone else could be too. I'll reset the password just in case," Jess said.

"Good idea," Mike said as he slid under the sheet beside her. Ask him to lock the accounts until you talk to him in person and let him know the FBI may be contacting him."

"Can he do that? Lock the accounts?" Jess asked.

"Absolutely, and ask him for references for an attorney and a tax accountant," Mike said.

"Why?" she asked.

"You have basically inherited twenty million dollars. Uncle Sam is going to want his share if you move the money back into the States. If you do or don't move the money, you need advice on how to keep as much of it as possible and where to invest it. I don't know the Belize laws or even the U.S. laws in this situation. You'll need an attorney and tax advice there and in the United States," Mike said.

"This is a lot more complicated than I thought," she said.

"And you may end up with a lot less than twenty million dollars," he said.

She leaned over and kissed him. "The money would be nice, but I'm happier with you."

"I'd rather have you, too. Now send your email. Then let's shower and go find some breakfast."

Mike got out of bed and rummaged through his luggage for clothes to wear.

"Mike?" Jess said.

Mike stopped and looked at Jess, noticing the bruise on her forehead and cringing inwardly. He reached for his own forehead.

"Yes?" he asked.

"I love you!"

He smiled, stepped over to the bed, leaned over, and gently kissed her on the lips. He felt the sexual arousal in his body but knew they had things to do. He broke away, knowing they had plenty of time for sex on this cruise. Besides, he was sore from the attention they had already given each other.

"I love you, too," he said.

They took separate showers. There really wasn't room for two in a cruise ship shower. Jess said she needed to shave her legs and she didn't need any distractions.

They left their room at 8:15 a.m. and found a *Do Not Disturb* sign on Bobby and Angela's door. They slid a note under the door letting Bobby and Angela know they had gone to the breakfast buffet around 8:20 a.m.

"Have you ever been to Belize?" Mike asked Jess.

"I've never left the U.S.," she said.

"What about you? Have you been out of the States before?" Jess asked.

"Apparently, I've been to Hong Kong. But I was just a baby. I don't remember a thing. Angela wasn't born yet," he replied.

"Some world travelers we are," she said.

They found the buffet line and grabbed some trays. Mike loaded his plate down and Jess tried to find some healthier options like fruit but failed. They each got a glass of orange juice and a cup of coffee and headed for the first empty table they saw.

They ate in silence for several minutes.

"What's on your mind?" he asked.

"I'm thinking about us. Your offer to buy into BAM, the money, and everything we've been through the last three days. Everything has happened so fast, and not the way I envisioned it at all."

"Do you know how many times I wanted to tell you '*Let's forget about waiting for graduation, let's date now*'?"

Jess smiled. "I wish you had."

Mike leaned across the table and put his hand on Jess's. "Look. You don't have to rush into any decisions. Bobby and I were going home to run the family business. Angela will graduate in another year and start law school. You were planning to start graduate school this fall. There's no reason for any of that to change unless we want it to change. Let's get through this week, make one decision at a time, and see how we feel after this Benji thing is over."

Jess frowned. "This Benji thing, as you just called it, is pissing me off."

"Hope I'm not interrupting a serious conversation," Angela said, as she sat beside Jess.

"We're just griping about this, quote, Benji thing, unquote, as Mike has called it," Jess replied.

"Good morning," Mike said to Angela. "Where's Bobby?"

"Making waffles," replied Angela.

"They have waffles? That son of a biscuit eater. I'll be back," Mike replied.

Angela smiled at Jess. "How are you this morning?"

"I'm confused, Angela. Your brother tells me he wishes we had gotten together sooner, then tells me I don't have to rush into any decisions. Let's see how this Benji thing works out, he says."

Angela laughed. "I'm sorry. That's a guy thing. They try to say what they think we want to hear. They aren't very good at reading people, especially women. Mike loves you, or he wouldn't be here. If you asked him to fly to the moon, he would find a way. He's trying not to pressure you."

"I would go anywhere with him. I want to be with him. If he asked me to give away all this money, I would," Jess said.

"Have you told him that?" Angela asked.

"No. You walked up before I could even think of what to say," Jess said.

Angela said, "There are two things you need to know about Mike. The first is that he has been a protective big brother and best friend his whole life. Meaning, he looks out for me and Bobby. The second thing is that he will not hesitate to use physical force to protect you, me, or Bobby. In fact, he tends to go berserk when fighting. That guy at the police station the other night is not the first he has put in the hospital."

Jess just gawked at her, not sure how to respond. Angela noticed her expression and laughed.

"Don't worry. He would never hurt you. But he would hurt someone who tries to hurt you. It's nice to have him beside you in a rough area."

Bobby approached the table with a tray of food and sat across from Angela.

"Good morning, Goldilocks. Your bear is having fun with the waffle maker," Bobby said.

Looking at Angela he asked, "Has he ever made waffles before?"

Angela giggled. "I doubt it. He was always too busy eating them." She looked at Jess. "In case you haven't noticed, these two can eat everything you and I eat and still be hungry."

Jess's phone chimed; she had received an email. She read the notification and then opened the email.

Angela asked, "What is it?"

"Mike encouraged me to email the bank in Belize, and let the banker know that we would be there Tuesday, and to lock the accounts until we arrived. Mr. Rollo says that he looks forward to meeting me and my new husband. I told him I was recently married to explain the name change and to explain Mike's presence. He also says that they have in-house counsel that will help us with legal and tax issues."

"That's good to hear," Mike said, as he sat down at the table with a plate containing four waffles.

"Did you have fun with the waffle maker, bro?" Bobby asked.

"I think I worked up an appetite." Mike deadpanned.

Angela and Jess grinned at each other and shook their heads.

Chapter 51

Benji was fussing over details. He was dressed as the blond girl and was wearing a dress with a little extra padding around the hips and breasts. The padding helped to make him look more feminine. He had spent the last two hours on the makeup and hair. It was perfect. It was time to go withdraw twenty million dollars.

If Jess were alive, he would never attempt this. She was his best friend. She had stopped him from committing suicide after his mother overdosed. She had given him a purpose in life. They had made promises to each other. He had promised he would find Staci and take care of her. She had promised that she would find the man who had abused them both. That was why he had put the monitor in her duplex. He knew she was getting close, but she wasn't telling him anything. She didn't want to bring back memories that would cause him to break down, she had told him. But he wanted to know. After years of thinking about it, he wanted revenge.

Now that Jess was dead, he wanted revenge even more. To get that revenge, he needed money, Jess's money.

This was the biggest scam he had ever tried to pull. If he had only managed to get the four account numbers to where Jess had moved the money, he could have transferred the money using the same app that she and Mike had written and never had to show his face. Or in this case, her face. He had finally managed to get the original account number, but Jess had transferred the money immediately after she had finished the app and then deleted it from her phone and her computer.

But Jess hadn't been in her apartment when she made that transfer. She had been somewhere else. Possibly the bank branch where her trust fund was managed. He could easily hack into her checking account. But she kept very little money in that account.

He knew she paid her bills each month as soon as the money was transferred from the trust fund to her checking account. Then she withdrew all but two hundred dollars from her checking account. That meant she had been withdrawing a little over a thousand dollars each month for the last six months. She had probably been doing it for longer than that. She had at least six thousand dollars in cash stashed. He had watched her closely. He had seen no evidence that she had spent the money on anything.

He took a deep breath and summoned his courage. This was very different from skimming cards and stealing credit card info. He could do that and remain anonymous. This, he had to do in person.

He left the Radisson Hotel with a large oversized black purse on his shoulder, dark sunglasses, a large floppy sun hat, and a yellow short-sleeve sundress that came down just above the knees. He was smiling. He knew the disguise was working because he had caught the eye of several men in the lobby.

He caught a cab outside the Radisson. In as feminine a voice as he could muster, he asked the driver to take him, or her, to the Caribbean Bank on Albert Street. It was a short trip from Marine Parade Blvd across Haulover Creek to Albert Street. He was dropped off at the Albert Street taxi stand, a half block away from the Caribbean Bank.

He walked to the front doors of the bank and stepped inside. He stopped just briefly to take the sunglasses off and get the layout. Then walked straight to the nearest available teller.

"Good morning, ma'am. How may I help you?" asked the teller.

"Well, I hope you can. I seem to have misplaced some of my account numbers. This was the main account," Benji said, sliding a piece of paper across the counter to the teller. "And I recently divided it into several different accounts. But I've lost those numbers. Can you help me?"

"Certainly," replied the teller.

Taking the paper, she logged into her computer and started typing.

"May I see your identification please?" the teller asked Benji.

Benji reached into the purse and pulled out a perfectly forged Arkansas driver's license with his picture in the blond wig, and the name and address of Jessica Benelli. He smiled and slid that to the teller as well.

The teller smiled back and said, "Excuse me a moment, I need to make a copy of your ID to update our records. I'll be right back."

There was a row of offices behind the counter where the tellers were stationed. The teller walked back to an office that had a man's name in small letters, he could make out Rollo, and in slightly larger letters said 'Vice President.'

Benji's gut dropped. Something was wrong. He didn't hesitate. He walked toward a sign that pointed down a hallway that read Restrooms/Banos. He glanced back just in time to see the teller and the Vice President step out of the office and look for him. He was a step away from disappearing into the hallway when he heard someone yell, "Stop that woman."

Benji raced into the Men's room, found an empty stall, and locked it behind him. Quickly, he pulled the hat and wig off, and then the dress. He pulled a roll of clothes out of the purse. There was a pair of shorts, a T-shirt, and a pair of sandals. He put those on. Reached into the purse again and pulled out a backpack and a Kansas City Chief's ball cap. He folded the purse and stuck it into the backpack. Then he crammed the hat, wig, and the dress into the backpack. His wallet and hotel room key were in the outer pocket of the backpack. He stepped out of the stall and went to the lavatory sink. He reached for a paper towel and wiped most of the makeup from his face before the door burst open and a security guard came in.

"Excuse me, sir? Has a blonde woman come in here?" the guard asked.

Without looking up, Benji asked, "Why would a woman be in the men's room? Look for yourself."

While the guard checked the two stalls, Benji grabbed his backpack and walked out of the restroom. Reminding himself to act relaxed, he walked slowly out of the bank and turned toward the Albert Street taxi stand. He turned abruptly and walked across Albert Street and entered the Downtown Shopping Mall.

Benji was breathing hard, nearly hyperventilating, after he walked through the mall. He was fighting off a panic attack. He found a bench and sat down. He put his hands behind his head and bent forward, forcing himself to catch his breath.

When he finally settled down, he forced himself to think calmly. What was his plan B? This was his plan B. And it had failed.

He dug into his backpack and pulled out a cell phone. He dialed a number from memory and waited for an automated system to answer. He punched a series of numbers. A phone rang on the other end and soon a man's voice answered. Benji stood up and started his walk back to the Radisson. He should have made this call before he left Fayetteville. He should have made the call as soon as he saw the report that Jess and Mike were dead.

He said, "Dad? It's Benji."

Chapter 52

The bank vice president had the teller call the police after they had left his office to talk to the blond and saw her running away. He had received the email from Miss Benelli, now Mrs. Bennett, early that morning. He acted on her instructions immediately and locked the accounts. He was rattled by the morning's events. Miss Benelli and the FBI had contacted him months ago, informing him that someone was trying to illegally gain access to her account. But he had not expected someone to walk right into his bank and pretend to pass herself off as Jessica Benelli. Had it not been for the email that he had received that morning, that lady might have gotten away with stealing twenty million dollars.

When the police arrived, he was searching through the bank's video surveillance footage. He was thoroughly confused. He showed the police the video of the blonde woman walking into the bank and then the young man walking out. None of the tellers remembered seeing the young man walk in. They had to be the same person he told the police.

It was 10:30 a.m. before the police left the bank. There was not much they could do they had told him. No crime had occurred. The blonde had asked about bank account numbers and the bank had prevented her from getting those numbers. The bank had prevented a crime from occurring, so there was no crime.

He went back to his office and read the email again. He confirmed that his memory was correct. Miss Benelli said she and her husband would arrive from a cruise ship on Tuesday and asked for references for legal and tax advisors. She had asked for an appointment to meet with him also. That confirmed to him the blonde was an attempted thief.

He searched through his computerized address book and found the FBI agent's phone number and called him. Special Agent Carson answered on the third ring.

Carson was still in Fayetteville. But Green, also known as Dr. Haygood, was on his way to Belize with another FBI agent and planned to visit the banker as soon as he arrived. The FBI was currently working with the Belize Police Force to decide how to proceed with the case. It would be mid-afternoon before Green arrived.

It was 10:55 a.m. Mr. Rollo sent a short email to his client, Mrs. Jessica Bennett. He explained that someone pretending to be her had tried to access her accounts that morning, but thanks to her email, they had prevented any access to her accounts. He looked forward to meeting her on Tuesday.

He had already canceled one appointment and a second was waiting on him now. He went back to work, still wondering about the morning's activity.

Chapter 53

The two young couples explored the cruise ship after breakfast. They found guest relations and shore excursions down on the third deck. There they also found the formal dining rooms and the theater. They asked several questions at guest relations, explaining it was their first cruise, and developed a plan for the next two days. They decided they would explore and experience as much as possible. That's when they weren't back in their cabin exploring other things.

Their favorite spot on the ship became a table at the back of the ship on the lido deck. It was close to the bar, the Pizza Pirate, the Seafood Shack, and close to the hot tubs. For a little while, they sat at the table, just holding hands, and watching the waves created by the ship.

It didn't take long for the four of them to start talking about shore excursions and what they wanted to do on Cozumel. They discussed snorkeling, shopping, or just sightseeing during the stop on the island. Mike and Jess knew their day would be taken in Belize with meeting the banker and the advisors. This conversation was interrupted by a ding from Jess's phone.

"Speaking of meeting with the banker. I just got another email from him," Jess said.

"Oh, my God! Mike, he said a young woman pretended to be me this morning and tried to get account information. But she ran and disappeared before they could hold her for the police."

"Could it be Benji?" Mike asked.

"It's possible," Jess responded. "I'm glad I sent that email. She might have gotten the money if Mr. Rollo hadn't put a hold on the accounts."

"Do you think Benji knows the account numbers?" Mike asked.

Jess said, "He might have gotten the original account number from an email, but there's no way he could have gotten the other four. They were never put in an email."

"He might have gone in with the original account number and tried to get the others," Mike said and hesitated slightly before continuing. "He probably pretended to be you and claimed to have misplaced the new numbers."

Jess continued the speculation. "If he had gotten the account numbers, he could have transferred the money without anyone stopping him."

"It's possible. But I'm sure there are more stipulations in place for further identifying who you are," Mike said.

"Like what?" Jess asked.

"Security questions for one," Mike replied. "Some banks might require fingerprints or a retinal scan, but I highly doubt that."

"What if I don't know the answers to the security questions?" Jess asked.

"We will deal with that when, and if, it occurs," Mike replied. "You have a working relationship with this banker and that's what matters."

Angela said, "What matters now is what will Benji do? Will he walk away, or will he do something stupid?"

Bobby added, "You mean, more stupid than walking into a bank and claiming to be Jess?"

After they stopped laughing at Bobby's comment, Jess looked at Angela and answered.

"He will call me. Belize is not one of the safest countries in Central America. It's in the top ten countries in the world for homicides. Mostly gang-related, but a few Americans have been killed. We will need to take care of the banking business and get back on the ship. His father may have some contacts in Belize. It's on the smuggling route between Columbia and the U.S."

Mike looked at her and said, "Robbery is not an option, you won't have the money on you. Kidnapping and extortion might be a possibility, but that's not Benji's style. He doesn't know we are alive."

"Now, what do we do?" Jess asked.

"As much as it pains me to say it, I think we need to call the FBI," Mike said.

"No!" Jess nearly shouted. "I called them when this first started, and look what's happened. I've been followed, my home broken into, my phone and laptop stolen, I was almost kidnapped, and your apartment was blown up. As far as I'm concerned, we can do better than they can. And Haygood, or whoever he is, is an idiot."

"Okay," Mike replied. "Then we will contact your banker. Tell him we feel we need some security leaving and returning to the ship. We tell him we are willing to pay for security and ask him if he can arrange it."

"I have a better idea," Bobby said. "We need a blond wig. Angela and I will pretend to be the two of you, and catch a cab to the bank. You two come after us, and use the security guards to get to the bank."

Jess said, "I can't ask you to put yourself in danger because of me. It's a good idea. But it's too dangerous. I think it's better for us to stay together. Four of us and a couple of security guys would be hard to overcome."

Mike noticed Angela had been quiet, but listening intently. When she spoke, they all listened to her questions.

"Who knows we are on a cruise ship?" Angela asked. Then, answering her own question, "The banker, DEA Agent West, and possibly the FBI. Benji doesn't know where we are. He may even think we are really dead."

Angela asked her next question. "Who, in Belize, knows what we look like? No one! Look at how we are dressed now. Shorts, T-shirts, and halter tops. Typical college students on a cruise. We can change how we look quickly."

"What do you mean, change how we look?" Jess asked.

Angela smiled. "If anyone is looking for us in Belize, they will be looking for college students. When we get off the ship in Belize, we dress as professionals. The guys can grow their beards in the next few days for an older, harried professional look. They can wear their suits. We can dress professionally and put our hair up also. With enough makeup and serious expressions, we can look several years older."

"I like it," Bobby said. "We are about to assume business roles anyway. It's time we started dressing for success."

"And, you are a millionaire. A multimillionaire," Angela said, looking at Jess. "Stop running. Start planning. I know you are having a honeymoon of sorts with my brother, but in our family, business comes first. You have a responsibility to take care of that money and make it grow. Be a good steward, as Dad says."

Jess frowned at Angela. "Do you always slap people around with common sense?"

Bobby, Angela, and even Mike laughed. "Always!" Bobby said. "That's why she's going to law school."

"Okay, my head is suddenly spinning. Let's go get some lunch before we resume this conversation," Jess said.

The phone that Jess was using for emails rang. Mike picked it up and answered.

Chapter 54

Benji had been walking the city. He was pissed. Dad had told him to drop his scheme and leave Belize immediately. He didn't mean walk away either, he meant to run away as fast as possible. He had made mistakes and he would never know what they were. If he had made one mistake, he had made several.

Benji had made mistakes that identified him, alright. He still couldn't believe the authorities were closing in. Even if he couldn't identify his mistakes, he couldn't believe they knew he was there. He hadn't used his real identity or any of his own credit cards.

This was all bullshit, Benji thought. He had covered his tracks. No one knew who or where he was.

At least, he thought that until he got off the elevator in the Radisson. He had walked around a corner and saw Dr. Haygood, really FBI consultant Green, standing in the hallway outside his room. That woke him up to the reality that Dad was talking about.

He'd made mistakes. They had followed him to Belize. How? What did he do wrong?

Now the FBI had his laptop. If they managed to break into that, he could spend the rest of his life behind bars if they caught him. He still had several IDs in his backpack and credit cards in his wallet. He could slip away. Run like Dad had told him. And he would run, but not yet. Things were too hot.

He needed another room and another hotel. He needed to lay low for a few days and plan a way out of Belize.

He had turned back around the corner and caught the elevator before the doors closed. There was an older couple in the elevator and they looked at him oddly. He apologized and told them he had pressed the wrong floor. He wasn't thinking clearly because he and his girlfriend had just had a fight.

They smiled at him and got off on the next floor. He had the elevator to himself and hit the button to go to the lobby. He looked in his backpack and found a pair of sunglasses. He put on the sunglasses and pulled his ball cap down to cover his face even more.

The elevator stopped at the lobby. He resisted the urge to run out of the hotel. He had always been a step ahead of the authorities. He couldn't understand what had happened. He took two steps out of the elevator and looked around.

There was a sitting area away from the elevators and the front desk. He forced himself to walk slowly and normally. He walked over, sat down, and picked up the Daily News newspaper and pretended to read while he scanned the people in the lobby.

His first look was for cops. He didn't see any. Did Belize have plainclothes cops? He looked around the lobby again. The younger woman in the black pantsuit looked familiar, but she certainly wasn't a cop. He scanned the room again. He came back to the young woman. She was talking on a cell phone, and looking in his general direction without looking at him. She looked familiar, but he couldn't place where he had seen her.

He looked at the woman again. This time he was sure she was looking directly at him. The hair stood up on his neck. He stood and put the paper down. He headed for the hallway where the restroom was located. It also led to a back door out of the lobby.

He glanced back to see the woman following him. He hit the back door at a run. This was the way to the hotel's marina. Going straight was a dead end, right into the Caribbean Sea. Benji turned right and ran down Marine Barracks Blvd. He turned right onto Cork Street and crossed the street. He headed to the Great House Inn and ran between the Inn and the neighboring cafe.

The woman was still behind him. But far enough that he should be able to shake her. She was still talking on the phone though. That meant she was talking to the police. He had to disappear.

He angled right down an alley and turned left on a side street. He ran through the tourists and the vendors set up on Fort Street and into the Tourism Village. The Tourism Village was where the water taxis from the cruise ships dropped the tourists off. And this was where he hoped to blend in with the crowd.

He glanced behind him before entering the village. The woman was still behind him. He was breathing hard, not used to running that much. He had to find a hiding spot.

Entering the village, he could hear the drums and Indian musicians playing haunting melodies on their flutes. The smell of cooking food and the chatter of small groups of people assailed his senses. He dodged around two tour groups returning to their cruise ships and headed back to the street at another entrance to the village.

He stopped and studied the street, then looked back at the village. He did not see the woman. He took his backpack off and carried it by the shoulder straps. He was hot, sweaty, and still breathing hard. He spotted a vendor selling tie-dyed T-shirts and bought one.

He removed his sunglasses and ball cap and changed into the tie-dyed shirt on the spot. He put the sunglasses back on and stuffed his sweaty shirt and ball cap into the bulging backpack. He looked over the vendors and the noisy crowd. He didn't see the woman in the suit, so he walked away down the street.

Chapter 55

Monday, 4:00 p.m. Carnival Cruise Ship Freedom

Over a long lunch, Mike, Jess, Bobby, and Angela discussed many things. The trip to Belize City was the primary focus. They wanted some protection. Guards of some kind. Jess didn't consider herself rich and was having a difficult time accepting the twenty million as her responsibility. It should be her and her mother's responsibility, she argued. They tabled that discussion for the second topic.

The second was the FBI. Why had they screwed things up so badly? Her first experience with the FBI had been very formal when she'd hacked into the ACT website. Her second experience had been when they had asked her to make online contact with a couple of hackers. The FBI's cover had been blown and they needed someone established to keep tabs on them. That had failed because the hackers disappeared. If they had changed their names, they did not come back to the same online haunts.

Her third experience was this time. The undercover agent working as a professor and using her as bait was something she knew nothing about. She thought it was possible they were looking for someone else, and she had been a person of interest.

She and her mom had talked to Special Agent Carson about the money in Belize. The FBI had contacted the bank and that was about all that had happened. Until recently.

The third topic was the DEA's involvement. It was decided that Agent West was telling the truth. His interest in the case was strictly about his son-in-law, or getting him out of trouble. Jess still did not mention Agent West's warning from Benji's Father. They decided to email Agent West and ask him about private security firms. They had come to realize that Jess's mom might be in danger too. If someone threatened her mother, Jess would hand over the money in a heartbeat.

The fourth topic of conversation was about BAM. What they planned to do with the company. Who was going to do what, and what their future goals were? This was an animated discussion because Mike and Bobby had big dreams, but very little in the way of actionable plans. Angela was quick to point this out by asking about new product ideas, updates for existing products, etc. This topic got tabled also because the guys clearly had no plans.

Somewhere during all the conversation, they had moved to their favorite table at the back of the ship. The ladies had ordered margaritas and the guys drank beer. When they realized what time, it was, they started thinking of dinner. The girls wanted to dress up and eat in the formal dining room. The guys had no objections, as they wanted to see their ladies in their finest dresses.

Angela and Jess headed back to the cabins to start getting ready for dinner. Mike and Bobby decided to stay and talk for a few minutes.

* * *

"Angela is right," Bobby said. "We haven't talked about BAM seriously since high school."

Mike said, "I've had some thoughts, but it's going to take your help. You're the engineer."

"I'm listening," Bobby said.

"We're already selling the calendar and the picture frames. How difficult would it be to get into the cellphone and tablet business? Using Android operating systems?" Mike asked. "Look at the junk phones you bought and what we have now. There has to be a market for medium to good quality products at a decent price."

"I think it's something to look into. Let's check into what's selling in Cozumel and Belize," Bobby said. "And maybe we need to look into other markets around the world."

"Maybe both. Let's go get ready for dinner," Mike said.

As they rose from the table, Bobby asked, "Steak or lobster tonight?"

"Are you kidding?" Mike replied. "Both!"

"Can we have both?" Bobby asked, as they started walking to their cabins.

"Absolutely, we may have to pay extra, but we can have both," Mike replied laughing.

"Dude, we've got to make our business grow or we will both be writing resumes for real," Bobby said.

"We need to ask Angela what she thinks," Mike replied. "She had the first two ideas."

As they reached their cabins, they said they would see each other shortly. Mike stood in the hall outside his room and emailed Agent West, asking about security. Agent West was the only law enforcement person he trusted right now. He entered the cabin and stopped short after closing the cabin door. Jess was sitting at a table applying make-up. He stared at her long, blond curly hair which hung down mid-way between her shoulders and her waist.

"You are gorgeous. Who are you, and what did you do with my computer nerd girlfriend?"

"Flattery! That will get you everywhere." She laughed. "You better shower. I suggest a cold shower from the looks of things."

Chapter 56

Monday, 5:30 p.m. Belize City, Belize

Benji had walked away from the Tourism Village. He found a small bar and grill not far from the main bridge which crossed Haulover Creek. He realized he had not eaten lunch and was suddenly starving. He found a small patio area at the back of the grill overlooking the creek. He had learned from a map that Haulover Creek was really the last four to five miles of the Belize river, right before it reached the Caribbean Sea.

The bar was playing reggae music through a hidden speaker system. There was the faint smell of the ocean, which was just a half mile down the river. A waiter stopped by and handed Benji a menu and asked what he could get for him. Benji ordered a Belikin beer and panades for appetizers while he studied the menu. When the waiter returned with the beer and the panades, Benji ordered the fried chicken and rice.

Benji ate his food and thought about his situation. He needed to get out of Belize, but he was sure the airport was being watched. His immediate concern, now that he had eaten, was getting a room for the night. He needed to find a place to hide for a few days.

Benji spent an hour eating dinner and thinking about his situation. He always thought better when sitting in front of a computer. But the FBI had his computer now. Other than finding a place to stay overnight, he had found no answers. He paid for his meal and left the bar.

He crossed the bridge to the South side of Belize City and walked several blocks. He didn't care where he was going. He didn't like walking but didn't want a cab driver to possibly recognize him. And he figured the FBI was starting to figure out his disguises. That's the only way they could have tracked him this far.

It was approaching seven p.m. The sun was sinking low in the west. The temperature was in the upper eighties, but the breeze off the Caribbean Sea made it seem cooler.

He had not seen the female agent following him since the Tourism Village. But to be safe, he stepped into a dark alley and looked over the streets. She was there. In the middle of the street on her phone. She was not looking in his direction, but straight ahead as she walked across the street.

He turned back into the dark alley and stood face to face with two young men who were staring at him and grinning.

They were teenagers, he realized. Young, dumb, and braver than they should have been. The one on the left was short, maybe five feet four inches tall to his six feet. The one on the right was taller, but still not as tall as Benji.

"What's in the backpack, pussy?" the little one said.

Benji noticed for the first time that he held a knife in his right hand down by his leg. The taller one had his arms crossed and seemed content to watch the smaller one. Maybe this was kind of a gang initiation, Benji thought.

"Clothes," Benji replied. "They belong to my sister," he added.

They had no need to know that the dress and wig were his. They might be useful yet.

The little one stepped forward and raised the knife to point at Benji's face.

"I doubt it, pussy. Probably got drugs in that bag." The little one spit at him.

That was the kid's biggest mistake. Not only had Benji's father taught him how to hack computers, he had taught him how to fight and defend himself.

Benji moved swiftly. He grabbed the kid's right wrist with his left hand, twisting the wrist and knife point away from him. He turned his back to his attacker and ducked for leverage. Using both hands on the left wrist, he flipped the kid over his shoulder in a karate throw. The throw was designed to break the arm, but the height difference made the move difficult. He removed the knife from the kid's hand as he hit the ground.

Benji had the knife in his right hand. He still held the kid's wrist in his left hand. He drew the knife across the kid's throat, shocked at how sharp the knife was. It cut almost to the bone.

Benji turned back to the larger young man. The grin was gone. His expression was one of horror. The young man reached behind his back. Benji knew he was reaching for a gun.

Benji lunged for the young man's chest with the knife. The young man's pistol came up and exploded. Benji's knife struck home, right into the heart. The force of his lunge carried them both to the packed dirt of the alley. Benji's left hand knocked the hand with the pistol away and he jabbed the knife in again. The young man stared at him and blinked his eyes.

Benji was breathing hard. He could smell dirt and gunpowder. He could hear people running and yelling.

"Police! Don't move!"

Benji tried to move. But he couldn't, for some reason. He felt weak and tired. It was hard to breathe, his stomach hurt. He looked down at his stomach. He was covered in blood.

"Stand up slowly. With your hands in the air."

He started to stand up. But collapsed forward on top of the young man who shot him.

Chapter 57

The Belize Police Department had received much of its training from FBI agents on loan from the U.S. When the department received a request to work with Green and Special Agent Henderson, they quickly agreed.

Special Agent Renee Henderson was a rising star in the FBI. She had been an officer in the Army military police for six years after college and had been recruited by the FBI for the cyber-crime's unit. After months of training at the FBI academy at Quantico, Virginia, she had been assigned to the Little Rock field office to help with this specific case. She still looked young enough to fit in on campus as a grad student. She was tech-savvy, very fit and well trained in hand-to-hand combat, and knew police procedure.

She knew she had not been Green's choice to make this trip. She had been the director's choice because she was the only agent who had seen Benji as both a woman and a man. She was the only person who might be able to identify Benji in disguise.

Green had reluctantly brought her to Belize, but he had no intentions of letting her anywhere near the important parts of the case. He had let her know that he had screwed it up once, he certainly wasn't going to allow a rookie to screw it up for him. That's why he had left her in the lobby. Her assignment was to watch for Benji.

She had missed him when he came in. She had been on the phone with the Belize Police Department asking questions about their handling of the incident at the Caribbean Bank that morning. She kept getting the same answer. No crime had happened, there was nothing to investigate.

She had spotted Benji when he exited the elevator at the Radisson. She followed him for several blocks into the Tourism Village. She had glimpsed him again when he was changing into the tie-dye t-shirt. Then she lost him again when she had to work her way through a group of tourists returning from a tour of Mayan ruins. She was in awe of how he used simple clothing changes to disappear or blend into a crowd. She mentally went over the tricks he had used. The blond wig with a little makeup at Starbucks two days ago; the blond wig and the dress this morning. Then the ball cap, and sunglasses. And now the tie-dye t-shirt. If he had another wig and more women's clothing, he might lose her completely.

She had called Green to give him an update. He had been pissed and told her to keep looking until she had Benji in custody. Use the Belize Police, search the city, and do whatever it takes to find him. She knew he wanted to keep her away from the hotel and the laptop. But she knew she was in a better position to capture Benji where she was.

She had spotted him an hour later crossing the swing bridge to the south side of the city. She managed to stay behind him and out of sight. She called the Belize Police Department for backup and was crossing the street when he ducked into an alley. She took off running as fast as she could.

She was standing at the corner, about to peek into the alley, when she heard scuffling. She turned into the alley and caught sight of Benji throwing the kid in midair.

Stunned, she watched Benji grab the knife and slash the kid's throat. She recognized that as a military move. She then saw Benji turn, and for the first time noticed the second assailant had a pistol and was raising it.

She reached for her weapon and remembered she didn't have one. She was visiting a foreign country and wasn't allowed to carry.

She heard the blast of the pistol. Saw Benji stab his assailant. Then they both fell. A Belizean police officer appeared beside her yelling. His weapon was drawn and he was yelling for Benji to stand up and put his hands in the air.

It didn't matter. Benji collapsed on top of the other gang member. Special Agent Henderson flashed her badge at the officer, then ran down the alley, stopping to check for a pulse on the first kid.

"Dead," she said. The officer moved past her and was holding his pistol on the other two. Henderson moved to them and she reached for Benji's wrist. He did not move, but she felt a pulse.

"This one's alive," she said. She rolled him over and off the attacker. There she saw the bloody hole in the tie-dye t-shirt low down on the left side. She then checked the pulse of the second attacker. It was very weak. She noticed the bloody stab wounds were centered around the heart.

"I've got a weak pulse on this one. We need to get them to the hospital," she told the officer.

He had already radioed for backup. Now he radioed for an ambulance. Henderson was looking at the two dying young men and thinking what a waste.

She spotted the pistol and pointed it out to the officer. It was still in the second attacker's hand. The officer picked it up, using a handkerchief, and stepped back.

She knelt beside Benji. She needed him alive. She raised the blood-soaked t-shirt he was wearing to inspect the wound. Blood wasn't pouring out, but it hadn't stopped either. Using as much of the t-shirt as she could, she put it against the wound and applied pressure. She knew applying pressure was supposed to reduce the blood loss, but didn't know if she was helping or not.

It took five minutes for the ambulance to get there. Benji was still alive as it pulled away. The other two participants in the attack, however, would never wake up. Special Agent Henderson looked at her hands. They were covered with Benji's blood.

Chapter 58

Special Agent Green went cold when he received the phone call from Henderson. He was thinking back to the phone call he had received earlier from the director. He told Henderson to get to the hospital and protect Benji. He said there was more going on than they knew. He would call her back in twenty minutes with an update.

The director had called him thirty minutes earlier and informed him about a conversation he'd had with the NSA director that afternoon. The NSA believed Jessica Benelli and a group of her friends had stolen millions of dollars from a criminal organization. The NSA director would not explain how they had gotten that information. But it was solid. The director had told him that Benji wasn't the person behind the attacks. If anything, Benji might get attacked himself.

Green needed to talk to Jess. But he didn't have her current phone number. He thought about Steven and Bets, Jess's hacker friends. He called the number for Bets's duplex. There was no answer.

Then he remembered Agent West with the DEA. Agent West answered on the second ring.

"West, we've been used," Green said. "Those kids we have been protecting are in real trouble. We believe they have stolen several million dollars from some very bad people. I need to talk to Jess right now. Benji Smith has been shot in Belize. And I believe Jess and Mike will be attacked as soon as they are located. I need Jess's number."

"I'm sorry," West said. "They don't trust you."

"I don't care if they don't trust me. I've been chasing the wrong person. And now he may die in a foreign country," Green said. "I need to know what's going on and I need to know now."

"Fine," West huffed. "Let me call her. And I will have her call you."

"Thank you," Green answered and hung up before West could respond.

It was a long five minutes before Green's cell phone rang. It was West calling him back.

"The cell number she gave me must not have an international plan. I called the cruise ship directly. The ship's crew will deliver them a message shortly. It's the best I can do."

"Thank you, West. I appreciate it. Once I figure out what is going on, I'll let you know," Green said.

"I would appreciate that," West answered.

Green paced the floor of his hotel room in the Radisson. He had Benji's laptop, but he had not tried to access it or even open it. He knew he wouldn't be able to log into it. If it was set up like Jess's laptop it would be very difficult to get into. To start with, it would have a two hundred and fifty-six-character password. It would take days to try all the possibilities. He would leave that to the lab techs.

His cell phone rang. But no number showed on his phone. It was blocked.

He answered the call, "Green."

"Is it Special Agent Green, or Dr. Haygood?" the male voice asked on the other end of the line.

Green sighed deeply. "It's FBI consultant Green, Mike. Is Jess with you?"

"You know the answer to that question. West said it was an emergency. What do you want?"

Green had lots of questions. But they would have to wait. Green was guessing about some of the things, but he took a shot in the dark.

Green replied, "We have Benji in custody. He's been gut-shot. He's probably in surgery now. I have an agent at the hospital. She thinks he will lose a kidney. He might not live, Mike." Green waited for a response, but Mike said nothing. Green waited, thinking he who speaks first, loses. Green thought, damn it, Mike, say something.

Finally, Green broke. "Mike, we know you and Jess stole money from some bad people. We know they're after you. We know it wasn't Benji behind the attacks. You're in trouble, Mike. I can help."

"Okay," Mike said. "I'll have to call you back with some details. But for now, Benji cannot stay in that hospital. If they know he's alive, they will attack again."

"Who is after you, Mike?"

Mike ignored the question and went on to lay out a plan for what to do with Benji. It was incredibly simple, Green thought. And to have planned this far in advance indicated a very high level of intelligence.

"Ok," Green replied. "I will go along with that. I think it's a good plan. When will you call me back?"

"Put our plan into action. I have to get information from Jess and someone else. I don't have all the details you need. Give me fifteen minutes," Mike said and hung up.

Chapter 59

Mike, Jess, Angela, and Bobby were back at the table on the Lido deck. They had changed out of their dress clothes after dinner and were relaxing over beers and margaritas after stuffing their bellies with steak and lobster.

They looked at Mike expectantly.

"What's going on, Mike?" Jess asked.

"Benji's been shot," he said slowly. "He's in surgery. They are afraid he may not make it."

They had listened to his side of the conversation but had not heard Green's.

Angela said, "We have a cousin who works as a missionary in Guatemala. He and his wife help drug addicts and abused women and children there. That's where you want them to take Benji?"

Mike nodded. Then he looked at Jess.

He asked, "I need to know two things. Where is the evidence from the websites you took down? And how much money did you take from the accounts you traced?"

She gave Mike a worried look. "I'm sorry, Mike. I got carried away. I took down five sites. It's all recorded on the thumb drive that I left with Bets and Steven."

"And the money?"

Mike could see the concern on her face when Jess swallowed hard. "Most of the accounts I traced from the sites had a few hundred dollars. One site led me to accounts with over one hundred and fifty million."

Angela and Bobby just stared at Jess with their mouths open. Mike looked like he was going to be sick to his stomach. Jess looked at Mike and flicked a little smile at him before getting serious again.

Jess said, "I followed the money like you taught me to. It went from one account to another. From one bank to another. In all, I found over five hundred million dollars. But I could only get access to some of the accounts. I moved it around the world and put it all in one account in a bank in Hong Kong."

Mike was starting to recover now and asked, "Why Hong Kong?"

"I have a friend there," she replied. "He withdrew the money as a cashier's check. Walked down the street to another bank and deposited it there. He then transferred it to a bank in Antigua. It's there now."

Mike looked at the three of them. Angela and Bobby were still in shock.

Mike said to Angela and Bobby, "I'm sorry. We never dreamed there would be more than a few thousand dollars in any of the accounts."

"This explains why they are trying to kidnap or kill you, Jess. You should have told me," Mike said.

"I know, Mike, but we agreed that we would keep our parts of the plan to ourselves. You said it was safer that way if no one knew the whole plan," Jess said.

Bobby finally got his tongue back. "It's all fun and games until someone gets hurt."

Mike and Jess were still staring at each other, ignoring Bobby.

"Bets and Steven are working on getting the other three hundred and fifty million," Jess said.

Mike's face turned red. He got up from his chair and walked to the back rail and stared at the water being churned by the ship. He was angry and conflicted.

Jess had followed the plan to the letter. He admitted to himself, that the mistake was his. He had not made a contingency plan in this case. The truth was, he never saw the possibility of millions of dollars. The plan was to take down websites and try to bankrupt the people behind the sites. They never dreamed it would lead to this much money. A few thousand dollars maybe, but not millions.

Jess had stumbled onto something much bigger. Much more dangerous than they had expected.

Mike turned around to find his sister, his best friend, and his girlfriend staring at him with concerned looks on their faces.

"Mike," Jess said.

Mike held up his hand. "You followed the plan; I never dreamed you would find that kind of money. It's my fault for not having a contingency plan. It won't happen again. From this point on, we are all in. Everyone at this table knows everything. Everyone is expected to look at alternatives to the plan. To think of ways our plan won't work so we can have an alternative plan. What do we do if something goes differently than expected? Okay?"

Angela and Jess nodded.

Bobby looked blank. But then said, "Who the hell is really after you, or us?"

Mike shook his head and said, "I need to call Haygood, I mean, Green back. We need to reevaluate things afterward."

Jess said, "Bets and Steven were to mail the contents of the hard drive to Agent Carson at his Little Rock office after they left town. We were afraid they wouldn't be safe after they tried getting the rest of the money. Someone had some very powerful software to track me back through three VPNs and my firewall."

Mike took out his phone and called Special Agent Green. He was five minutes later calling Green than he had planned.

This time the voice on the other end of the line just said, "Hello."

Mike started by saying, "Jess took down five child porn websites Friday morning. The plan was to trace their money trail and clean out their accounts. We expected to find a few thousand dollars, nothing more. But Jess stumbled onto something much bigger. She found several accounts with millions of dollars in them and in her anger, she cleaned them out. She intends to turn the money over to the FBI, but we've been a little out of touch. "

Mike stopped talking for a moment. He had to be careful what he said and how he said it. "Jess copied the websites onto a thumb drive, it's being mailed to Agent Carson at his office in Little Rock. Whoever is behind the attacks on us and Benji has some powerful software. You saw Jess's laptop. You know it's very secure."

Green replied then, "Yes. And I have Benji's laptop now. And I'm sure it's as secure as Jess's. Maybe, more so."

"Whoever is after us tracked her movements through three VPNs and her firewall, got her phone information, my phone information, and who knows what else in the matter of a few hours after she hacked their websites. And they organized the attack on us, which means they have contacts."

Mike was sure Green was following his logic now when he asked, "So you think the only people with that kind of sophisticated software have government connections? Mike, I haven't even tried to access Benji's laptop because I know it will take days to break his encryption. I understand your thinking, but it's absurd."

"That's why we haven't trusted you or Carson," Mike added emphatically. "It may sound absurd, but think about how many people you know who could do that. You taught us cyber security. You told us it can't be done. It takes millions of dollars to stay on the cutting edge of security. The only agencies that can do that are the NSA or the CIA."

Mike was almost shouting at Green when he saw Angela waving at him with one hand and putting a finger to her lips with the other.

Green was quiet for a full minute before he said anything.

"Mike, I need to call you back. Can I have your number?"

"No," Mike answered. "Tell me when to call and I will call you back."

Green sighed heavily. "Ok. Call me in an hour, if I don't answer, wait an hour and call again."

"Okay," Mike replied and hung up.

He was still standing and looked at the table. Bobby said what he was sure they were all thinking.

"We're in deep shit, bro. What do we do now?"

Chapter 60

Green was cool and collected most of the time. But now he was thinking very hard and he was sweating furiously. Weighing what Mike had said against the phone call from his director, he knew Mike had hit a home run with his analysis of the situation. The NSA knew more than they were telling the director. Mike knew more than he was telling the FBI. And he was left in the middle trying to put together a puzzle that was missing half the pieces.

Green called Henderson. She answered on the first ring and must have anticipated what he was going to ask.

"Benji just came out of surgery. He lost a kidney and a lot of blood," Henderson said. "They really don't want us to move him tonight. I explained that it was urgent that we pronounce him dead, and get him out of the hospital before someone showed up and hurt more people."

"Good," Green said. "I know you want to go with him. But you can't. We have to sell his death. We will have to trust the Belize Police to protect him. Were you able to reach the missionary?"

"Yes," she replied. "He didn't want anything to do with Benji until I mentioned Mike's name. Then he reluctantly agreed. He said they had a doctor volunteering there now, but they were low on medical supplies. I told him we would help with the medical supplies and he softened tremendously."

"Good," Green replied. "Take care of things at the hospital and get back here as soon as you can. It's getting very interesting, and tonight is going to be a long night."

Green's next call was to Agent Carson.

"I've been waiting on your call," Carson answered.

Green filled him in on Benji, and what he had learned from the director and Mike. He asked Carson to find and protect Bets and Steven.

Carson replied that they had personally delivered the thumb drive and Jess's laptop to him and left in a hurry. He said they had taken the battery out of Jess's laptop because it kept turning itself on.

Green cursed at this news. "It seems our young friend may be onto something. Analyze that thumb drive, but focus on the financial information. We need to follow Jess's tracks if that's possible now."

"One more thing," Carson said. "Benji called 911 about 10:30 Friday morning and reported a female neighbor's overdose. He kept the woman's son in his apartment until the Department of Human Services could get there and take the child into custody. Apparently, it wasn't the first time Benji had looked after the kid."

"One day he's Mother Teresa, the next day he turns Rambo in an alley," Green replied. "Thanks, Carson. Let me know what you find on that hard drive."

Green's third call was to the FBI director's office. It took a few minutes before the director answered. He updated the director on what he had learned from Mike. Then he explained Mike's suspicions about the software.

"That's ridiculous," the director replied.

"I wish it were, Director. Where did you get your information about the kids stealing millions of dollars?" Green reminded him.

The director sighed heavily. "The NSA," he admitted.

"Sir, we need more information. I think these kids can help us. These kids are working as a team. They are compartmentalizing information in case they get caught. They have planned ahead in ways that threw us off course. Sir, they haven't admitted it, but Benji was bait to make us look the other way while they took down these child pornographers."

"And how can they help us, Green? What are we looking for? Once you get into this Benji kid's laptop, you will find the person you've been looking for this past year. Make arrangements to bring him back home as soon as possible. And then arrest these others for wire fraud."

"But, sir!"

"That will be enough, Green! Finish this and come home."

The director hung up. Green was perplexed. The director was ignoring all the attacks and the attempted kidnapping of Jess. He wanted them arrested and brought home. It didn't make sense.

There was a knock at his door. He looked through the peephole and saw Special Agent Henderson standing in the hallway with a backpack in her hand. He opened his door.

"Come in. We need to talk," said Green.

* * *

Special Agent Renee Henderson tensed at Green's tone. She was expecting a verbal lashing because Benji got shot. Instead, he walked to the mini-fridge and took out a beer.

"Would you like one?"

"No," she replied. "Actually, yes. Although, I would prefer a shot of tequila."

"Why are you here, Henderson? I know the director handpicked you. Why?"

Henderson thought about the question. There were so many things they should be talking about, and he asked this. She liked Green but despised how he operated. He was so old school he didn't trust her. That's what this question was about. Trust. She dropped the backpack on the little table by the window and sat in one of the two chairs. It had been a long day. She took the beer that Green handed her, twisted the top off, and answered.

"He thinks you're a bit of a renegade. That you and Carson together are unpredictable. He thinks you will be more apt to go by the book if I'm here," she said.

Green nodded and asked, "What do you think about Benji?"

Henderson hesitated. "I saw him throw one attacker and take away his knife, cut his throat, then stab the second attacker while being shot. He knows how to fight better than a lot of my army buddies. He didn't hesitate. If his second attacker hadn't had a gun, I think he would have killed him and survived without a scratch."

"What about his internet and credit card scams?" Green asked.

Henderson reached for the backpack. She unzipped a small pocket on the back and withdrew a half-sized notebook. "You know," Henderson said, looking at the notebook from Benji's backpack, "it looks like he has been making monthly payments to a mental health hospital in Fayetteville for over a year."

Green asked, "Why would he be doing that? Is he seeking treatment?"

"No, these amounts look like he has been paying for someone to stay there," Henderson said.

"This is a diary of sorts," she said. "He paid his way through college, with scholarships, financial aid, and theft. He implies that he only stole what he needed. He even admits that he got a thrill from the thefts."

"But he's still a thief," Green said.

"He's still a thief that sees himself as a modern-day Robin Hood," Henderson said.

"So, he's hiding something."

"Looks like it."

Green sighed. "The director wants us to bring him in as soon as possible.

She looked at him incredulously. "Does he know we just had him pronounced dead and sent him to Guatemala?"

"No," Green replied.

"Great!" Henderson groaned. The word practically dripped from her tongue. "Now you've got me going cowboy with you."

"Let me bring you up to date," he said.

He told her about his earlier call with the director, then his call with Mike, and finally, the last call with the director.

Henderson stared at Green and finally said, "Now I understand why you and Carson go renegade. You've got good guys, or kids, who have gone bad and are stealing from even worse guys. You've got Benji, who is a thief, working with them, I think, to be a distraction."

"Yes," Green said. "And the question still remains, who is after them? We can arrest them all, and they still wouldn't be safe."

Henderson asked, "How much money did they steal?"

"I don't know. The director doesn't know. But the NSA implied several million," Green answered. "Mike said they intended to turn the money over to the FBI, but they have been out of touch. They're on a cruise."

She whistled at the amount. "So, we have no evidence, just third-party information that they stole some money?" Henderson asked.

"Yes. And the fact that they admitted to taking down several child pornography websites. God, I can't even say that without shuddering," Green said. "And following the money trail to try to bankrupt them."

"But he said they intend to turn over the money, so was it really theft?" Henderson said. "Plus, Agent Carson was aware that the young lady was searching for those types of websites. Did she keep any evidence?"

"Put on a thumb drive and in Carson's custody now. And I think I like where you're going with this. Go on, please."

Henderson said, "You said they never expected to find millions of dollars. If they turn the money and evidence over to the FBI. They were doing us a favor."

"True. Except we never authorized the theft of money," Green said.

"If it weren't for the NSA, we wouldn't know about the money," Henderson said. "I believe they stumbled onto an NSA operation, and the NSA wants us to shut them down."

Green sighed deeply and sat down at the small table across from Henderson. "And we could end this if the NSA would tell the director who was behind this."

Henderson asked, "What do we do?"

Green smiled. "It seems our guilty party died in the operating room tonight. That case will be closed tomorrow."

"We let him go free?" Henderson asked.

"We can charge him again when it's discovered he miraculously survived the trip to Guatemala," Green replied. "Right now, he won't be doing much running for a few weeks with his injuries."

Chapter 61

Mike knew Angela was the one who was always steady and asked deep probing questions. But this time, she was the emotional one. The plan they had made protected everyone but Mike and Jess.

"Mike, I don't like this," Angela said. "I don't want you and Jess taking all the risks."

"Can we trust the FBI?" Mike asked.

"No," she replied.

Jess had the same look in her eyes as Angela. "Call Haygood, or Green, I mean."

Mike picked up his smartphone and punched in the number for Green.

The phone rang once on the other end. "Green here."

"It's Mike."

Green said, "Mike, I believe you were correct about the NSA. I believe Jess stepped right into the middle of one of their operations. The director wants me to bring in Benji, and you and Jess."

"Why me and Jess?" Mike asked.

"Wire fraud. It covers all kinds of things including illegal internet activity," Green replied.

"Now I'm finally starting to believe you," Mike said.

"Mike? Carson has the thumb drive and Jess's laptop. He's reviewing the information now. Bets and Steven delivered it to him in person. They would turn Jess's laptop off and it would turn itself back on. They are still trying to find you. And now they may be after Bets and Steven. Are they okay? Have you heard from them?"

"No," Mike said. "We haven't heard from them."

Mike hesitated for a moment. He was thinking of Bets and Steven. He had dropped the ball there, too. He had not planned to cover Bets and Steven. He was beginning to feel out-maneuvered.

"Mike? Are you still there?"

"Yes," Mike replied. "What can you tell me about the NSA software?"

"Nothing. I can't even tell you it exists. But your theory makes perfect sense," Green answered. "The director got his information about you and Jess from the NSA. And they wouldn't tell the director how much money you stole, who you stole it from, or how they knew."

Green hesitated a few seconds. "Mike, as far as I'm concerned, if you turn the money over to us, we don't have a case against you and Jess. The NSA wouldn't give us any evidence. Without evidence, we have no case. Benji is a different story, though. We will be keeping our eyes on him."

"Are you saying you're not coming after us?" Mike asked.

Green said, "I think it would be a waste of time. But Mike, you need to send me an email ASAP. I have a link to a website you need to check out. It may help you figure out what's going on. I can't do it. I've been instructed to wrap it up and come home. Then you can let me know so we can wrap this up."

"No," Mike said. "No email. Do you have a pen and paper?"

Mike gave him the email address that Jess had created the day before and the login password. He told him to create a draft email and save it. He would log in later and read the draft.

Mike ended the call with Green. He looked at the others and then at Jess.

"Have you heard from Bets and Steven?"

Jess shook her head.

Mike told them what Green had said about dropping the thumb drive off and leaving Jess's laptop with Carson. He told them that Green wasn't pursuing them, but the FBI director wanted them brought in for wire fraud.

* * *

Jess took the phone from Mike and checked for emails. There were none. She checked for drafts and found nothing there yet. She was worried about Bets and Steven now. She struggled around the filters the cruise line had on their WIFI and was finally able to log into her Tormail account. She had three new emails, two from Harvey and one from Bets.

The first email from Harvey showed a deposit slip and transfer slip for over one hundred and fifty million dollars. The second was from Bets and it said that she and Steven were on the run. They were scared and would be in touch when they felt safe.

The last email from Harvey said that he was going black. He was giving up his title of number one hacker god because he couldn't stop whoever Jess had pissed off.

Jess was worried now. Benji had been shot, and they were all on the run.

"This is not good," Jess said. "Bets and Steven are on the run, and my friend in Hong Kong has gone black. If he can't block them, we're in trouble."

"How can we find out who's after you?" Angela asked.

"Green said he had no idea, but there was a website we needed to check. He is supposed to leave a draft message under our email account," Mike said. "He couldn't confirm the existence of NSA software, but he thought it was the logical conclusion since the NSA contacted the FBI. He thinks we stepped right into the middle of an NSA operation."

"Why would someone who has five hundred million dollars have a dark child porn website?" Bobby asked. "That's a rich sicko."

Angela said, "Pedophiles don't do it for the money. Some claim they should be classified with the LGBTQ community."

"Don't even go there," Bobby said. "Children don't know enough to make that decision on their own."

"I agree," Angela said. "And the psychological abuse can affect them for the rest of their lives."

"Let's move on," Mike said. "That's why we did this. To stop a predator. Now he is trying to stop us."

"Okay, what do we need to do to stop this pervert?" asked Bobby.

Mike asked Jess, "Has Green written that draft email yet?"

She nodded.

"Let's go to the ship's computer lab," Mike said.

Jess said, "I need to get a thumb drive out of our safe first."

Chapter 62

Jess had told Bets about the one hundred and fifty million dollars right before they left town. Bets and Steven used Jess's laptop to make a try at the rest of the money Jess had found. They had found a possible way into the banking software program, but Steven wanted to discuss it with Mike and Jess before trying it.

When they realized someone was checking out Jess's computer while they were on it, and there was little they could do about it, they shut it down. When it turned itself back on, Steven flipped it over and took the battery out of it. At that point, they decided it was time to leave Bets's duplex and get out of town.

They thought a little fun on the beach might be just what they needed after four years of hard studying. Jess had mentioned Antigua, so they had decided to fly there and then contact her. Whoever she had pissed off was not taking it lightly.

Bets and Steven had planned to drive straight through from Fayetteville to Miami. They had not taken the route suggested by Maps on their phone. They had, instead, gone through south Arkansas and through Northeast Louisiana, crossing the Mississippi River on Interstate 20 at Vicksburg. They turned south at Jackson and east on Interstate 10 at Mobile. And then took the straightest, most obvious route to Miami. They believed if anyone was following them, they would try something long before they reached Miami.

Steven and Bets were going into their third straight day with less than five hours of sleep. The continuous hum of the tires on the pavement and the flashing white stripes between the lanes were starting to dull their senses. Steven was driving and had been talking for five minutes straight when he looked over and found Bets sound asleep.

It was nearly midnight. They needed rest. Their flight left at 8:15 a.m. Tuesday morning and Steven decided to find a hotel and get some rest and a shower. Bets was already sleeping, and he wasn't reacting as quickly as he should have been. He had that drunk feeling that comes from staying awake too long.

They were still thirty minutes from the Miami airport. He looked for freeway signs showing motels and took the first exit showing three motel signs. The first two showed no vacancy signs. The third one was an old motel that allowed you to park right in front of your room door. It also advertised rooms by the hour, giving Steven an indication of the type of motel it really was. He was so exhausted, he didn't care. They could at least get a shower before heading to the airport.

There was no one in the lobby when Steven rang the bell. The desk clerk, who appeared from a back room, was an older Hispanic man, who looked like he was high or drunk. Steven couldn't tell which. Steven asked if he had two rooms, and was informed two people only got one room. He asked for a wake-up call at six a.m. and the man told him no wake-up calls. Too tired to argue, Steven paid in cash and took the room key. They were in room twenty-one.

There were two cars parked in front of their room. So, he parked in front of room twenty. He woke Bets up and told her what they were doing. He got out, unlocked the room door, and carefully turned the lights on. He was shocked to find the room clean. The decor was at least thirty years old. He figured the wallpaper was older than him, but there was a king-size bed, a small table, and two chairs.

Bets grabbed her suitcase out of the back seat and told Steven she was taking the first shower. Steven found himself looking at the motel parking lot and asking himself why did he stop here. His tired mind gave him the answer. They had the only room available at this exit. He grabbed his luggage and both of their laptop bags and headed to the room. He used his key fob to lock the car behind him.

Setting the bags on the floor, he closed the door behind him. The bathroom door was slightly open and he could hear the shower running. He reached for the curtains to close the crack in the middle. Movement in the parking lot caught his attention. He pushed the curtain back with his left hand and peeked out.

A black car drove through the lot. Steven couldn't tell what kind it was. The driver and three passengers seemed to be checking out the license plates on the cars. He thought he saw one of the passengers point toward his car. When the passengers leaned out the car windows with guns Steven couldn't believe what he was seeing.

Steven yelled, "Bets, get down! Get down!"

He yelled again as he busted into the bathroom. Bets pushed the shower curtain back to yell at Steven for intruding on her shower just as the first sounds of automatic gunfire started. She dropped down into the old tub, just as Steven dived and tore the shower curtain off the rod.

He pushed Bets down and flattened his body on top of hers. The shooting stopped, but they didn't move to get out of the tub. The hot water from the shower head was pounding on Steven's back. He was shaking so badly he could hardly move. He managed to stand up and turn the water off.

"Are you okay, Bets?"

When she didn't reply, he grabbed the shower curtain and threw it out of the tub. He saw a naked Bets curled up in the bottom of the tub, shaking. She stared wide-eyed at him and nodded.

"Come on," he said. "Stand up."

He reached down and took her hands, helping her stand up. As soon as she stood up, she threw her arms around him and started sobbing. They stood like that for a minute. As thrilled as Steven was to have a naked Bets holding him this tight, his mind was on the gunshots. He didn't see bullet holes anywhere. So, what were they shooting at, he wondered.

Steven was wide awake now; he was still shaking. His heart pounded and he was breathing quickly. He put his hands on Bets's face and gently tilted her head to look into her eyes. When he was sure he had her attention, he started talking.

"We need to get out of here and get to the airport. The police will be here shortly. I'm soaked, so I need to change, too," he said.

Bets nodded but did not move or let go.

"Bets! We need to move now," Steven said.

She was still looking up at him and holding on tight.

"Are you okay?"

Still no response. He bent over and kissed her, then swatted her naked butt with his hand. That woke her up. She let go and tried to slap him, but he brushed her attempt aside.

"Bets, we have to go."

"Okay," she whimpered.

Steven started to step out of the tub, but Bets grabbed his shirt front, stood on her tiptoes, and kissed him.

They left the motel room and found Steven's car riddled with bullet holes. The motel room in front of his car was demolished. He hoped no one was hurt. They turned and hurried away from the motel, down the street to a Waffle House.

Fifteen minutes later, an Uber driver picked them up and headed to the Miami International Airport.

Chapter 63

Harvey didn't leave his apartment often. He leased time on a mainframe computer, which was a few blocks away. When he realized someone was tracking him online, he just turned his terminal off. He went black, as he called it. He still had his personal laptop, if he needed it, and a separate internet access that he used for personal business.

Later, after lunch, he would walk down the street to an internet cafe and send a few emails. He was not concerned about someone finding him in a city of seven million people.

It was an inconvenience that he had expected to happen. His Russian friends were watching and waiting, though, and they would trace the person who was tracking him. When Jess had contacted him about moving the money, he agreed, thinking it would be several thousand dollars. When Jess told him he would be transferring one hundred and fifty million dollars, he knew someone would be tracking the money. They had probably logged Jess's keystrokes, invaded her computer and were tracking all her recent contacts.

He had intentionally set himself up by contacting Jess's friends. He thought it would be Jess he would be talking to, but it was her friends. The setup worked, either way, and it only took a few minutes.

He had contacted his Russian friends immediately after returning from the banks. They were experts at hacking and tracking. Now he just had to wait for the Russians to contact him.

Chapter 64

Jess had retrieved a thumb drive which allowed her to reboot a computer and restart it using the operating system found on the thumb drive. It used only RAM in the computer and never used the hard drive. The Tor operating system was very secure and private and allowed them to view whatever Agent Green wanted them to see without leaving a trace on the computer they were using.

Jess loaded the website and found several discussion boards and links to research papers and articles on encryption, tracking internet use, and protecting against hacking. She and Mike browsed the site for an hour before finding what Green must have wanted them to find. It was a research paper on theoretical financial tracking and information gathering. It didn't look interesting until they Googled the authors and found they all worked for a think-tank located in Washington D.C.

Angela and Bobby had moved to another computer and were looking up information about the island of Antigua. Mike and Jess were about one hundred pages into a two-hundred-and-fifty-page paper when they found what Green had apparently wanted them to find. It was about methods that could be used to trace online money transactions and how to locate the computer that was used to make the transfer. It also talked about getting other information from the computer and identifying the owner of the computer.

"That's it," Mike said. "It's not theory, it's fact."

"This was written six years ago," Jess said. "There's been time to program it and test it. The question is how to defend against it, or track it."

"Let's keep reading," Mike said.

It was in the last section before the summary. There they found a section on tracking the tracers and defending against the use of similar software. Mike and Jess were thoroughly engrossed in reading the theories when Bobby scared them to death by simply whispering 'hey' in their ears and making them jump.

"It's nearly two in the morning and we have to be up early to catch the water taxi. You need to wrap it up," Bobby said.

"I think we just did," Mike said.

"And?" Bobby asked as Angela joined him.

Jess answered for them. "The concept is simple. The programming may be complicated."

"May be complicated?" Angela asked.

"It depends on how much prewritten code I can find. Considering this paper was written six years ago, that may not be difficult."

"Mike, you're being awfully quiet," Bobby said.

"Yeah, you guys go to bed," Mike answered. "Make sure we're awake in time to shower and eat in the morning, please. Jess and I need to look at one more thing. It won't take long. I promise."

They said their good nights and Jess looked at Mike.

"What are you thinking, big guy?" she asked.

"One of my finance professors talked about cyber security systems for banks. He went in-depth on the systems used for credit card security and mentioned that the banks used a program to trace users back to their computers to reduce fraud. Most users use the same phone or computer system so if a new computer was used to access account information, it will ask for verification."

Jess said, "So the software we are looking at could do the same thing, only it doesn't ask for verification, it steals information instead."

"Exactly," Mike said. "And getting the banking software is easy, modifying it will be a cinch for you."

"But how does that help us stop the tracking?" Jess asked.

"We don't," Mike said. "We provide fake information instead. Then it will lead whoever is after us somewhere else."

"And who do you suggest we lead him to?" she asked.

"I think the director of the NSA will do, for starters," he replied.

Jess smiled at him, leaned over, and kissed him.

"Let's go to bed," he said.

Chapter 65

The sky was overcast and promised rain, but Belize City was on the edge of one of the world's largest rainforests. A little rain was to be expected now and then.

Mike, Jess, Bobby, and Angela arrived in Belize City aboard the water taxi. When they disembarked, they found three professionally dressed people awaiting them. A man and woman stood holding a sign that said Bennett's and a third man stood beside them holding another sign that said Phillips.

They had all dressed in their best professional attire that morning. The guys wore their khaki slacks and navy blazers with ties. The ladies had found business attire in Houston and wore knee-length skirts, white blouses, and blazers.

Angela looked at Mike and said, "You've been busy, big brother."

"Too much has happened, it's time for some professional security," Mike replied.

Mike moved toward the man holding the sign that read "Bennett's".

They were carrying their luggage. They had informed the cruise line when they left that morning they would not be returning. They had told them they had an emergency and needed to return home as soon as possible.

As they approached the three holding the signs, Mike held out his hand and introduced himself and his group. Their suits made them stand out, as did the earpieces each of them wore for communication purposes.

The older man of the three said, "I'm Robert Black, this is Gayle Becker, and the gentleman to my left is Diego Gonzalez. Now, before we get started let's step to the side so we can discuss a few things quietly."

They moved out of the way of the crowds exiting the water taxis. The crowds were being herded right through the Tourism Village before they were allowed to escape to their excursions for the day.

"First things first," Black said. "We are here to provide protection. Which means we put your lives ahead of ours, and because we do that, we expect full cooperation. Am I understood?"

"Yes, sir," Mike responded.

"Secondly, because we put our lives ahead of yours, we get paid very well. We are here because Agent West assured us you could afford our services," Black said.

Jess spoke up then. "Our first stop today is the Caribbean Bank. If you have an invoice, I will pay for two months of service upfront, then we will mutually decide if we need to continue at the end of that period."

Mr. Black looked from Mike to Jess, then said, "Okay, then we have an agreement. Now, we have a right to know what we are getting into. West told us everything he knew. What can you add?"

Mike explained the situation. He held nothing back, including their theories about the NSA.

He ended by saying, "We stepped into something much bigger than we expected. We aren't thieves. We intend to transfer the money to the FBI when it's safe for us to do so. But we are determined to see this through. We started by simply hunting down a pedophile and trying to shut him down."

Black nodded, looked at Mike hard, and asked, "I understand you got that broken finger from the hammer of a gun?"

"Yes, sir. Dumb luck, that I didn't get shot. I'm no fighter. In a fistfight, I can hold my own, but this is far beyond my abilities."

"Good," Black said. "Let us do the fighting, then. Have your plans changed any since our first contact?"

"No sir," Mike answered.

He pointed to Angela and Bobby and indicated they would be going to an electronics store and then to the airport. And told them he and Jess would be going to the bank and then to the airport.

"And where will we go from there?" Black asked.

Jess said, "Forgive us for being paranoid, Mr. Black. But we will tell you in the car when we are on the way. May we get going? Our appointment is in a few minutes."

"Of course, we have two cars waiting out front. Follow me, please."

Chapter 66

Their trip to the bank only took five minutes, and they discussed leaving Belize and flying to Antigua. Black told them there were much better hiding places back in the States where they could set up much better security. Mike and Jess both said they would be willing to discuss it after today. Right now, they had business to take care of and reservations in Antigua.

Black opened the door for Jess and Mike to get out in front of the Caribbean Bank. He entered the bank with them, while Becker went to park the car. She would follow them in and stay in the lobby until they were ready for the car.

Mike noticed that Black's eyes were everywhere and seemed to take in every individual. He also noticed that he kept a hand on the lapel of his jacket and wondered if there was a weapon holstered there. He found himself hoping there was.

Mike opened and held the door for Jess to enter the bank. They stopped just inside the door to orient themselves. The lobby area had a counter with several windows for customer service. One of the tellers greeted them and asked how she could help them.

Jess said, "I'm Jessica Bennett. My husband and I have a 10 a.m. appointment with Mr. Rollo."

"Just a moment," the teller said.

The teller reached for a phone and dialed a number.

She said, "Jessica Bennett is here to see you, sir."

"He will be right with you," the teller said and smiled.

A middle-aged gentleman came from a hallway on their left. He walked swiftly toward them and introduced himself. He shook hands with Jess and Mike as Jess introduced them and then she introduced Black as their security.

"A lot has happened recently, we don't feel safe right now," she explained to Mr. Rollo.

"I understand," he said, frowning. "Please follow me to our conference room. We will be more comfortable there."

Once in the conference room, Mr. Rollo introduced them to an attorney who specialized in forming corporations and American taxes.

The attorney told them they did not, under any circumstances, want to move the money back to the U.S. She could be charged with tax evasion, for the past twenty years, and interest and penalties could add up to more than the amount of money she had.

If the money were left in Belize or another Caribbean Island country, they would have full access to the money with no penalties. The attorney said he could quickly set up a corporation and the bank could set up a corporate account; they could be ready to start business the next day.

Mike and Jess quickly agreed to this and started signing the paperwork. Mr. Rollo left the conference room and returned a few minutes later with another folder and a form for Jess to fill out.

"Before I can authorize the transfer of money to the corporate account, you must fill out this form to verify your identity," he said.

* * *

Jess frowned as she took the form. As she read the paper Mike watched the frown turn into a smile. She quickly answered the questions and handed it back to Mr. Rollo.

He removed a sheet of paper from the folder, compared it to the form, and smiled. "Everything seems to be in order. We can proceed."

It took a little over an hour to set up the corporation. The bank account was set up so that either Jess or Mike could access funds, and Mr. Rollo handed them each a new Visa debit card.

As they were finishing their business, Black spoke quietly into the earpiece. He asked Becker to get the car.

Jess was beaming as they walked out of the conference room. She hugged Mike tightly as they walked down the hallway.

Jess said, "Thank you for being here, Mike. I don't think I would have had the strength to do that by myself."

"You're welcome, dear. Now what was on that form you had to fill out?" Mike asked.

"Do you remember telling me that I might have to prove who I was somehow? Well, that was a list of questions about my childhood that only three people would know the answers to," she said.

"And that was you, your mom, and your dad," Mike replied, smiling.

"Yep," Jess answered. "Now, what are we going to do with a corporation that doesn't do business?"

"We will think of something," Mike replied.

Black was ahead of them as they approached the front door of the bank. He motioned for them to wait as he stepped through the door. He looked up and down the street and found Becker standing by the car door.

She nodded at him; he turned and said, "Let's go quickly, there's something Becker doesn't like."

"How do you know?" Jess asked.

"She wouldn't get out of the car otherwise," he said.

Mike and Jess followed him from the bank. The car was parked fifteen feet away. It was only six to seven steps away. Mike heard rushed steps behind him, and Becker yelled, "Gun!"

He saw her pull her pistol from inside her jacket. He reached for Jess to get her on the ground. Something hit him in the head and knocked him away from Jess. He tried to regain his balance, but couldn't stop himself from falling. The sound of gunshots finally reached him. He searched desperately for Jess. He saw Black shoving her in the back seat of the car. They were above him for some reason, he must be on the sidewalk. He heard her screaming his name. Then he blinked and everything went black.

Chapter 67

Mike had made arrangements that morning to charter a flight from Belize City Municipal Airport to VC Bird Airport in Antigua. He had barely had enough money left on their temporary visa card to pay for the flight.

Bobby and Angela were to arrive ahead of them and take care of their luggage and any other details before their scheduled departure at noon. That was after they stopped by an electronics store and bought a couple more phones and some international SIM cards. Bobby would also check out what kinds of phones they were selling in Belize and their prices.

Bobby, Angela, and Diego were standing outside the plane and had been talking about the different types of phones sold in Belize when Diego's smile disappeared and he held up his hand for Bobby to be quiet.

"Shit! You guys really did need us. Come on. I need your help, Mike's been shot. Angela, tell the pilot we need to go as soon as they get here. Bobby, help me get the medical kit out and set up on the plane."

Angela was already moving, but Bobby stood motionless.

"What?" Bobby said.

"Move!" Diego shouted.

Bobby moved but still appeared to be stunned. Diego shouted at Bobby again.

"Get the two stainless steel boxes that look like toolboxes out of the luggage compartment. They are medical kits."

Bobby understood then. Their plane was a fifteen-seater with luggage compartments on the outside. He remembered seeing Diego unload them from the car and ran to get them.

Diego grabbed the boxes and put them on the plane. Bobby was back to being in shock. Angela was with him now and was beginning to cry.

Diego grabbed them both by their shoulders.

"Do you want to help Mike?" he asked. "Then pull yourself together. Angela, as soon as they get here, I need you to take care of Jess. She's hysterical and doesn't want to let go of Mike. Mike has a scalp wound that isn't life-threatening, but he could lose a lot of blood. It did knock him out. Bobby, when they get here, you and I will get Mike out of the car and onto the plane where I can work on him. Okay?"

"Are you a doctor?" Angela asked.

"No, I was a corpsman in the Navy. A medic. Now, tell me what you are going to do when they get here," Diego demanded.

Bobby and Angela repeated his instructions to him. He needed their help but he needed to keep them busy and keep them from going into shock when they saw the blood on Mike's head.

Diego saw the car coming and heard the plane start at the same time.

"Becker is going to pull right up to the door here, so be ready. Okay?"

The car stopped right at the stairway leading to the plane. Black opened the back car door. He had Mike's legs in his lap while Jess held his head. She had taken her jacket off and was holding it against the wound on Mike's head to help control the bleeding.

Diego orchestrated everything. He instructed Angela to focus on Jess and to ignore her brother. He was afraid she would lose control if she looked at him. Then he instructed Bobby and Mr. Black to carry Mike onto the plane. Becker got out of the car, ignoring everyone and everything around her. She unloaded some bags from the car onto the plane. She got back into the car and drove away.

"Jess! Jess, look at me," Angela instructed.

Jess slowly looked at Angela. She was still sobbing hysterically. Angela took her by the arm and pulled her out of the car.

"Come on. They're putting Mike on the plane. We have to go," Angela said.

"It's my fault," Jess whimpered.

"No, it's not. Now, snap out of it," Angela said. "We need to be useful and productive. How do we stop this maniac?"

Angela led Jess toward the plane.

"Where's Mike?" Jess asked.

"They have loaded him onto the plane. Diego is a medic, he's going to take care of him," Angela replied.

Chapter 68

July Fourth, 11:00 am. Antigua

The small resort appeared abandoned, except for eight people. It had become run down and had needed major repairs since a hurricane damaged it a couple of years before. The previous owners had failed to make a premium payment and their insurance company denied the claim. The bank where Harvey had parked the money had owned the property until Jess bought it a month before. The resort, if it could be called that, consisted of a main building and twelve bungalows. The main building held the office, a cafeteria, two small meeting rooms, and a laundry or maintenance room used by the staff, and the reception area. When it was bought the month before, it had been shut down completely for renovations. The bank was going to renovate and sell, but Jess made them an offer they couldn't refuse.

Steven and Mike were sitting on the veranda of bungalow number five, sipping on their beers, listening to the waves hit the beach. They were wearing shorts, T-shirts, and sandals. Mike wore a ball cap to cover the scar on his head. Jess, Angela, and Bets were in the kitchen of the bungalow making lunch. Mike and Steven had been sent to get more tables and chairs so they could have lunch outside. They were expecting Bobby back at any time. Whether his trip had been successful or not, they would not know until he returned.

The last four weeks had been the hardest of their lives. They were all computer geeks. Some, more than others. They were used to being on their computers, their tablets, or their phones. Outside of doing some very dark research, and setting up their operations center, they had stayed off the internet.

They had all stopped using their Facebook, Twitter, and Snapchat accounts. None of them had established another online identity. They had not checked their emails, text messages, or called anyone. Their phones had been turned off and locked in a safe. Mike and Jess had the only access to the safe and they had the only phone. And it was another burner phone. They were staying dark for a reason.

Mike and Steven heard car doors from in front of the bungalow. They looked at each other, stood anxiously, and took the well-beaten path around the small building. They recognized Bobby immediately, but not the brunette, who was turned away from them.

They were getting a small amount of luggage from the taxi when Bobby looked up and saw them.

"Hey, bro. Hey, Steven." Bobby grinned at them.

The brunette turned toward them then.

"Steven, you know Benji. Benji, this is Mike," Bobby said.

"Hi, Dad," Benji said, using Mike's code name and holding his hand out to shake Mike's.

"Benji." Mike hesitated for just a moment. "Why the hell didn't you listen to me when I told you to get out of Belize?"

* * *

Mike and Benji had never met in person. But they had talked on the phone several times. Mike reached for Benji's outstretched hand and then pulled him into a bear hug.

"Are you okay?" Mike asked Benji, still holding his hand as he pulled away and looked him in the eye.

"I am now," Benji replied. "You guys are the family I've never had. Except for Jess, she's always been there. And to answer your first question, I've always had an issue listening to parental figures."

Mike smiled at him. "I'm glad you made it. Let's get you settled into number six and go see the girls. They'll be happy to see you. Lunch should be ready soon."

Bobby chimed in, "I'm ready for lunch. Hurry up, Benji!"

Steven added, "Me, too!"

It only took them five minutes to drop off Benji's small amount of clothes. Benji took a couple of minutes to take off the wig, wipe the make-up off, and change the dress for khaki shorts and a t-shirt.

Steven had started asking questions, but Mike stopped him by reminding him they all had questions and they could ask and answer them at lunch.

Mike could tell that Benji was moving slowly. He wasn't completely healed from the gunshot wound. He started telling Benji about the resort.

"This resort is now owned by Jess. She used her money to buy it and start the renovations. It has a main building and twelve bungalows," Mike said.

"Bungalows seven through twelve are on the other side of the office, most of them are still being repaired. They were damaged in a storm last year. One through six are in better shape, and we are using them," Mike continued.

Steven added, "We saved six for you because it has the prettiest sunset views."

Benji had finished pulling on a plain white t-shirt and they headed out the door to the veranda facing the beach. Jess was standing on the veranda of number five looking in their direction. When she saw Benji, she yelled and started running toward the group.

* * *

Benji grinned from ear to ear when he saw Jess. She was the one true friend he had had in life until now. She had understood him and accepted him as he was. She was the one who stopped him from committing suicide on two different occasions in high school. Only the two of them knew about that. She was the one who had helped him find a mission in his life, and he loved her dearly for it. And even though he had been shot and could have died, the last six weeks had saved his life.

They met under the outstretched fronds of a palm tree that was leaning toward the sea. Jess and Benji hugged and kissed each other on the cheeks. There were tears and smiles on their faces as they sobbed and clung to each other.

Finally, Jess pushed him away but kept her hands on his shoulders. She looked him up and down.

"My God, Benji!" Jess frowned at him. "You're pale and skin and bones."

"Yeah," he said. "Getting shot and having to stick to a liquid diet for thirty days will do that. I thought you were dead."

"Come on. The food is done. There is plenty of beer and we have mixed up two pitchers of margaritas." Jess winked at him and took him by the arm, leading him to number five.

Angela and Bets emerged from the bungalow carrying plates and pitchers. Bets sat her plates down and rushed to Benji for another round of hugs. She let Benji go, stepped over to Steven and put her arms around him. She laid her head on his chest.

Benji looked at them and grinned in confusion. "What is this? Did you two hook up?"

"Yeah, kind of," Bets said. "We had a little inspiration from Mike and Jess."

Benji snapped his head around, looking at Mike and Jess. He found them on the other side of a large table where they were holding hands and watching. He gave them a questioning look, raising his eyebrows. Jess raised Mike's left hand and raised her left hand beside it.

"Wait! You got married?" Benji asked.

"Not officially," Jess said. "We do have a marriage license, so we decided to make it look real."

Mike added, "The rings and our intentions are real. I proposed to her right out there on the beach during a beautiful sunset. To my surprise and joy, she said yes."

"Come on. Let's eat. We have lots to catch up on after we eat," Jess instructed.

With the guys helping, Angela and Bets brought food from the bungalow and set it on the table. Mike and Jess got Benji settled into a chair.

When the meal was over, Mike and Jess got up and served everyone another beer or refilled a margarita glass.

When Mike and Jess sat back down, everyone got quiet and looked at them.

"No one at this table knows the whole story of the last few weeks. You knew a part of the plan, but the plan changed and we had to wing it," Mike said.

"I discovered how deep Jess's love and friendship is when I caught her looking at porn online last semester. That sounds strange, doesn't it?" Mike asked. "It turns out, she was running a facial recognition program through pornography databases. They weren't just any pornography databases; they were child pornography databases. Disgusting stuff. Horrible stuff that I could never imagine any child having to go through."

Benji watched and listened to Mike carefully. He had tears in his eyes, took a deep sobbing breath, and then exhaled. He looked at Mike and nodded.

Mike continued, "The face she was trying to match was Benji's. Jess swore me to secrecy, and I agreed. But I asked her why she didn't take the websites down? Why didn't she destroy them? She replied that that wasn't good enough. They would have a new website up the next day, with the same or new pictures and videos. She did turn them into the authorities and let them handle the prosecution.

"I was disturbed for a couple of weeks when it dawned on me that I should help. Angela and I have a cousin who went through some rough stuff when we were in high school. So, I knew if I ever wanted to have kids of my own,

I needed to protect them from predators like this. That's when I went to Jess with an idea."

Jess spoke then. "I went to the FBI. They were leery at first, but said they would follow our progress. It got dangerous the week before graduation when I found over a hundred files and pictures of Benji."

Benji looked at her and the tears and sobs started coming. His face screwed up in pain. He grabbed a napkin and covered his face. Bets reached over and put her arm around him and pulled him toward her.

"You never told me!" he sputtered.

Jess smiled softly. "There was no time to tell you. The twenty-four hours after I found the site has been the craziest twenty-four hours of my life."

Jess looked at Benji and asked, "Why were you monitoring my internet use?"

"I'm sorry. I knew you had to be getting close to finding those pictures if they were still out there. I wanted to know where they came from because I wanted revenge. I still want revenge," Benji said.

"Then you tried to access my account in Belize?" Jess asked.

"I thought you were dead. The money wasn't really yours, and it would have helped with my plan to get revenge. I know I should have called sooner, but I believed that damn police report," Benji said.

"We're going to get revenge, Benji. I promise you," Jess said.

Mike picked up the story again. He told them, "Jess found the files, she downloaded them and saved them to a large-capacity thumb drive. She followed the web links, like I taught her, and followed the money trail. She had found corporations, owners, more websites, and more money. The Friday before graduation, Jess destroyed their websites and transferred their money to the bank in Hong Kong. At this point, it should have been over. But she found a lot of money."

He told them that Jess had informed the FBI of what she had done. And that's when things went crazy. Somehow the people backing the porn business had tracked her down.

"So those attacks at school were really from this person you took the money from?" asked Bets.

"Yes, we believe he was responsible for all the attacks," replied Jess.

Mike continued his story. "We were literally shocked. Everything happened so fast, there was no planning. Except for Green and Carson. Green got a tip that they were coming after Jess. I don't know where that tip came from, but it probably saved Jess's life. We thought it was random, too, until we went to the hospital to see Green. He let us know immediately that he thought it was Markowitz."

"What was all that talk about Markowitz?" asked Angela.

"Jess had mentioned the Markowitz money to Carson when someone actually called the bank to ask about the money. It was a coincidence that Green knew Markowitz," Mike replied.

Mike explained the firebombing of the apartment forced them to run. He went on to explain that DEA Agent West had really known Markowitz's family and assured them that Markowitz's family were all dead. West was only involved because he was trying to get his son-in-law out of trouble. He didn't know his son-in-law was an informant for the FBI.

Bets picked up the story. "Then we got involved," she indicated herself and Steven, "and almost screwed things up."

"Yes and no," said Jess. "We needed a distraction to get away. The DEA helped with that. We needed someone to help us figure out who was after us. You and Benji helped with that. What we didn't expect was for the FBI to track Benji down. We just needed them looking the other way when we left town. We had no idea that they were really interested in you."

"How did they follow me?" Benji asked.

Jess looked at him and frowned. She raised a finger and pointed at him. "You were supposed to lay low. Instead, you went to Starbucks in Rogers and stole credit card information from an undercover FBI agent. And you used that card to buy airline tickets to Belize."

"Shit!" Benji exclaimed.

Bets added, "The same female FBI agent made the connection after they raided your apartment that Sunday morning. She saw you at Starbucks on Friday morning and followed you to your repair van. She saw the blond woman get in the van, and then she saw *you* drive away. The DEA followed your Jetta to your apartment, and then saw you leave as a blond woman and get into your van and drive away."

"Oh, man!" Benji sighed.

"They found your van and all the tools you used to make credit cards and other things. Apparently, you've been one bad boy," Bets said.

"I'm sorry guys, it's how I paid my bills," Benji told them.

Mike spoke again. "Look, we forgive you. But they followed you to Belize. We had to stop you at the bank. We had to warn you to get out of Belize. The FBI was on your trail for credit card fraud and who knows what else. Their trailing you led whoever was after us to find you in Belize and attack you."

"No," Benji said. "I'm pretty sure the attack in Belize was purely chance. I turned down the wrong alley and ran right into two teenage gang members. One started threatening me with a knife and calling me a pussy. I hate that word. It's what I was called ... never mind."

Benji stopped and looked at Mike. Mike finished his statement for him.

"When your attacker came at you with the knife, you somehow took it away from him. Killed him and turned to the other one who shot you?"

Benji nodded. "Something like that."

Jess spoke then. "Your attackers weren't random, Benji. They were lookouts for a drug-related gang that operates in Belize."

Benji nodded. "How did I get to the hospital, and then to the mission?"

Mike looked at him. "We had to come clean with the FBI. Special Agent Henderson, the agent who was following you, was the first on the scene. She got you to the hospital. As soon as you were out of surgery, they were able to sneak you out to the Mission and hide you there."

"So, they know all about my crimes," Benji stated.

"Some," Jess replied. "But we think we have a way to keep you out of prison."

"Y'all weren't involved in that part of my life. I don't want you getting into any more trouble for me," Benji said.

"We aren't," Mike said. "We have our own troubles. Bank robbery and wire fraud are no small issues. We've been making a deal though. Agent Green and Agent Henderson will be here this evening to give us their final offer. We think it will be something we can all live with."

Benji stared at Mike. "What do you mean, bank robbery and wire fraud?"

"Mike and I had been working on a program for me to access and move my money at the Caribbean Bank," Jess said. "Mike learned a few tricks about the software they used and somehow it gave me admin privileges. When I found your pictures and videos, it pissed me off. I had written down the banks and the account numbers, so I was like, what the hell, let's try this. Out of the four hundred million that I tracked down, I was able to move and transfer one hundred and fifty million. Plus, I erased their websites. That was early Friday morning. By Friday evening they were tracking me and Mike down. We couldn't figure out how they tracked me past the three VPNs I went through."

"They tracked the money back to us somehow," Mike said.

"Fuck!" Benji shouted. "One hundred and fifty million? We are dead!"

Benji stood and walked to the edge of the veranda and the pergola which covered it. He looked out at the Caribbean Sea thoughtfully before turning back to the table.

He looked at them carefully. "I appreciate all of you trying to help me, but these people will not stop until we are dead and they have their money back.

"Who are we dealing with Benji?" asked Angela.

Benji snorted. "The Mafia, a cartel, I don't know! But, if you took that much of my money, I would come after it."

Mike quietly answered, "They already have Benji. Several attempts were made on us in Fayetteville. There were the attacks on you and us in Belize City. And Steven and Bets in Miami."

"We aren't hiding in a closed resort in Antigua because it's beautiful and we want to. We are here because attempts have been made on our lives because we stole money from them," Jess said.

"Okay, but y'all didn't get shot," Benji said.

Everyone at the table got very still. Mike reached up and took his ball cap off, revealing a nearly shaven head and a still-healing four-inch scar along the right side of his scalp just above his ear.

Jess spoke very softly. "That's not true Benji, Mike was shot in Belize City also. We had just hired some security to protect us. They went to the bank with us. We were attacked as soon as we left the bank. If Mike had not moved to protect me, the shot would have hit him in the back of the head and he would have died there. Mr. Black and Miss Becker took out the three attackers with three shots and saved our lives. They had us loaded in the car and on the way to the airport so fast it was a blur. Diego, the third member of our security team, is also a medic. He cleaned Mike's wound and sewed it up while the plane was flying from Belize to Antigua. It knocked Mike out and he didn't wake up for twenty-four hours."

"I'm sorry," Benji replied. "I didn't know." He looked at Steven and Bets. "Y'all were attacked too?"

"Well, Steven's car was, and the hotel room we parked in front of," Bets replied. "We had just checked in, and I was taking a shower when Steven busted in yelling for me to get down. He was barely through the door when the shooting started. Thankfully, we weren't able to park in front of our room, or we wouldn't be here."

Mike asked, "Benji, have you ever heard of someone called The Bookkeeper?"

Benji leaned back in his chair. His pale face went even whiter. He couldn't hide his shock.

"I don't know, maybe, yeah," he said. "It's been a long time."

"We've been busy doing some coding, and with a little help from some friends of a friend, we've located and learned a few things about our attacker," Mike said.

"Friends of a friend?" Benji asked.

"Russian hackers," Jess said.

"Anyway, they have been monitoring his computer activity. We figured out the software he was using to track us and basically reprogrammed it for our use," Mike said.

"It is some really sneaky software that we are pretty sure was written by the NSA. It has a backdoor reporting system that the Russians are ninety percent sure leads back to an NSA server. But with a few tweaks, it now leads back to us."

"How do you know it was written by the NSA?" Benji asked.

"Long story made short," Mike said. "The NSA informed the FBI that Jess had stolen several million dollars and they wanted her arrested. But they wouldn't tell the FBI how they knew she stole it, who she stole it from, or how much. So Haygood, I mean Green, gave us a tip to figure out how the program tracking works."

"Wait," Benji said. "Are you telling me that Haygood was an FBI agent?"

Jess answered, "Oh I forgot that you didn't know. Haygood was undercover looking for you. You really pissed them off with your income tax return scam."

"Shit! This is getting worse and worse," Benji answered.

"Tell us what happened to you," Jess said.

"It sounds like you know the story already," Benji said.

"What happened at the mission? What have you been doing for the last six weeks?" Mike asked.

"Mainly recuperating. Playing with kids, and teaching them and their mothers how to use computers. I've learned some Spanish, enough to speak to the natives and not get confused by the words I don't know. Thanks to Mike's cousin and his wife, I've learned a lot about Christianity and giving back to people," Benji said.

"It was an amazing few weeks. With all the problems I have; that *we* have," he corrected himself, "we have *no* problems compared to the women and children there."

He looked at Mike and said, "Your cousin and his family are amazing. They help people who have nothing learn how to get back on their feet and live again."

Benji looked at Mike and said, "What? Why are you grinning like that?"

"You are starting to sound just like cousin Ben. If you start preaching, we will send you back," Mike laughed.

"It's not a bad place to go to, honestly," Benji replied.

"Let's get this table cleaned up and then we can meet in the main building at three. We have a lot more to discuss and to do," Mike said.

Chapter 69

July Fourth, 3:00 p.m. Antigua

The cafe area of the main building had been converted into a large computer lab. One wall was covered with computer monitors, which could be synced to one large twelve by sixteen-foot big screen or operated as twenty-four individual screens. Bobby, with the help of Angela, had been working for two weeks straight setting up the computer lab.

Everything was connected to a satellite system, giving them the fastest internet service available on the island. Bobby had tested the system until it worked to perfection. Mike had insisted on having no glitches. There were backup computers in case one went down. Each computer was connected to the others and each had its own firewall just in case. There was a backup generator for the backup generator, just in case the island's power was interrupted.

Mike had insisted on going over and over everything several times, and looking at their system from the outside in. He had Bets and Steven play the hackers and challenged them to break into the system. They used every trick they knew and actually broke into it several times. The group then worked together to develop solutions.

They had deemed it unbreakable two weeks ago. But they knew, in the hacking world, everything could be hacked eventually. Their primary concern had been to protect their system from the software that was used to find Jess the first time. Thanks to Jess, money had been no issue. Getting the equipment to Antigua had been a small challenge, but they eventually found a way to deal with that also.

Harvey, their Hong Kong connection, had managed to secure most of the equipment they needed. Jess had invited him to come to Antigua, but he had declined, saying he didn't do planes, trains, or ships. He said he would live vicariously through Mike and Jess. As long as they sent pictures, that was.

There were seven computers in the room. All had their own desk and they all faced the monitors on the wall. Each computer could control the wall monitor as a single screen or as a split screen making it easy for each person to communicate what they were looking at to the group without everyone gathering around a single computer.

Mike and Jess did not know if they would use this very much. But they planned to use it tonight.

Mike and Bobby had arrived early and turned everything on. The rest of their group were starting to arrive. Benji entered the room with Steven and Bets and looked at the setup.

"What in the world is this? It looks like something right out of a sci-fi movie," Benji said.

Bobby stepped forward and said, "Let me be the first to welcome you to JAMB International headquarters. We have seven computer stations, all linked to a mainframe computer in the next room, and a twelve by sixteen-foot monitor."

"Wow," Benji said. "What is JAMB International?"

"In high school, Mike, Angela, and I started a little company called BAM. Now that Jess is with Mike, we've renamed it JAMB," Bobby said.

Benji looked at them with new appreciation. "I suspected you two were more than dumb jocks," he laughed. "What is JAMB International doing now?" Benji asked.

Mike answered by pointing to the door and saying, "I'll let Jess answer that question."

"Today, we are going after the man who had the pictures of you and who tried to kill us. With the help of the FBI, this will be over very soon," Jess said.

Jess had stopped in the doorway to answer Benji's question. She entered the room, followed by FBI consultant Green, Special Agent Henderson, and Angela.

Jess moved to where Mike was standing. "Everyone, let me introduce Professor Haygood, or Green and Special Agent Henderson of the FBI.

Green said, "I think I know just about everyone here, but please, introduce yourselves for Henderson's sake."

They went around the room and introduced themselves. Benji went last. When Benji had introduced himself, Henderson stepped forward and stuck out her hand.

"You are an interesting person, Benji Smith. I have something for you."

She took a large bag off her shoulder and reached into it. She pulled out an old backpack and handed it to Benji.

"Your laptop is in there," Henderson said. "We were, uh, umm, unable to break into it." And she winked at him.

Green said, "More like, unwilling to break into it."

Henderson added, "I have a letter for you from a young lady named Staci. She said to tell you she's ready to leave."

"You met Staci?" Benji asked.

"Yes," Henderson said. "After Staci told us her story and your story, Green and I tried to close your case. According to FBI records, you died in a hospital in Belize. We know you ran all those credit card schemes and the income tax scheme to pay her hospital bills. After investigating everything she told us, we felt our government should have covered her expenses. Anyway, after seeing Staci and learning about what you did for your neighbor's son, we knew what kind of person you were. When you return to the States there will be some charges brought against you. But I think if you agree to repay the money you stole, pay a fine, and agree to some community service, you can avoid jail time."

Benji nodded, "It's better than I expected. How did you find Staci?"

"Your notebook from your computer bag. You kept track of what you paid," Green said.

Jess had been watching Benji and was very surprised. "Benji? Who is Staci?"

Benji's eyes became moist. "Staci is the girl I told you about. She was two years younger than me. The man who abused us had both of us at the same time. We shared a room. I tried to protect her, but got whipped for my efforts. When I finally escaped, I took her with me. We ended up with different foster families. I was reunited with my mom eventually. She stayed in the foster system and never got the treatment she needed for being abused. When I found her two years ago, she was on drugs and had been abused even more. I promised her I would get her help and somehow, I would pay for it."

"So, the scams were actually to pay for her medical bills, not for college?" Jess asked.

"Every bit of it," Agent Henderson said, answering for Benji.

Mike looked at Green and asked, "What about the case against us?"

"There is no case," Green said. "You have done exactly what Jess promised Agent Carson she would do. You have turned over the evidence and the money you took. We've already arrested four of the five people behind the websites."

Green said, "Our Chicago office is about to raid The Bookkeeper's house. I think you guys have some work to do while I pull up a live feed of the raid. Which computer can I use?"

Bobby moved quickly and said, "This one. The feed will also show on the wall."

He sat at the terminal next to Green and said, "I think we need a little music in the meantime. How about *Whatever It Takes* by Imagine Dragons."

Mike, Jess, Angela, Bets, and Steven all joined Bobby at their own computer terminal until all terminals were being used. Henderson and Benji leaned over Steven's shoulder to see his screen better.

"What are you doing?" Benji asked. "I've never seen this software before."

Steven said, "You are about to see a man lose two hundred and fifty million dollars in just a few minutes. Each of us has gained access to three or four accounts that we will bounce around the world before it is all deposited into a single account in Washington D.C. where the FBI will assume responsibility for it."

Green said, "I've got the feed up. It looks like they are just about ready."

Jess said, "Go on the count of three. One. Two. Three!"

The keyboards started clacking. All six were hackers now. They had practiced for this moment every day for the last week. They could hack into every bank where The Bookkeeper kept money. They should be able to move all of his money in less than six minutes.

* * *

The words of the Imagine Dragons song blared through the speakers on the front wall.

Benji watched Steven's computer screen. He was amazed at what his friends were doing. He wanted to know how they had managed to hack into so many banks. How did they get the account numbers? He had so many questions. Then he looked up at the screen on the front wall and was stunned. His stomach lurched and he felt himself getting sick.

"I know that house," Benji said, turning pale.

"How do you know that house?" Henderson asked softly. She put a hand on his shoulder to get his attention.

"That's where Staci and I were," he said.

"Green, this could be Benji's abductor," Henderson said.

Green was reaching for his cell phone. Jess was the first to say "finished." Quickly followed by the others.

The screen showed men in FBI jackets rushing to the front door of the house.

Green said, "I don't have a signal."

Mike handed Green his phone and quickly looked at Jess. "What's going on?"

"I've got someone who has been inside the house," Green said.

The agents on the screen busted in the front door. Benji gasped. The recognition was complete now.

"Where do they need to go Benji?"

Benji put his hands on the back of Steven's chair, he was leaning forward and trembling.

"First room on the left is a library of sorts. Go to the mantle above the fireplace."

He waited for Green to repeat his words.

"In the center of the mantle, underneath is a button. It opens a secret door to the right of the fireplace."

He watched the screen as an agent followed Green's repeated instructions.

"The first door on the right is a bedroom. The second door is a stairwell. Don't worry about the doors on the left. That's the playroom and the camera room."

He watched as the agent hesitated at the stairwell door.

Benji continued, "The stairs go down several flights. I don't know how far down. It was a long way when I went down it. He has a garage down there. He had an ice cream truck and an old Volkswagen bus. It comes out into a sewer tunnel. That's how we got out."

He could see the agent had stepped aside and let two more agents go ahead of him.

Green said, "No one is in the house. But signs show he was there not too long ago."

The screen went blank and Green said, "I lost signal, they're too far underground."

"Was there anyone in the bedroom?" Benji asked.

"No," Green said.

"But there was before, wasn't there?" Benji asked.

"Yes," Green said.

Chapter 70

July Fourth, 4:00 p.m. Chicago, Illinois

The Bookkeeper had owned multiple security systems, but he always relied on motion sensors and video cameras. They sent notices to his cell phone when someone approached his house from the front sidewalk or the back door. This time, he received a notice from both doors. He didn't bother to look. He had just watched all the money that he managed disappear. He knew it was the police coming for him.

He turned the computer monitor off out of habit. He took two steps to the mantle and hit the button for the hidden door then stepped through and closed the door behind him. He unlocked the door to the bedroom.

"Johnny, we must go now," he said.

Johnny stood and slipped his house shoes on. Pajamas and house shoes were all the clothes he had. The Bookkeeper took him by the shoulder and pushed him toward the stairwell door. He opened the door and took a flashlight from a shelf just inside.

"We're going to take the stairs, Johnny. Be careful, there are a lot of steps," he said as he shined the flashlight ahead of the boy.

The man was trying to remain calm. His mind was racing. He had planned for this event but never expected it to happen. They had just reached the bottom of the stairs when he heard the stairwell door open far above him.

He looked back at the stairwell, frightened now. How had they found the hidden rooms so fast? He hurried the boy up.

"Hurry, Johnny. To the ice cream truck," he said.

"Stop right there," a man's voice came from the darkness.

"Johnny, go back up the stairs," Malichi Smith said as he stepped out of the darkness holding a pistol. They watched the boy turn and head back up the stairs.

"Who are you?" The Bookkeeper demanded.

"I'm the father of one of the kids you abused. I'm the man who tracked you down. When you found out that I tracked you down, you had your people attack me. You forced me to choose between killing my wife or my son."

"Benji's dad."

"Revenge is swift," Malichi said as he pulled the trigger that ended the life of The Bookkeeper.

Chapter 71

Special Agent Green ended the call and handed Mike his phone back. Green started logging back into the computer.

Benji, who had been anxious and jittery, said, "Well, what happened?"

Green grimaced and said, "We got him. He's dead. Someone killed him in his garage and disappeared. They recovered a young boy though."

Everyone in the room smiled and cheered. Mike and Bobby high-fived each other. Jess couldn't conceal a knowing smile.

Green said, "We aren't done yet, we need Benji's help hacking into his phone. He left his computer on, but there wasn't much on it besides accounting programs and the tracking software that he used to find Jess. Can you help us out, Benji?"

"Gladly," Benji said.

Thirty minutes later, the FBI agent had unlocked the cell phone and was looking at contacts and phone logs. Most of the time was spent downloading the software Benji used. The firewall the FBI used didn't want to let it through, so the agent ended up using someone's personal laptop to hack into the phone.

Green insisted on letting the Chicago office do its job and signed off the Zoom call.

Bobby said it was time to celebrate and started playing Queen's *We Are the Champions*. Then he slipped out the door and disappeared. Jess and Henderson went to the kitchen and started getting snacks and drinks. Jess said they kept it stocked for the days they spent in their computer lab.

Bobby returned with the security team. He said it wasn't right to celebrate without them.

Henderson's phone rang and she stepped aside to answer it. She looked at Green and said, "The director wants to talk to you."

Green answered the phone and listened to what sounded like a very angry voice on the other end of the call.

Finally, Green looked at Mike and Jess and winked at them. He said into the phone, "Sir, if the NSA says the money was transferred using one of their computers, then they must have been responsible for transferring the money. Are they saying their system was hacked?"

This time Green smiled and shook his finger at Mike and Jess.

"No, sir, I don't know how it was done. Yes, sir, I will try to find out. Good night, sir."

Green busted out laughing and handed the phone back to Henderson.

"You guys were slick, I never noticed that you ran all that money through the NSA's computer system," Green said.

Mike said, "Actually, we didn't. We cloned the IP address of an NSA computer and that is the IP address for our mainframe for tonight."

Mike looked at Bobby and Bobby said, "I'm shutting the clone down now, before they track us down."

Mike said, "If things failed tonight, we didn't want the operation traced back here, we wanted it traced somewhere the Bookkeeper wouldn't attack."

"Smart thinking," Green replied. "And you got a little revenge, too."

Mike smiled. "Yes, sir."

They celebrated until almost midnight when Green and Henderson excused themselves to go back to their motel for the night.

Mike and Jess found themselves standing beside Benji. Jess asked Benji if he was okay.

"I'm fine. But I need to go get Staci," Benji said.

"Bring her here. You can stay here for as long as you want," Jess said.

"That sounds great," Benji said. "But I'm broke. I have no money, and I still owe the hospital for her last two month's stay."

"Benji, you don't have to worry about money," Jess said.

"Jess, I know you're rich. But I can't accept your money."

Mike said, "Benji, do you remember us telling you about the one hundred and fifty million Jess took?"

"Yes," Benji replied carefully.

"The FBI never knew how much she took," Mike said, "and we never told them. We gave them a hundred million back and kept fifty. We figure it belongs to you, or you and Staci for what you have been through."

Benji was stunned. "Fifty million?"

"Something close to that," Jess said.

The rest of the team gathered around.

"Did you tell him?" Steven asked.

"Just told him," Jess said.

"Wait, you were all in on this?" Benji asked.

"Benji," Jess said. "We talked and we want you to have the money. And this was before we knew what you did for Staci."

"But y'all went through so much, you almost got killed so I think y'all deserve the money," Benji said. "All of you."

Mike looked at Benji and shook his head.

"Let's do this, let's split the money," Mike said. "You and Staci split twenty-five million. We'll split the other twenty-five million seven ways."

Jess saw Benji look around the group, and then frown slightly.

"We're including Harvey, from Hong Kong. We couldn't have done this without his help," Jess said.

Chapter 72

Benji rented a car at NWA Regional Airport. He drove directly to the NWA Psychiatric Hospital. It was past time for him to have gotten Staci. He was on his way through the parking lot to the main entrance when he heard a male voice call his name. He turned to find his father, Malachi Smith in the flesh, leaning against a pickup truck and watching him closely.

"Dad? What are you doing here?" Benji asked.

The hurt in Benji's voice was obvious. His father had abandoned him and his mother. He barely made it to his mother's funeral.

"Checking to make sure my child is okay," he responded.

"What does it matter to you? You abandoned me and Mom."

His father said, "I had to. To keep you alive. I tracked down The Bookkeeper, but he got to me before I got to him. Your mother didn't die from a drug overdose. The Bookkeeper killed her and made me watch her die while the killers videotaped it. Then they showed you asleep in your room. He was tempted to kill you while you slept. He told me he would kill you unless I went to work for him. The last two months, I've done everything I could to protect you and your friends."

"Protect? We were almost killed!" Benji said.

"I'm sorry. I sent the dumbest, the most untrained idiots I could find after you and your friends," his father said.

"That was you?" Benji asked.

"Yes. Charles Anderson worked for me. He was keeping an eye on Jess while I watched you. I didn't think she would find anything about you on the internet, so I gave her some leads. When she did, all hell broke loose."

"How did you know about that?" Benji asked.

He said, "I'm a hacker, too, remember?"

"I guess so. What do you want?" Benji asked.

"I wanted to make sure you were okay. I wanted to say I'm sorry for not being there for you and to ask you to forgive me. And I wanted to warn you and your friends."

"Well, I'm okay," Benji said. "As for forgiveness, I'm not sure I can do that yet. And The Bookkeeper is dead, what do you need to warn me and my friends about?"

Benji's father sighed deeply. "I understand if you can't forgive me. I haven't forgiven myself yet. I still love you, and I loved your mom."

Benji was growing tired of his father. He never understood why he wasn't there when he needed him. He wasn't sure he bought his father's explanation.

"What's this warning?" Benji asked.

"The Bookkeeper had other people who worked for him. They were like me. He blackmailed them and used their families against them. Some of them may come after you thinking to getting revenge or to get some of his money back. Others will relax and settle down to a normal life. I don't know. But I do know you and your friends are not safe yet. If I can find you, they can find you. Tell your friends not to get rid of their security team."

Benji was shocked. He hadn't thought about how his father had found him.

"How did you find me?"

"The FBI talks too much," his father said.

His father opened the truck door and started to get in. He looked at Benji and said, "Go spend some time at that mission in Guatemala with your friend there. It will do her good to see that other people have suffered and that helping them will help her. Take care of yourself, Benji. I will contact the mission if I need to reach you."

There were no hugs. No proclamations of their love for each other. They just nodded at each other as his father got into the truck and drove away.

Benji stood there for several minutes thinking about what his father had said. He still had questions. His mother was murdered? That explained a lot of things. But the biggest question was how did his father know he was here? The FBI talks too much? He needed to talk to Mike and Jess. They were definitely still in danger.

He headed into the hospital. He wanted to get Staci and get her out of the country as soon as possible. His father's idea of going to Guatemala was a good one. But first, he had to go back to Antigua.

Chapter 73

Saturday, August 3, 12:00 Noon. Antigua

The little resort had been busy with preparations for a double wedding for two days. Mike and Jess were getting married, as well as Angela and Bobby. Jess had hired new staff to run the resort and it was scheduled to open to the public the following Monday. The staff was preparing almost everything, with the help of friends and family.

Their computer friends were all there, but Steven and Bets were no longer together. Bets had made up with an old girlfriend and dumped Steven. Steven said he had been upset for a few days before getting over it.

Benji had shown up with the most beautiful girl any of them had ever seen. They quickly learned that this was Staci. Staci was short and slender with a pixie haircut. Steven was already in love with her. Benji was very protective of her, saying Staci was like a little sister and he would protect her with his life. Steven knew what he meant. Benji and Staci were planning to go to the mission in Guatemala and spend some time volunteering there. Benji had already arranged to set up a charitable fund to support the mission.

Benji had also told Mike about his meeting with his father. He passed on the warning his father gave him. Mike assured him they planned to keep the security team for a while longer.

The elder Brocks were there, with Grandma Williams, and Mrs. Benelli. They had all become close friends after the ordeal they had gone through.

The security team was still there. Although they were less formal about their roles now. Green had also recommended keeping them on board in case the Bookkeeper had managed to reach out to another friend and send some more attackers. The Bookkeeper was still unidentified. They didn't know his legal name. He owned everything under fake names and shell corporations. His fingerprints were not on file. He was simply a non-existent person. The FBI continued to work on that, though.

Green, special agents Carson, and Henderson had all taken vacation time to come to the wedding. How could they resist? Mike and Jess, paid all their expenses. Green had announced the night before that he was retiring as an FBI consultant and was planning to go back to teaching. He said grading papers was much less stressful than working for the FBI. He was a few months away from retirement and had recently been diagnosed as a type two diabetic.

Harvey wasn't coming. But insisted they set up a video feed so he could be there in spirit.

The wedding was on the beach, with Mike and Angela's cousin, Ben Brock, presiding. He and his wife, Amy, and their three children had traveled from Guatemala to perform the wedding and take a short vacation. The first vacation they had taken in three years, since moving to Guatemala.

The two oldest Brock children were all over Benji as soon as they saw him. He picked them both up in his arms and gave them hugs and kisses. He introduced them to Staci and soon they were all over her as well.

The wedding went smoothly, with only two hitches, according to Grandma Williams. "Those kids are hitched now," she laughed. Professor Green kept his distance from her, however.

The reception was a long affair with much visiting going on among the family and friends. Mike noticed Green looking at his cell phone and thought he must have bought an international cell plan before this trip. Green motioned to Henderson and Carson and they stepped outside of what had once been their computer lab.

Mike prodded Jess and said, "I wonder what that's about."

"I think we are about to find out," Jess said as the three FBI agents came back inside.

Carson and Henderson took their seats. Green walked to the head table and leaned between Mike and Jess.

"They've identified The Bookkeeper," he whispered.

Mike grabbed a knife and his wine glass and tapped the glass, getting everyone's attention.

Mike said, "We have an announcement to make."

Green said, "I guess this does affect everyone here. The Chicago office has identified The Bookkeeper."

He hesitated as if not believing what he was about to say.

"The Bookkeeper was Bennie Markowitz. They identified him from old fingerprint records that didn't make it into the national database. They had to manually match the fingerprints which is why it took so long to identify him."

Mrs. Benelli gasped. "I thought he was dead."

Mike looked at Jess and said, "That must be who was checking on your account. I wonder who killed him?"

"I guess we'll never know, will we?" And she smiled a knowing smile. That would be a secret kept between her and Malichi Smith.

The End

A note from the author.

This story is 100% fiction. The characters are all fictitious and are in no way meant to resemble or implicate any living or deceased persons. Child sexual abuse and child pornography are real. So are the verbal, mental, and physical abuse, and neglect children experience from it. We don't have to be superheroes and step into the middle of family situations when we suspect something is going on, in fact, I would discourage getting directly involved. But we can report our suspicions to the right authorities and let the professionals investigate.

The National Center for Missing & Exploited Children says in 2022, there were more than 31.9 million reports of (CSAM) child sexual abuse material in the United States.

Their CyberTipline also includes:

18,336 Child sex trafficking reports

80,524 Online enticement, including "sextortion"

12,906 Child sexual molestation

46,029 Other, including child sex tourism, misleading domain names, misleading words or images, and unsolicited obscene material sent to a child.

This does not include reports made to local, state, or federal authorities. Nor does it include the unreported cases.

For more information go towww.missingkids.org[1].

Many cases of child molestation are perpetrated by a person the child and the family know and trust. A perfect example is the case of Heath Stocks and Jack Walls. Mr. Walls was known as a pillar of the community, a long-time scout leader, and voted Lonoke's Man of the Year once. What people didn't know was that Mr. Walls had been molesting his scouts for over twenty years.

---

1. http://www.missingkids.org

When Heath's family found out, Walls told Heath to kill the situation. And Heath killed his parents and his sister, he was ashamed of everything he did but couldn't find the nerve to commit suicide. He is currently serving life In the Tucker Unit of the Arkansas State Prison.

The psychological power a molester has over his victim is incredible. A child will lie to his parents because he may think he is protecting them from harm.

To learn more about Jack Walls and Heath Stocks go to:abusedinscouting.com/a-predator-in-our-midst-the-jack-walls-story/[2]

Heath Stocks was one of my 4-H members when I was a County Extension Agent in Lonoke County. I helped him prepare a presentation on Wildlife Conservation to compete at the Arkansas 4-H O'rama one year. Like his parents, coaches, and teachers, I did not see the signs and never dreamed he was being sexually abused.

Cyber crimes

To protect yourself from cybercrimes, follow these tips:

1. Change your passwords regularly. Use two-part authentication where possible. Two-part authentication is where a site sends you a second code to enter before it allows you to proceed with logging in.

2. Use a VPN, Virtual Private Network, to protect your phones and home WIFI systems.

3. Do not open unsolicited emails, or documents within those emails. Report those emails as junk or phishing emails and delete them unopened.

4. Avoid public WIFI where possible.

---

2. http://abusedinscouting.com/a-predator-in-our-midst-the-jack-walls-story/

About the Author

Tony C. Franklin was born and raised in the Southeast Arkansas town of Hamburg. He grew up on a small farm one-half mile from the Arkansas/ Louisiana state line. One set of grandparents lived in the Delta town of Wilmot, Arkansas; the other set lived on Hopkins Hill, west of Jones, Louisiana, and the renowned Bayou Bartholomew. Tony tries to pay homage to the South he remembers growing up in.

He currently resides in Fort Smith, Arkansas. He is a poet who also writes fictional "grit lit" and "southern noir" short stories and creative non-fiction stories. He is currently working on his second novel.

Read more at www.tcfbooks.wordpress.com.